PRISONER

The Fenrir Series

Karla Rose

KDP ISBN: 9781794123083
ISBN: 9780473526573 (paperback)
ISBN: 9780473526580 (digital)

Cover design by: Karla Rose

For Estelle, whose bright personality, fun, and positive attitude have turned many a bad day on its head.
For my Beta readers Rebecca Frost, Sheryl Wilson, Brittany Shaw
and for God who puts all the right people into my life.

COUGHEE. IT CURES WHAT AILS YOU

The strong scent of coffee was a constant companion in Coughee the cafe that declared their coffee would 'cure what ails you'. Of course in Jem's opinion it was a gimmick, but try telling that to her boss Jenny, or the customers who swore by it. Coughee was a small, intimate according to Jenny, cafe that was always packed with people. Wrought iron tables overflowed from the shop into a long front courtyard and out onto the footpath until they sat in front of Mrs. Grover's Flower shop. Which of course the elderly business owner did not appreciate, and which in turn had led to Jem's foul mood. Apparently Mrs. Grover thought she should yell at Jem until Jem moved the tables instead of taking her complaints to Jenny the cafe owner.

Jem dragged each of the three incredibly heavy tables from in front of the florist back closer to the cafe. People could be so disgusting, Jem hated working here sometimes. Okay most of the time. Honestly, why would someone screw up their sugar sachet and their dirty rotten snot rag and jam them inside of their coffee cup? Surely they knew Jem was going to have to get it out, and it wasn't like Jenny gave the staff gloves.

One of the cups on the table Jem was moving was lined in coffee foam and lipstick. Lipstick that incidentally had been at least two shades too dark for the woman wearing it. Naturally the cup slipped forward on the table as Jem moved it, tipping just enough of the leftover coffee out from under the revolting tissue to slop down the front of Jem's apron.

That was great, just great. Now Jem was all sticky, and the tepid coffee was running down her chest and soaking into her clothing.

She ground her teeth. Why would anyone order a large coffee if they weren't going to drink the darn thing?! There was probably three dollars worth of coffee just in what had gone down the front of Jem's shirt.

Sighing Jem acknowledged that maybe she should have cleared the tables first. Then she wouldn't be wearing some customers' coffee. Of course, if Jem had done that she could pretty much guarantee someone would have sat down at the table so she couldn't move it. Then she would have had that nasty old bat, Mrs. Grover, from the florist yelling at her again. Honestly. Weren't old ladies meant to be kind? Obviously Mrs. Grover had missed that memo.

Jem forced her body upright and felt the muscles in her back protesting sharply. Her whole body hurt thanks to the never-ending barrage of dishes. She'd been hunched over the sink out back for far too long, and once again she'd missed out on her morning tea and lunch breaks.

She was so freaking hungry that her tummy was growling impatiently, it was only being made worse by the sweet scent of pastries, and the aroma of sandwiches that kept wafting from the plates of customers.

After a little manoeuvring, Jem finally managed to clear the cups and get them out to the kitchen, then she went back out into the courtyard to drag the last of the heavy tables from in front of the florist. She could really have used a second person to help her shift them. Either that or Jenny should consider putting the monstrously heavy things on wheels. That would have made it easier if nothing else.

Jem placed her hands absently onto the last table and prepared to move it, only to find another cup. She could have sworn she'd cleared the table. The table had definitely been clear when she looked two seconds ago, she was sure of it.

She grabbed the cup in frustration and her hand

came into contact with something warm. Jem lifted her eyes to really look at the cup and a pair of hands came into view. Then a pair of arms. The empty cup was actually full and attached to someone. No, not just someone. The hottest man Jem had ever seen.

Hot as in looks like his should be illegal. It was safe to say he made tall, dark, and handsome look short, pale, and grotesque. So hot.

He had long strong legs, clad in faded blue jeans showing off muscles that would no doubt ripple as he walked. Muscular arms, and a chest wrapped in a soft brown leather jacket. His hair was shoulder length and black. He had aristocratic features with just a hint of feral masculinity. Jen was particularly fond of the light stubble, leading into a small brush of hair at his chin, which joined the hair above his lip, and his dark green eyes that appeared to somehow fade to yellow near the iris. Then he smiled at her and all Jem could see were lips and teeth. She dropped the cup, shocked at the inexplicable fear and attraction that rocked her, sending hot coffee slopping over the rim of the cup and nearly landing straight on his lap.

Dan shot nimbly to his feet. He was, yet again, thankful for his wolf reflexes. They were the only reason he managed to avoid hot coffee scolding his crotch.

He'd obviously been expecting a woman when his Dad and eldest brother Thomas had sent him out to find the next Valkyrie. After all, Valkyrie were exclusively women. They knew Freya was going to claim her for her cause. She always did. The Valkyrie were Freya's private army. What Dan hadn't been expecting was her.

At all of five foot four, the woman just barely came to his chin. Mousy blonde hair and built like he thought a woman should be, all soft curves and lush lips. His eyes couldn't help but be drawn up and down her curvy frame.

Her name badge clearly stated her name was 'Jem'. But from the moment he caught her sweet blossom fragrance the only word that entered his mind was MINE. His wolf wanted to claim her as its mate right then and there.

She hadn't realised he'd sat down at the table. He'd watched her scowl as a cup of coffee tipped down her front. Then he'd watched her sigh, clean the table, rush the dishes into the shop and then move towards him completely unaware of his presence. She was shooting nervous glances over at the florist, and he couldn't help but wonder why she was so worried? Was it the elderly lady bustling around inside that concerned her?

He felt his wolf growl in male satisfaction when Jem's eyes finally met his. Her pupils dilated minutely and he knew the gold of his wolf was showing in his eyes. He smiled his 'two hundred and fifty-kilowatt lady killer' smile, as his brothers, the twins, had dubbed it, and was shocked when she practically leapt out of her skin dropping his coffee cup.

He moved out of the path of the steaming hot coffee, while his wolf lunged at the reins desperate to protect her from the unknown threat. At least until Dan realised he was the threat she was reacting too.

Rolling his eyes internally at his ridiculously territorial wolf, Dan drank in her sweet scent. Was this what all male Fenrir went through when they came across a compatible female? No wonder the guys all seemed so out of control when the females hit their heat. The pull this little female had over him was intense, and she wasn't even Fenrir, she was Valkyrie. Though at this stage it seemed as though she was completely unaware of what she was. But whether she knew it or not she was dangerous. For all Dan knew, everything he was experiencing could be some kind of trick to lure him in. Maybe Freya had created a new ploy to destroy his people. Maybe this Valkyrie was already Freya's and she had some magic over her to make her smell so appealing.

"Oh my gosh. I'm so sorry!" Jem said panicking

as she attempted to lap up the spilt coffee on the table with the cloth she had tucked into her apron.

She surveyed his clothes for wet patches while wiping frantically at the coffee that had spilt all over the table.

She was so cute when she panicked. Surely she couldn't be Freya's yet?

Dan almost wished he'd gotten some of the coffee on himself, having Jem's hands on him seemed like it could be a very good thing.

He drank in her every feature. There was no way he could kidnap her now, and he certainly wouldn't be using her as bait to draw out the rest of the Valkyrie. Even if it were to find out if the rumours of Freya amassing an army were true. This little Valkyrie was the only female his wolf had ever reacted to, and if there was even a chance that she was his mate he wasn't going to do anything to endanger that. There had to be another way to do this. Mates weren't that common, you couldn't just throw one away if you came across them, and Dan wanted her as his mate, not as his prisoner. Dad and Thomas would understand. He wasn't just going to grab her, not until he knew for sure. Not even if snatching her would help them draw out Freya and her cronies. There had to be another way. Dan was going to have to call them. Jem's scent changed everything and nothing. If it were true and Freya was gathering up the descendants of

Valkyrie and convincing them to join her army then he needed to stop it. But kidnapping Jem or any of the other women just wasn't going to cut it. As far as Dan was concerned this woman may as well have been his mate, at least until she flat out turned him down, and until then he couldn't do anything less than protect her. The problem was if he didn't figure out what to do to get her to join the Fenrir against Freya, she was also quite likely to be one of the tools used to destroy the Fenrir the next time Freya attacked. If that happened, loyalty to pack would come first for him, just like it came first for any wolf who wasn't mated. Even for mated Fenrir, the safety of the entire pack was of paramount importance, often having to come before the life of any single individual.

The thing was protecting Jem had suddenly become of paramount importance to Dan, but if his Dad gave him an Alpha command Dan would have had no choice but to do whatever his Father wanted. Whether he wanted to do it or not. That was just how it worked when you were part of a pack, and although he was an Alpha in his own right, and part of the Alpha family. He wasn't 'The' Alpha in control of the den.

Dan caught Jem's hand and stilled her frantic wiping "Calm down little dove it's only spilt coffee. I didn't even get any on me." He said.

He was impressed, he'd actually managed to hide

the note of disappointment from his voice. Her touching him was definitely not something he was likely to complain about.

Jem ignored him. "I'll get you another." she said, then spun around, attempting to go back into the shop, only to suddenly realise he still had hold of her hand. Dan smiled.

Jem felt her heart skip a beat as the guy smiled at her. He'd called her little dove, and it was kind of nice. Even if he was a perfect stranger. Not many people knew, but Jem was short for Jemima, and Jemima meant dove. Jem had a thing about names and their meanings. So she had obviously found out what hers meant. Maybe this guy was interested in the meaning of names too?

The guy's thumb started to trace a lazy trail along the back of Jem's hand, and suddenly all her senses were on high alert. Her skin was tingling, and he just seemed to be standing there with a satisfied smile plastered on his face.

Cocky guys usually made Jem angry, but with this guy, her heart was beating double time. Her hearing and sense of smell started going crazy. It was as though she could smell everything, and he smelt divine. Like sandalwood and a strong musk that made her feel like a swooning teenage girl. Her face flushed in embarrassment and she saw his nose twitch just slightly. He seemed to draw in a deep breath, and she could have sworn she'd even heard a low growl coming from his direction. She offered again to replace his coffee.

"Don't worry about it." he said pulling her in closer.

He was so tall and cute, and it was taking everything in her to fight the sudden urge to do something completely out of character, like give him a quick kiss. Heat rose to her cheeks and she dropped her head in embarrassment, realising she was considering kissing a perfect stranger in front of a cafe full of people. A stranger who was undoubtedly out of her league.

"Jemima Andrews!" Mrs. Grover admonished. "How crass! I thought you were moving these tables from in front of my store, not throwing yourself at your customers. If you're going to behave like a little harlot I'll have to speak with your employer. Maybe you'd find working in a brothel a more appropriate occupation."

Jem was so shocked at the accusation she didn't know what to say, then she felt the guy's body tense noticeable against hers. It was almost as though he were preparing to pounce. His grip tightened on Jem's hand and he spun around to face Mrs. Grover, pulling Jem behind him in an almost protective manner.

His jaw tensed angrily, and right when Jem was expecting him to lunge or yell at the unsuspecting Mrs. Grover he started speaking calmly to her.

"Good Afternoon. You must be Mrs. Grover the owner of the Florist. Jem here was just raving about your work. I understand you put together all the arrangements yourself? You have quite a talent." he said smiling.

He was all teeth and charm as he bent down to kiss Mrs. Grover's hand in a courtly fashion.

The old lady flushed pink, looking flustered as the incredibly sexy guy started talking to her as though they were close friends.

"I uh.." Mrs. Grover stuttered.

"I was actually about to say that it was a brilliant idea to have the cafe put their tables out in front of your store. I imagine a lot of people sit here looking in the window while having their meals then come in and buy your arrangements. I was actually considering purchasing a bouquet myself." He smiled. "How can I resist when they make such a strong statement from your window, and they smell just heavenly. You must have a real nose for scents." he said cocking his head in an inquisitive, almost animalistic manner.

Jem stepped away relieved to be out of the arms of this very attractive, cuddly stranger. She slipped her hand out of his and spun around while he spoke flirtatiously with the now blushing Mrs. Grover.

Goes to show she wasn't so special after all. If he could speak to Mrs. Grover like that, then he was probably just some skeezy guy trying to cop a feel. Or maybe he simply liked to flirt with everyone. Either way, Jem had better replace his coffee.

Rushing back inside the cafe, Jem slipped behind the front counter and quickly slid a cup under the coffee machine. Jewel gave her a look that in best friend speak loosely translated to 'What's going on? You're as red as a tomato and rushing around like a headless chicken'.

"I'll tell you after." Jem said rushing back through the crowd of people to the still incredibly sexy guy.

Apparently she hadn't been seeing things before. He was most definitely one of the hottest men she'd seen outside of the movies. As she approached she heard Mrs. Grover chatting animatedly to the guy about her great-nieces. Hope and Bree, who sometimes helped with her arrangements, and whom she'd 'LOVE' to introduce him to. An angry bubble of jealousy rose at the mention of the two girls, which was weird since Jem was really quite fond of both Hope and Bree, despite their Aunt. For some reason either of the very pretty young women, heck any pretty girl being anywhere near this guy made Jem want to beat someone senseless. She'd only been in the guy's presence for like two seconds, said about three words to him, and aside from trying to scald him with a boiling hot cup of coffee, barely even interacted with him at all. But for some reason, she was acting as though she owned him. Jem was actually becoming one of those crazy obsessive girls. Jewel was right. Jem had gone too long without a date. The whole waiting for the right guy thing was completely overrated. Was there even such a thing as the 'right' guy? Maybe if she was actually getting out and dating she wouldn't be having to fight to stop herself from jumping this guy right here and now. Jewel was right. Jem needed to take a leaf out of her book, and just find someone to have fun with. Get a little male attention before she turned into a crazy cat lady.

Jem placed the coffee cup carefully down on the table beside the guy, and then she made a break for it. She needed to get out of there as quickly as possible, before she did something to really embarrass herself. If Jem were honest she knew he was way out of her league. Jem may as well have been a potato for all the romantic appeal she would garner from him.

Jem swept past the outside tables, clearing them as quickly as humanly possible, and took all the dishes out the back. There was no way she was going back out there to make a fool of herself. If she had to she'd pay one of the others to let her stay out the back until he left.

"Please tell me you'll let me take over washing the dishes." Jem begged Marty as he wiped his sweaty forehead.

His face lit up. "Are you serious? Yes please! Yes. You're not messing with me are you Jem?" Then he looked at her downcast face. "What's wrong?" He demanded.

Jem forced a smile. "Nothing really. I was just an idiot that's all. I had a run-in with Mrs. Grover. Then nearly scalded a guy with boiling hot coffee. I just think it's time to do something out of sight for a bit."

Marty wiped his forehead again. "Babe. It's hot as Hades back here, are you sure you want to do the dishes? You're already looking a little pale on it."

"I haven't had a break yet." she admitted.

"Geez Jem. You're meant to have had morning tea and a lunch break by now!" he scolded.

"I know." Jem said. "Ginny quit, and Barb called in because one of her kids is sick, and she couldn't get a sitter. So I haven't had a chance."

"That's ridiculous Jem. I got my breaks. You can guarantee Jewel got hers. Go and take a lunch break, then if you're still masochistic enough to want to do the dishes I'll jump out front."

Jem nodded her head in relief, tapping her hand to her forehead in salute. "Yes Sir!"

"Just get your cute butt out the back to have some lunch before I change my mind" Marty laughed.

Oh my gosh, Jem moaned, this had to be the best chicken sandwich she'd ever eaten. Ever. She inhaled her lunch, jamming it into her mouth as though she hadn't eaten in days. She was shocked that by the time her mind had wandered back to the hot coffee guy, which was pretty much as soon as she sat on the back step of the cafe, her sandwich was more than half gone. Her stomach cramped painfully. Maybe she should have taken a little bit longer eating her sandwich. Chewed it or something.

Leaning back on her arms Jem stretched her bare legs out, hiking her knee-length black shorts up, exposing said legs to as much sunlight as she could. It was never going to make her pasty white legs brown, but all those experts went on and on about how good vitamin D was for mood and health, so she would do it. Besides, it felt nice. Needless to say, before Jem even had the chance to really enjoy the summer sun for more than five minutes Jewel burst out the back door squealing like a schoolgirl.

"Oh my goodness Jem! Where did you find him? Where can I get one of my own? Is he what the blushing was all about? You've just got to come and see!"

Jewel's high pitched, excited voice reminded Jem of a dozen dates they'd got ready for together, or talked about after the fact. Not to mention countless chick flick marathons comprised of loud singing and swooning over sexy actors.

Knowing someone since childhood should really make you immune to their emotions, but somehow, even after almost twenty years of knowing each other Jewel's excitement was as contagious as it had been at eight. Jewel was a regular ray of sunshine, and no amount of age or heartache had changed that.

Jem's shoulders bobbed up and down, as laughter shook her frame "What are you squealing about you dingbat?" she asked.

Jewel brushed Jem's teasing aside or ignored it completely. Grabbing her hand, Jewel yanked Jem to her feet. "Oh you have to come look!" she squealed.

"Hey!" Marty protested as Jem was dragged in the back door of the narrow hot kitchen. "There's no way Jem's finished her half-hour lunch break." He said checking his watch. "It hasn't even been fifteen minutes. Now get back out the front and leave Jem in peace." He scolded.

Jewel pouted, pushing her plump bottom lip out. "But Marty she has to come see!" she whined practically stamping her foot.

"See what?" He demanded.

Jewel sighed in a way that clearly announced she thought Marty sucked the fun out of everything. "Fine, spoil the surprise. It's just, the sexiest guy I have ever seen in my entire life just came up to the front counter and left you flowers." Jewel squealed.

"What guy?" Marty asked a little defensively.

Jewel rolled her eyes at him. "I told you. The sexiest guy I've ever seen. Ever." She grinned.

She turned to Jem the massive grin still on her face. "So spill. Who is he? Where did you meet him? If you don't want him can I have him? Oh my gosh Jem, he's so cute!"

Jem laughed. Trust Jewel to take a situation she had personally been feeling embarrassed about and making it into something fun.

"Wait. What? Did you say flowers?" Jem asked, "I never get flowers."

"You did todaaay." Jewel said in a sing-song voice.

Weird. Jem had never received flowers before. Not a single one of the guys who had decided to call themselves her boyfriend had ever even given her daisy from the grass, let alone actual flowers. To be fair the three or four guys she'd gone out with weren't really given a chance. The shortest of those relationships had lasted just a week, the longest six months.

Jem just didn't see the point in staying with a guy if it was obvious it would never work out. She was looking for forever. One of those, in sickness and in health, have a family, for richer or poorer, grow old together type relationships. While the guys she'd dated were looking for... Well, it involved coming together, just not in the long term sense, and that just wasn't her. She wasn't confident enough in her body to let just anyone see it, and then there was the whole spiritual aspect. No matter what the current culture suggested about sex, Jem believed that it was one of those things that was special. That you were linked to the people you had sex with, even if you were only with them the once. Besides, when it came to sexiness, Jem just didn't feel like she was. Most of the time she felt kind of frumpy. The guys she'd dated hadn't exactly helped with that. Once she had actually been told by a boyfriend, after seeing her in a swimsuit, that she 'wasn't as fat as people thought she was'. That was the quality of compliments she'd received from guys so far. Actually, when she'd told Jewel about that conversation her friend had been ready to track down and castrate the guy. Even now Jem wondered if Jewel had actually tracked him down and told him off because any time she saw him these days he made a super quick exit.

While Marty glowered by the sink and Jem contemplated what Jewel could possibly have done to her ex, Jewel bounced merrily from the room and came back carrying one of Mrs. Grover's largest and most expensive arrangements.

"Someone left these? For me? Are you sure?" Jem asked.

Disbelief radiated from Jem. People, guys, especially hot ones, did not leave her flowers. Tips, yes. Flowers, no. Jewel on the other hand. She positively dripped sex appeal. She had flirtation down to an art. She knew when to flip her hair. When to cock her hip. When to pout. When to giggle. Men fell all over themselves to have a chance to date her. People wouldn't realise it, heck Jem wouldn't know if they hadn't been besties, but even a girl as beautiful, charismatic, and seemingly confident as Jewel, doubted her appeal. From years of late-night conversations, Jem knew that Jewel questioned whether she would ever get a guy that wanted forever with her. She wanted the Cinderella dream, and so far all she'd had were toads in bad prince costumes.

Meanwhile, Jem usually seemed to be the recipient of the pity date. Whenever Jewel insisted she wanted to double, Jem would be forced to accompany her. She was always partnered with a friend of Jewel's date. On the few occasions Jem thought it had gone well and the guy had asked for her number, he had eventually called and spent the whole time chatting about Jewel. Wanting to know the best way to get her attention. More often than not the guy would be out on a date with Jewel a few weeks later, after drilling Jem for information, and sometimes ringing her while the two of them were dating to get advice. Jem was silly enough to let the guys do that to her, all the while dreamily wishing a guy would someday like her enough to do the same for her. Well, maybe not exactly the same. But the whole making an effort to find out what she liked thing was kind of nice.

Of course from watching the life cycle of Jewel's relationships, just because the guy went to the effort of finding out what Jewel liked didn't mean that the guy didn't lose interest, or that Jewel didn't. Jewel, though seemingly flighty, was just as perceptive as Jem when it came to boyfriends. The only difference was she was happy to subsidise her living costs by accepting a free meal out. While doing that just tended to make Jem feel guilty, she usually offered to go dutch rather than let the guy pay.

Jewel rolled her eyes again. "Of course I'm sure. They came with a card, and this." she grinned wriggling a small and expensive looking black cell phone back and forth in front of Jem's face.

"What kind of a crazy stalker gives someone a cell phone?" Marty exclaimed. "He's probably a serial killer, or someone who's going to use the GPS in the phone to follow you home."

Jewel fanned herself. "He can follow me home any day." She said with a sigh.

Taking the flowers, Jem read the card. Of course Jewel read it aloud over her shoulder.

"To my dear little dove. It was a delight to meet you. I hope to have the pleasure of your company again very soon, Though perhaps without spilling coffee. Yours truly, Daniel Lovell." She read in her best impression of a guy voice.

"Oh Jem, how romantic is that." Jewel gushed.

"That's creepy if you ask me." Marty said drying his hands on a tea towel and walking over.

Jewel poked her tongue at Marty. "So how did you meet him?" she asked.

FLOWERS AND PHONE CALLS

J em shifted uncomfortably. "He's just a customer." She answered.

A customer she wanted to jump and had jealous reactions about when someone started trying to set him up with their nieces.

"Sure he is." Jewel grinned.

"No really. I was shifting the tables because Mrs. Grover was ranting about them moving in front of the florist. Then I nearly tipped a hot cup of coffee all over him. Today is the first time I've ever seen him before. Really." Jem said.

"Are you serious?" Jewel looked a little bit confused.

"See." Marty said, "Creepy. He's probably nuts. You better not be walking home alone again Jem. He'll probably burst out from behind a bush and kill you or something. You should wait in the store for Jewel to finish and walk home together. Neither of you should be walking home alone anyway. There are crazy people all over the place."

"Gee Marty, way to bolster her confidence." Jewel said shaking her head at Marty, "Ignore Mr. party pooper over there. Jem, this Dan guy probably just saw what we see every day. That you're beautiful, smart, hard-working, amazing and to top it off can get him free coffee." Jewel said.

Jem laughed. "Yeah maybe."

"Take it as a win babe. It's not often a gorgeous guy gives a girl flowers like that just for being her, and you my dear deserve flowers." Jewel said.

"I'm not saying she doesn't." Marty huffed. "Just that if some guy you've never met buys you expensive flowers and leaves you a cell phone so he can ring you, be on your guard. Normal people don't do that kind of thing."

Jem couldn't disagree with that.

"Maybe he's loaded?" Jewel offered, then sighed. "Okay. Yeah. That is a bit weird. But still flattering."

The thing was, it wasn't unusual for customers to get Jewel flowers, or for them to ask her out on dates for that matter. Jewel was bubbly, happy, gorgeous. Jem sometimes felt a little less than when she was next to her. She couldn't figure out why the guys were interested in Jewel, but not her. Jem and Jewel actually looked quite similar. Both about five foot five, both blonde and blue-eyed, though Jewel kept her hair cut and coloured in whatever the current style may be. They were both friendly, both chatty, they were both fun to be around. Or at least Jem thought she was fun. Mostly. The biggest difference Jem could think of between the two of them was that maybe it was obvious Jem wanted forever, while Jewel could be mistaken for just wanting to have some fun. It didn't take a genius to realise the whole 'this chicks looking for marriage and babies' thing did have the ability to absolutely terrify a bulk of guys. Like they thought she was going to insist they marry her after the first date or something. While Jewel's naturally flirtatious manner attracted guys like bees to honey. The funny thing was, Jewel wanted forever just as much as Jem did. She just had one major ability Jem didn't. She knew how not to scare guys away. That, and she loved to go out and socialise. While as much as Jem liked people she was a lot happier to sit at home and paint, or read a book, or watch a movie. Maybe she really was boring after all.

"He was cute, wasn't he?" Jem said.

Okay, cute was putting it mildly. But Marty was being all disapproving and Jem didn't want to seem too keen. She didn't want to get her hopes up over something that she knew could never happen. Guys just weren't interested in her. They were interested in girls like Jewel. Fun girls.

"Are you serious? He was smoking hot!" Jewel said.

"Do you really think he was a serial killer or

something?" Jem asked.

"Yes." Marty said, at the exact time Jewel said. "No."

Jewel scowled at Marty. "He didn't look like a serial killer to me."

"Yeah cause you can tell a serial killer just by looking at him." Marty said rolling his eyes at Jewel, "Someone being hot doesn't mean they're not crazy. I mean look at you for example." He said, then started grinning at his joke.

Jewel took a second then twigged to what he was saying.

"Hey!" she said, hitting him half-heartedly. Marty had said Jewel was hot, so the compliment had removed at least some of her motivation to be truly angry at him.

Jem laughed as well earning herself a less than gentle smack from Jewel too.

"I'll show you crazy." Jewel growled snatching up the phone and dialling.

"What are you doing?" Jem asked apprehensively. "Who are you even ringing?"

"I'm calling Hotty McCoffee guy of course." She grinned evilly.

Jem didn't believe for a second Jewel would really ring. She hadn't believed it, and she had been mistaken. Cause the next minute the phone came flying Jem's way. She caught it without thinking and put it automatically up to her ear.

"Hello Daniel speaking." Came the voice on the other end.

'I'm going to kill you' Jem mouthed to Jewel, who was bounding gleefully back out to the front of the store.

Marty was frowning at her, so Jem quickly made her way to the little outside area behind the store again.

"Hello?" the voice sounded confused.

"Um. Hi?" She sounds like an idiot.

"Little Dove, it's you!" he said.

If nothing else he sounded pleased. She really hoped he wasn't some psycho killer after all.

"Yeah. It's me. Um, thanks for the flowers, they're beautiful." She said groaning inwardly, could she sound any lamer?

"I'm glad you like them." He said cheerily.

"You didn't have to. Get them for me that is. Thanking me for the coffee was plenty." That was brilliant, now she sounded ungrateful.

"How else would I get you to notice me?" He asked. "You were pretty focused on doing your job."

Had he never seen himself? Everybody who met him would notice him. How could they not?

"I guess... It's just... I don't get flowers. Ever. So I kind of wanted to make sure you're not some sexy psycho killer, who's going to lure me out on a date or something and then murder me."

"You think I'm sexy?" His voice was all male satisfaction.

If she could see him now, she didn't doubt he'd have a massive smile.

"I. What?" She asked.

Why had she said that? Saying a guy was sexy was something you said to your friends when the guy wasn't around. Not to the guy. What was wrong with her?

"You think I'm sexy?" He repeated.

"I also asked if you were a psycho killer." Jem said, at least trying to ignore the redirection to the sexy comment altogether.

He laughed. "I promise I would never hurt even a single hair on your head. But if you're worried you can invite your friend when we go out."

"What makes you think we're going to go out?" Jem asked, more than a little bit wary about why he would want Jewel to come along. There had been guys who had used that as a way to get in with Jewel in the past, and Jem had no intention of reliving that.

"I'm persistent, and apparently I'm sexy?" he sounded a little uncertain this time.

"Are you just?" she said, unable to keep the amusement from her tone.

The smile was back in his voice. "I am. So tonight?"

"I." tonight? "No, not tonight. I'm on the late shift. Actually, I'm working all day. I don't finish till six. There's no way I could be ready in time. I'd have to get home and have a shower or I'd smell awful. Like grease, coffee, and dish wash liquid." She said.

Besides if she took Jewel along to make sure he

wasn't actually crazy, then she was going to need to dress up or she'd be ignored completely. That and smelling like garlic butter had to be a first date no-no.

"You smelt alright to me." he said simply.

"Give me a few hours. It gets hot in the kitchen, and there's only so much deodorant can do before it's stink city." She said.

Oh good grief, had she just said stink city? Did she want to put this guy off before they even got started?

He laughed again. "Well then Jem. When would you like to have dinner? Or would a different meal be better?"

Maybe he really was keen?

"Dinner is good. Friday? Would Friday be okay?" She asked.

She couldn't believe she was accepting a date with him, all she could hope for at this point was that she didn't sound desperate.

"Great. I'll book us a table somewhere. Any requests?" He asked.

"No. Anything's good. Wait, do you have someone my friend can go with? Like a double date?" Jem asked.

"I'll see what I can organise." He said, "Hey, Jem?"

"Mhm." She said.

"Feel free to call me anytime." He said, and she would have sworn she could hear his smile.

"Okay. Thanks. Bye." She said, sounding like an idiot, at least to her ears.

"See you Friday, little dove." He said.

The phone went dead. Now Jem needed to check that she could get the afternoon she'd agreed to off, that and check if Jewel was keen.

"Are you serious?!" Jewel squealed. "Yes. Hell yes! He's got a date for me?" She said.

"He only said he'd try to get you a date. He didn't exactly guarantee he could get you one." Jem said trying to tamper down Jewel's enthusiasm just a fraction. She didn't want to be on the receiving end of Jewel's disappointment if Daniel didn't come through.

"Oh, I hope his friend is as hot as he is. If he is, I'll buy you lunch. For a week." Jewel enthused, completely ignoring Jem's attempts to calm her enthusiasm down.

"Generous Jewel." Jem said laughing.

Jewel looked at her funny.

"Jenny lets us have free lunches at work remember." She said.

"Oh. Right. Well, I'll pay for your dinner and movie next girls night." Jewel said, solemnly crossing her hand over her heart.

Jem laughed. "You're on."

"I can't believe you've agreed to go out with this guy Jem. He could be a nut job or something!" Marty groused carrying a tray of empty cups out back.

"I'll have Jewel with me." Jem said, sounding more than a little defensive.

"Yeah and he's bringing a friend. You two are about as tough as a pair of kittens. What if they're both crazy? They might just snatch you both up or something." He warned.

"If you're so worried why don't you come along

too?" Jem offered.

Surely Dan wouldn't care if she invited someone else. Would he?

"No thanks." Marty grumbled.

"Well if you're not going to insist on coming along then you can't be all that worried, can you?" Jewel announced, sashaying past the two of them with a tray of food and coffee.

"I think you're just jealous. If you wanted to go out with Jem so badly, you should have asked her before anyone else did." Jewel said staring purposefully at him.

Marty stood there his mouth ajar and turned beet red.

Jem hadn't even realised that Marty was interested in her, but couldn't help but wonder if it was true going by the amused look on her boss Jenny's face, who had clearly heard the comment from the front of the store when Jem had opened the door between the kitchen, and the horrified look on Marty's. Apparently Jem was the only one who was completely unaware that Marty liked her.

"Oh, there you are Jemima dear!" Mrs. Grover exclaimed rushing up to the front counter right as Jem stepped out of the kitchen.

For once not only was the older woman's voice friendly, but her entire demeanour was pleasant, and she was directing all her focus on Jem.

"I'm sorry Mrs. Grover. Have the table's shifted again? I'll go out and move them." Jem said, all the while praying Jenny would step in and defend her.

"Oh don't be silly my dear. I'll talk to Jenny about that soon enough. I have so many ideas. So many plans, and all thanks to the encouragement of your young gentleman. Oh, my dear. That Daniel Lovell. He is just wonderful." She smiled.

Jem had never seen Mrs. Grover so enthusiastic about anyone other than her great-nieces. She almost seemed like an entirely different person. Happiness just made her seem younger somehow.

"Did you get the flowers?" Mrs. Grover asked looking up and down the front counter.

Jem blushed. "Oh, yes."

Mrs. Grover didn't wait for Jem to continue.

"Weren't they beautiful?" she said. "He even brought my most expensive bouquet. Lovely boy. Lovely lovely boy."

"They were beautiful, thank you Mrs. Grover." Jem said.

She couldn't figure out where this conversation was going? Was this some kind of trap? Why was Mrs. Grover being so nice to her?

"Oh call me Rosemary, please. You're a lovely girl. Oh, Jenny, you're there. I want to talk to you about adding some windows between our stores and maybe putting your tables permanently in front of my shop. We could even set up some loyalty cards between our stores." Mrs. Grover… Rosemary gushed.

Jenny looked as shocked as Jem felt. Mrs. Grover was usually caustic towards the staff at Coughee, to say the least, but something had brought around a change in the woman, or maybe someone? Though what Daniel Lovell could have possibly said to bring about this kind of change was completely beyond Jem.

"Oh. Of course Rosemary. How about we go to my office and we'll talk logistics." Jenny said, sending Jem a stunned look.

Jenny led the radiant Rosemary Grover out back to her office, and Jem questioned if she had passed out from lack of food and was currently unconscious. Or maybe she'd entered the twilight zone. What else would explain the unprecedented change in both Mrs. Grover and in Jem's dating life? Maybe she had died or something?

An hour later Rosemary left the cafe and went back to her own store, where she presumably was making phone calls to builders and card printers to get her new plans underway.

"I don't know how you did it." Jenny exclaimed once Rosemary was safely inside the florist, "But that woman suddenly thinks the sun shines out your... well yeah. It's safe to say she thinks you're wonderful. You wouldn't believe what she wants to do. She wants to pull out the walls between our two stores, display her bouquets in here at no charge to us. Advertise for us in her store. Give coffee vouchers to her customers.

Offer discounts on her bouquets for anyone who is recommended from here and has proof of purchase. Her ideas could increase the sales of both our stores. It's brilliant. I really don't know what you did but don't stop doing it. That's the longest I've seen that woman smile since I set up shop here. I thought her teeth might fall out she was smiling so much." Jenny said.

"It wasn't me. I mean I didn't do anything." Jem said.

Nothing except stand next to her when she met Dan. What was with this guy that he could weave people under his spell so easily. Maybe Marty was right, what if he was a creep? Or what if he was dangerous? Maybe going out on a date with him wasn't a good idea after all.

Jem took a deep breath. She hadn't been on a date in forever, and for the first time in what felt like forever, she actually wanted to go out with someone. Which meant she needed to strike while the iron was hot, and if nothing else right now Jenny's good mood was a way for Jem to get off early Friday. Dan might have been a creep. But it was also possible that he was just an incredibly hot, charismatic guy, who just happened to like her, and Jem was going to give him a chance.

The day and a half before their date went quickly. Especially since Dan called the night before. From what he'd told her he'd had to travel home to see his parents about something. But he promised he'd be back and waiting at her front doorstep on Friday to take her and Jewel out, along with his friend Gerard. Jem had insisted he meet them at the restaurant, after all, he could still be a psycho killer. Also, he was still in the process of convincing Gerard to come. Dan told her his friend worked in some kind of security job and getting time off was almost impossible. Then he'd laughed and explained that Gerard worked for Andrew, one of his six (yes six!) older brother's. Andrew and Dan didn't really get on that well. He wasn't sure why. Maybe because they were both so competitive, or because Andrew was obsessive about getting everything perfect. Dan admitted to her that he tended to fly by the seat of his pants most of the time, and he knew it irked Andrew that despite his lack of planning things still tended to work out for him. Jem enjoyed chatting with Dan so much. She loved his voice and hearing about his family. She loved how he was interested in her, and especially how he didn't ask a single question about Jewel aside from discussions about getting her and Gerard together. By the time Friday finally rolled around Jem was in an excited flap about the date, and so was Jewel. Marty was much less enthusiastic.

Jem was gone and her scent had gone with her. Dan was positively seething that this florist woman had come along and ruined what had, in his opinion, been a rather successful first meeting with his mate. The old woman was the picture of feminine elegance. She actually reminded him of some of the older women from the den, which was rarer and rarer in town. Her hair was in a perfectly styled plait, that she'd rolled into a bun on top of her head. Her make up was bold, but tasteful. Between how she made herself up and what she wore, Mrs. Grover was a well put together lady, and Dan found himself thinking how getting angry at the woman was probably the most counterproductive thing he could do, even if that was how he felt. His best option was going to be being polite, treat her like a lady, and get her on his side. Some people were much better on your side than standing against you. Or in this case, standing against Jem.

After the florist had moved her focus from Jem to him, Dan had stood and listened patiently as she spoke about her great-nieces. Two girls who he was sure were lovely, but he had no interest whatsoever in meeting. He'd set his sights on Jem, and no one else would do. He was glad just standing and listening had taken the woman's hostile attention away from Jem, and if that was all he could do to protect Jem then he would listen to the woman go on about her nieces all day if he had too. Besides, in standing and listening to the woman he'd received the satisfaction of seeing Jem bristle when she returned with a fresh coffee and heard the woman mention the other girls. She was clearly jealous, and you only got jealous if you were interested in someone. Which meant she was interested in him.

"Mrs. Grover. Your shop, like your work, is Divine. But you really could benefit from placing some of your work in the cafe next door. Perhaps you could come to a mutually beneficial agreement with the cafe owner. Advertise for each other." He suggested.

Without realising he was doing it, a thread of alpha command slipped into his voice. With his Father being pack Alpha Dan had unsurprisingly been born with that same alpha potential. But with six older brothers and a younger sister, all with an alpha potential of their own he was unlikely to ever become the pack Alpha. So the ability, up until now, had been latent. Strange that it would make itself useful now. It was common knowledge that an alpha command didn't work unless the person you were speaking to was Fenrir, so the fact that his wolf had pushed his words out as an alpha command was odd. He was even more shocked when Mrs. Grover's eyes paled just slightly. Apparently Dan's wolf had picked up on something he hadn't. He sniffed the air. She definitely wasn't Fenrir, she didn't have the right scent, but given her nodding and her obvious desire to please him, not to mention the partial shift of her eyes, it was possible, if not likely, that one of her parents or grandparents had been a fully shifting Fenrir. It was rare to hear about pack member who had mated a human, but it did happen. Those pack members and their descendants were usually lost, and apparently, the ability to shift was lost eventually as well. He'd have to mention this all to his Father. If this woman was a non-shifting Fenrir there could be dozens more out there like her. It could also explain why her bouquets were so good. They weren't just beautiful, the scent combinations were also rather compelling. But whatever her Fenrir status was, it appeared she was completely unaware of it. If she had been aware, then there was no doubt in his mind that she would have known exactly what he was, and it was clear she didn't.

"Your scent combinations are wonderful." he acknowledged.

She glowed at the praise. "Why thank you..."

"Daniel." He said.

"Daniel." she repeated with a smile, "If you think I'm good, you should see what my niece Bree has come up with. That girl has real talent. She's only seventeen and she makes her own perfumes, soaps, shampoos. I'm trying to encourage her mother to let me pay for her to go to cosmetology school. Such talent. She could have her own line of scent and beauty products before twenty if she applied herself." Mrs. Grover gushed.

"Well. Mrs. Grover." He said.

"Oh, Rosemary please." she blushed.

"Of course. Rosemary. I would love to buy one of your bouquets. I think I need to thank that barista, Jem, for introducing us." He said.

"Oh yes." she gushed "Lovely girl. So hardworking, and always so polite. She gets on nicely with my nieces too. Such a good girl." She said.

He could have laughed at the woman's backpedaling. It'd been clear from watching her interacting with Jem earlier that she was not fussed on Jem at all. But now, as she worked to put together a spectacular arrangement, she shared every tidbit she knew about Jem. Both he and his wolf hung on her every word, greedy to garner any information they could about the woman they were almost convinced was their mate. By the time Rosemary was done talking, Dan was presented with an incredibly beautiful arrangement of lilies, lupins, roses, and carnations. It was truly a masterpiece. He paid the extravagant price, with a smile, even throwing in a little extra for the small card featuring a dove.

"Thank you Rosemary. Your work is beyond compare." He said kissing the blushing woman on the cheek. "I think I'll deliver these right now." He said.

"What a lovely idea. How romantic. Jemima is

very lucky. Very lucky indeed." She said, "If only I could find a young man like you for my nieces." she gushed "Oh and I really should talk to Jenny about those tables. Yes having them in front of my window may just increase my sales. I may even look at putting windows against the side of the building so Jenny's customers will be able to see more of my work."

Rosemary continued talking to herself about her new business ideas while Dan carried the flowers into the cafe. The scents of sweet pastries, coffee, and fresh bread assailed his senses along with the normal human smells. Of course, it was Jem's unique perfume that he was focused on. She wasn't out the front, she must have been in the kitchen, but she was close, and that thrilled him. A perky blonde barista greeted him at the front counter. She was pretty, and she seemed to be aware of that fact.

"Welcome to Cough ee. Can I help you?" she smiled as she looked at the flowers he held expectantly.

It seemed as though perfect strangers brought flowers into the cafe regularly. His wolf growled at the thought of other males attempting to stake a claim on his Jem. Though he had a feeling that Jewel, or so her badge named her, was the one used to receiving flowers, and not her co-worker.

"Actually. Yes." he returned her smile.

Flicking her straight blonde hair over her

shoulder, she leaned forward onto the counter accentuating her small chest.

"Whatever you want." She said, her smile was all invitation.

"I'd like to give these flowers to Jem if that's possible." He said looking her in the eyes and smiling.

He ignored the way she reeled back in shock. Apparently, Jem didn't get flowers often after all. If ever. He couldn't say he was upset about that fact, and his wolf was equally pleased. After only a moment's hesitation, a radiant smile lit up Jewel's face.

"Jem. My Jem." The girl was beaming.

He'd been expecting jealousy, but this girl was pleased, beyond pleased that Jem was the one getting flowers.

"I can't wait to tell her." Jewel exclaimed reaching out for the flowers excitedly.

"I was hoping to give them to her myself." he crooned, not letting go of the bouquet.

Smiling and twirling her poker-straight hair around her finger. "Sorry cutie, but she's on her break. I promise I'll pass these on though." She said pulling the bouquet a little harder towards herself.

She seemed genuine, but Dan wasn't going to chance Jem not getting his message "Give her this too." He said handing over his emergency burner phone.

Her smile and eyes widened. "Of course."

He turned to leave with a, "Thank you." and a wave.

"Your welcome. Oh. Wait! Here." she thrust a large muffin his way. "It was so nice to meet you." She said.

"And you." Dan smiled.

Now he just had to let his Dad know what had happened. Which was going to be that much harder without his phone.

UNDER A SPELL

The motel where Dan was staying in the small town of Ivaldi was wonderfully close to the cafe. When Dan looked out the window of his room he could actually see the cafe. He was really hoping that meant he would at least catch a glimpse of Jem throughout the day. The room, of course, had been chosen for its tactical advantage. The whole point had been that then he would be able to track the movements of his target before he grabbed her. When he thought about what he'd been planning to do to Jem, he actually felt like a bit of a creep. If he hadn't met her and realised she could potentially be his mate, he would have thought nothing of just grabbing her and taking her back to the Lovell den. What kind of person just grabbed somebody like that? He and his family hadn't even considered simply talking to her. Convincing her not to join Freya. Or even finding out if she'd been contacted by the Aesir Queen yet. Their whole focus had only been on preventing Freya from gathering her army. They'd forgotten that the women Freya had been recruiting were people, not just Valkyrie.

Granted grabbing Jemima had seemed a necessary evil when his Dad had sent him to get her. The pack was under a lot of stress. Fenrir were going missing or being attacked whenever they left pack lands these days. The only blessings they had encountered were that Freya and her Einherjar hadn't figured out how to locate any of the Fenrir dens so far. The fact that they were yet to be discovered was apparently thanks to a spell performed by the Dwarves back when the pack lands were first founded. The only thing was, the spell was starting to wear thin. It would only be a matter of time before it collapsed entirely, then Freya and her people would no doubt track the Fenrir down and eradicate them all.

Freya had spent the last five hundred years recruiting the descendants of her original Valkyrie. Not all of them of course, just the select few female descendants that had special gifts. Gifts passed down from mother to daughter. Gifts that allowed them, with the right tools and training, to not only have the ability to shift into swans but also to play a role as gifted warriors, healers, negotiators and magic wielders. The Fenrir couldn't afford for Freya's army to grow any larger. She had already collected many of her Valkyrie's gifted descendants, and the ranks of her Einherjar were swelling with each generation, with each human war. If she gathered any more there would be no hope for the Fenrir. When Freya and her war descended upon the world it would be a slaughter, and there was no doubt her first port of call would be to eradicate the Fenrir.

The day was close at hand, every Fenrir could smell war on the horizon. The winds of change had turned. It wouldn't be long before Freya made a real attempt at destroying them. But they wouldn't allow her to succeed. Not without a fight.

No Fenrir knew why Freya or Freyr hated them so much, but the brother and sister team they had dubbed 'the witch twins' had been after them ever since they discovered the existence of the Fenrir over two thousand years ago.

Dan was sitting at his desk preparing to video conference his father when his phone rang.

Strangely the call was blocked, no-one had this number. No-one except his Dad, and now Jemima.

"Hello Daniel speaking." He answered.

He could hear somebody fumbling with the phone.

"Hello?" he said.

Maybe it was a prank call after all?

His heart started beating double time when he heard a voice he instantly recognised as Jemima's greet him. He automatically looked out the window and over to the cafe searching for her, she wasn't outside. His reaction to her was embarrassingly enthusiastic. He needed to tone it down, he couldn't sound too pleased to get her call, he didn't want to scare her off.

She quickly thanked him for the flowers. Dan smiled, thank the Creator she liked them. He decided right then and there that he would bring her flowers every day if it made her happy.

Jem was clearly nervous. She insisted on trying to convince him that he didn't really want her. If she only knew just how much he did. With her every word Dan's heart swelled and his confidence grew. When she accidentally admitted that she found him sexy Dan had to push down the desire to simply run back to the cafe and claim her as his mate. As it was he teased her gently, using humour in an attempt to diffuse her obvious embarrassment. He loved that she found him attractive, especially since he thought she was gorgeous. He would have happily admitted this fact to her, only he had the distinct feeling that coming out and saying it wouldn't achieve anything positive. It would probably just freak Jem out. She could be one of those girls who just wouldn't believe him no matter how many times he told her she was attractive, so until he knew her a bit better he was going to make it into a bit of a joke.

His attempt at humour fell flat, and Jem's tone became a lot more serious. Maybe joking hadn't been a good idea after all. Clearly, he didn't have the skills boasted by Ben and Bobbie. He did the only thing he could do, he turned serious. Went into problem-solving mode. Safety in numbers seemed like the best option. If it made her more comfortable he would encourage her to bring her friend. He would much rather have been alone with her, but if having someone else around would make her feel safer, then he would just cope with that. He'd put up with almost anything if it meant he got to be around her.

As soon as he made the suggestion he could sense her agitation increasing. Now when she spoke to him she sounded even less happy. How could he be screwing this up so badly? He'd never had issues with women before. Of course, he'd never really invested any time in women, when he had it was strictly as friends, and exclusively within his pack. He had been led to believe that he could be quite charming, but maybe he wasn't. Maybe she really didn't want to go out with him.

He was running out of options and so he stuck with honestly, lacing it with humour once again while trying desperately to sound funny rather than creepy.

She seemed to perk up, and Dan released a sigh of relief. It was hard to tell if she was interested in him or not, which hurt his pride just a little. But even with hurt pride, he knew he'd ask her out as many times as it took until she agreed.

He was actually surprised when she agreed to

have a meal with him, even more so when she admitted the main reason she refused to go out tonight was because she was worried about smelling bad. He didn't say it out loud, but he knew he would willingly take her any way he could get her. He didn't care if she was covered in coffee. He'd take Jem out any day of the week. He'd take her out and he'd be proud of it. Nothing short of an Alpha command would prevent him from spending time with this woman. Even the prospect of finding a date for Jem's friend wouldn't stop him from accepting their date. He hadn't actually considered a double date. Of course, he hadn't really thought about someone else being there with them. Surely he could find somebody though. One of his brothers maybe? He had six, so it wasn't like there was a shortage. Then again he'd met Jewel and she would chew his brothers up and spit them out. Either that or one of those idiots would embarrass him in front of Jemima, and he didn't want or need that. Plus what if they fell for her? Sure it was unlikely. But there was no way he was taking that chance. Gerard might be keen to take out Jewel though, he could certainly use someone fun in his life. Gerard could be far too serious at times. It always struck Dan as odd that Gerard seemed to want a serious, dominant kind of mate. Dan had always thought he needed someone a bit more like Jem's friend Jewel. Someone happy, friendly, flirty. Someone who would challenge him to see more than just the rules and the job. Someone who would make him have fun.

He couldn't stop smiling after she said goodbye, he was so glad she had called, and let her know she could call him any time. He wouldn't care if she called him at midnight, he would talk to her whenever she was willing. For now, he was just excited that she'd agreed to date him. Friday couldn't come soon enough.

Dan hung the phone up quickly. He wasn't going to give Jemima a chance to talk herself out of going out with him. This date was going to happen.

All he had to do now was ask Gerard to come along so that Jewel had a date too. That and fill his Dad in on what had happened with the whole kidnapping a Valkyrie thing.

How did you even start to explain this situation? That instead of capturing the Valkyrie, you asked her out on a date.

The phone vibrated in his hand again. It was yet another blocked number? He grinned. Maybe she was calling back again? She'd better not be trying to cancel. There was no way he was going to let that happen.

"Calling so soon." He said, laughter in his voice.

"What do you mean calling so soon? You were meant to make contact over an hour ago!" Drew exclaimed.

Drew was not happy. He probably even had one of his rants all prepared.

"What the heck is going on there? You better have a good reason for not calling!" He ranted.

Just brilliant, Drew was building into his patented 'you're so irresponsible' tirades, fantastic.

"Yeah thanks Drew. I'm fine. Safe and sound. Haven't been captured by any crazed Aesir gods or anything." Dan said sarcastically, knowing that this tact was the last thing that was going to calm his brother down.

Drew paused. "Did you have trouble?"

"No but…"

"You had no trouble. So what kept you from ringing on time? Did you even find the Valkyrie?" He demanded.

Dan had most definitely found her.

"Yeah I found her." He said.

"Good. So when are you bringing her back to the den?"

"About that." He started.

"Please tell me you got her?" annoyance leached into Drew's voice.

"Not yet. There was a complication."

The line went dead.

"Drew? Drew?!"

What a dick. He hadn't even waited to hear what had happened. Well, Dan wasn't going to call him back, it was probably better to just conference Dad anyway, find out what he thought Dan should do.

The ring of the video conference trilled then

clicked off as someone answered the call. The screen flickered and then there was Nicolai, Dan's tech-savvy brother, staring at him on the screen. "Hey Daniel. Give me a sec, I'll just conference you in with Dad." He said.

"Thanks Nick." Dan said.

Nick smiled, he wasn't much for face to face. He was amazing with his tech stuff though. Working with technology was the one place Nicolai seemed to be confident, if it weren't for him Dan doubted the den would have power or technology of any kind.

The screen flickered again, and there was Dad. He was flanked, as per usual, by Thomas, Dan's eldest brother. Drew was suspiciously absent. Dan was going to take it as a win. If Drew was there it would just dissolve into a 'rage at Dan' call.

"Are you alright Daniel?" his Dad asked.

"Yeah. I'm okay." He answered, and this time he knew not to tease.

"You're late. Your Mum and I were starting to get worried. You know she'd kill me if her baby boy became the newest wolf to go missing." Dad said.

Dan laughed. "You know I'm too fast for Freya and her idiot Aesir." He laughed.

Thomas laughed, but Dad didn't look as amused. Thomas had always been Dan's favourite brother, and it's not like he had a shortage of them being the youngest male of seven. He was forever thankful that he was given a younger sister. It meant he didn't end up being the baby, and all the protective energy of his brothers fell on Peta rather than him. He did feel a bit sorry for Peta with that at times though. If she ever found a prospective mate they were all going to ride the guy so hard he'd likely run away screaming.

"So what happened. Why did you take so long to contact us?" Dad asked.

"I found her." He said, meaning his mate rather than the Valkyrie, though they were one and the same.

"Of course you did. We tracked the genealogy and told you exactly where this Jemima Andrews was." Dad said.

"No Dad. I found her. I found my mate." Dan clarified.

"There are Fenrir in Ivaldi?" Thomas asked. "Which pack is she from?"

"Um. No. Actually. It's Jemima. She's my mate." Dan said pushing his hair back, even though it wasn't actually in his face.

"The Valkyrie? Impossible." Dad frowned.

"I'm just telling you what my wolf is telling me, and as far as he's concerned she's our mate. Dad. She's the only female my wolf has reacted to. Ever. And that's not all I found either. While I was out today I found an un-shifting Fenrir."

Both Thomas and Dad's eyes shot wide open in shock.

"Are you sure?" Dad asked.

"She reacted to an alpha command. Her eyes even

attempted a shift." Dan said.

There was that, and then there were her scent combinations, there was no way they were the work of a plain human.

"You gave her an Alpha command?" Thomas asked.

"Not intentionally. That little surprise was thanks to my wolf." Dan said.

"Dan I need you to come home." Dad said.

"I can't. I have a date with her on Friday."

Dan's Dad's entire demeanour suddenly changed. "Come home now Dan." He commanded, and it wasn't just a Dad telling you what to do kind of command. It was an Alpha command. Dan had no choice, he'd be going home whether he wanted to or not.

"But." Dan disagreed.

"She could be manipulating you. We need to make sure nothing else is going on." Dad said, this time without the alpha command behind it.

"But Dad." He disagreed again.

"We'll talk about it when you get home." Dad said.

Dan had no choice. He was going home. He'd be back though, and by Friday, with a date for Jewel so Jem would be at ease. Then somehow he'd convince her that she was meant to be his mate.

The drive back to the den was uneventful and slow. But that was mostly because Dan spent the entire drive wanting to be in Ivaldi where he could convince Jem to go on a date with him sooner than Friday. Like right that second. He was almost bored the trip was so slow. He didn't meet any pack mates on the way, and he didn't see any of Freya's cronies. It was simple. He even drove straight into the den garage, and there was no welcoming committee. Which wasn't unusual since he was always coming and going. He had noticed Jaime, one of Drew's security team, as he drove in though. Jaime waved at Dan from his watch position before speaking into his walkie and letting the team and Dan's Dad know that he was back.

Dan left his bag in the car and made his way back to his family's home in the housing wing. He wasn't intending on staying long, now that he'd found Jem, he intended on convincing her that she and he were a good match, mates even. He was going to do whatever it took, he and his wolf were in total agreement about that.

"Dan!" his Mum exclaimed as he walked into the lounge.

She was sitting down for her afternoon cup of tea, and his sister Peta seemed to be working at the table on something with photos. That girl was crazy about her photo boards, every member of the family had one. Though now that he thought about it he realised she hadn't made any for friends in quite a while.

"Hey Mum. Hey Peta. Dad around?" He asked.

"He's with Drew. I think they found another Valkyrie." Peta said looking up from her board.

Dan pointed to the conference room. "In there?"

Mum nodded. "They shouldn't be long."

Dan knew that her comment was a hint for him to wait. Of course, it didn't stop him from just waltzing right in. He had never been one for respecting his Dad's private meetings. Besides, he was the one tasked with tracking and capturing the Valkyrie's, he should be in on the meeting.

The moment Dan walked in the room Drew spun around and glared at him. Dad and Thomas smiled.

He really couldn't figure out what Drew's problem was.

"Hey Dad. Thomas. Grumpy." Dan said.

Drew growled.

"Why did you order me to come home Dad? I found her. I'll get her. It'll just take a little bit longer. I'm not going to just snatch her when she's potentially my mate." He said.

Drew's face suddenly went pale. "What did you say?"

"The Valkyrie. She's my mate. At least she's the only female my wolf has ever taken an interest in. Why?"

The room suddenly went very quiet.

"You can't mate a Valkyrie Dan." Thomas said.

"Yes I can. As long as she accepts me that's

exactly what I plan on doing." Dan said.

He'd even leave his pack and live out in the human world if that's what she wanted.

"It has to be a trick or a spell. Freya must have gotten to her already." Drew said, ignoring Dan and speaking directly to their Dad.

"No Fenrir has taken a mate outside of the four packs in thousands of years. Not since the first Fenrir took their mates." Dad said.

"Well now I know that's not true. Like I told you earlier, the Florist in Ivaldi, Rosemary Grover. She was definitely Fenrir, or at least part Fenrir. There could be dozens more out there like her." Dan said.

It was so frustrating telling them this information over and over again. It was almost like they hadn't listened to a single word he'd said when he called them.

"We're going to need to confirm that information Dan. For now I want you to stay home. We'll check a few things before you go out there again. In the meantime I want you to go to the infirmary and get checked out." Dad said.

"What? Why? There's nothing wrong with me." Dan said in frustration.

All three of them watched Dan cautiously. Clearly they thought there was actually something wrong with him.

"I'm fine, and I need to get back to Jem." He said shaking off the minor Alpha command.

"I can't let you do that Dan. If this is a trap I'm not

going to just let you walk into it, and if it's not, well, if Freya has come up with some way to trick our wolves, we need to know." Dad said.

"But if she is my mate I need to have a chance to win her." Dan said.

His Dad and brothers shot each other a look that made Dan feel uneasy.

"This isn't a spell, and it's not an illness. There's nothing wrong with me." He said, starting to get angry.

"That may be the case. But we need to get it checked out all the same Dan. What if there is something wrong? We need to protect the pack. If you're wrong about the Valkyrie, then you could be wrong about the florist too. Freya has been much more active lately. We don't have any idea what she's got up her sleeve. All we know is that it's not good for us. She's preparing for something. Whatever it is, it's coming soon and all Fenrir are going to suffer for it." Thomas said.

"Fine. I'll get checked out. But I'm telling you now there's nothing wrong with me, and as soon as I finish up at the medical wing I'm calling her." He said.

"You can't tell her about us. About any of this." Drew snapped.

Dan rolled his eyes. "I'm hardly going to share any of this with her. Not before I know she's actually my mate, or that she can cope with it. At this stage she'd probably think I was nuts if I started going on about a race of shape-shifting wolf people."

"That's fine. Just don't tell her anything you don't need to. Protecting the den needs to come first." Dad said, and that was his last word, which meant the conversation was over.

Dan made his way to the infirmary. He couldn't figure out what his family's problem was. Yeah, he was acting a little obsessive. But to be fair, every Fenrir male he'd ever seen who'd met their mate, or even a potential one, acted a little bit obsessive. Especially once the female agreed to court them. Of course, Jem wasn't a Fenrir female, and she'd only agreed to go on a date with him, not to court him. But his wolf thought the two words were basically interchangeable. So as far as he was concerned it meant she was considering him, and that was nothing if not a step in the right direction. A step towards her agreeing to become his mate.

"Hello Daniel. Long time no see young man. Where have you been? I've missed having you over at my house." Hazel, Gerard's Mum, and the head doctor in the den said, pulling him into an enthusiastic hug. "Gerard's been acting all mopey without you around. Such a shame you're on different teams."

Dan laughed. "I don't think Drew thought he could trust Gerard and me to actually pay attention to our jobs if we were together. He thinks we cause trouble or something."

Hazel laughed "I wonder where he could have possibly gotten that idea from?" she said.

"I know right!" Dan laughed "ridiculous. Gerard and I are completely responsible."

Hazel laughed louder. "Of course you are dear. Now how can I help you today?"

"I met my mate today, but Dad, Thomas and Drew think it's some kind of trick, care of Freya." He said shrugging.

Hazel frowned. "Why would they think that? And how could you meet your mate, weren't you out of the den collecting one of the Valkyrie's?" she asked.

"That's why they think there's something wrong. My mate. She's the Valkyrie." He said.

"Oh. Oh my. Well. Okay. I'll give you the complete run down then. Though if it's a spell I don't know how they think I'm going to be able to tell." Hazel said, sounding worried.

"It's not a spell Hazel. She's my mate. I can tell. She just doesn't know it yet. Actually, I've set up a double date with her, and her friend Jewel. I was hoping Gerard would be my wingman on this one. You don't know where he is, do you? I'll need to ask him before he gets roped into doing anything else for Drew." He said.

It was almost as though Drew had been actively trying to keep Gerard and Dan away from each other ever since he became security head. It wasn't even like the two of them were that bad when they were together, well, except for that time when they decided to run the perimeter of the den without letting anyone know and they fell down that ledge. That was not the best. If Drew hadn't been keeping an eye on them, and how long they'd been gone they could have easily been in big trouble.

"Sorry Daniel I don't. He'll be around somewhere. Andrew's been having him track down some of the rogues. A few of them have gotten a little bit dangerous so he's been having to keep an eye on them." Hazel said pulling out some of her equipment. "Gerard's been absolutely shattered from all the running he's been doing."

Hazel spent the next hour asking Dan inane questions, poking and prodding him, and just generally making sure he was healthy. She even got him to shift and tested everything while he was in wolf form. Then she made him stick around while she tested his blood.

"Well Daniel. From a medical standpoint, you're fine." Hazel said, "You do seem to have higher testosterone levels than normal, but if you have met your mate it's not surprising."

"I did tell you I was fine." He said.

"The thing is Daniel, it's unusual for a Fenrir to react to a non-Fenrir." Hazel said frowning, "There really could be a magical component that I don't have the skills to check." She said.

"Hazel I'm fine." Dan said shaking his head in frustration.

He couldn't wrap his head around why everyone wanted to believe there was something wrong with him. Granted he was a little preoccupied with the idea of getting back to Jem, but otherwise he was just the same as he'd always been.

Hazel let him leave reluctantly. But only after

he promised to come and have dinner with her and Gerard soon, insisting she missed having her boys around. He wished he could be having dinner with them tonight. Dinner with Hazel and Gerard would have been relaxed. Meanwhile, he had to have dinner with his family. It was tense to say the least, at least to begin with. It was the first time in what seemed like forever that they had eaten as an entire family. They all knew what was going on with Dan, and they all thought there had to be something wrong with him. Like he was under some kind of spell or something. This was despite him insisting he was fine. Still, the whole awkward 'they didn't think the girl he was going to mate was right for him' thing wasn't enough to permanently damage the positive atmosphere that was created when his family got together. It was a great night, they caught up on what everyone was doing. The twins made inappropriate jokes that earned them smacks on the backs of their heads, and they all laughed, a lot. Sometimes being in a family with seven siblings was the best. Yes, it had its moments when it sucked, but overall it was awesome. Dan really wanted Jem to be a part of it. None of his siblings had mates yet. It was actually strange that none of them had mated. In this generation, none of the children from alpha families in any of the dens had taken mates. Even the ones who had reached mating age hadn't been able to find their other half. If Jem accepted him, he would be the first to take a mate. Not to mention it would be the first time he ever experienced something before his brothers. That was actually quite an appealing idea. Actually getting to do something before his brothers. Meanwhile, he would be happy to have Jem as his mate even if he was the last to take one. He'd be happy as long as he had her.

Now that Dan was back it kind of felt like he hadn't been home in forever, and he'd missed being here. He would have missed it more, and enjoyed it more, if he weren't so desperate to get back to Jem. He was so keen to get going that he spent the entire next day searching for Gerard so he could get him to agree to come on this date. Jewel was pretty so that would help. The only thing was, his friend tended to prefer his girls to be a bit... tougher, a little less girly. He usually went for the adventurous, low maintenance type girl, and Jewel, yeah. The likelihood of Jewel being low maintenance was minimal. Maybe Gerard would come along as a favour to Dan? No harm in asking anyway.

By lunchtime Dan was starting to get frustrated. He couldn't find Gerard anywhere and had no idea where he could be. In the end he gave up and went to visit Nicolai in the command centre. Nick always knew where everyone was, or he could find them in a snap. It was probably the first place he should have gone, and if he'd been really thinking things through rather than thinking about Jem he probably would have gone there first.

Dan walked in to find his brother with his glasses perched on the end of his nose while he looked at a dozen screens at once. The entire room was full of the fluorescent white glow of monitors and the hum of CPUs. Numbers and images danced across the screens quickly. Dan didn't see how

Nick could take in half the information from one screen, let alone the twelve he had running, but he did. He had a photographic memory or some such thing. Dan liked to think of him as a kind of walking computer. He was always desperate to learn more, to know how things worked.

"Hey Nick." He said plonking down in an empty computer chair.

Nicolai didn't even turn around. "Hey Dan. What have you been searching for all day? I think I've watched you traverse every tunnel in the den."

"Yeah. I'm looking for Gerard. You haven't seen him have you?" He asked.

"You're not going to find him in the den. Didn't Drew tell you?" Nicolai stopped what he was doing and turned to look at Dan.

"Tell me what?" Dan asked.

Nicolai looked confused. "Dan. Drew sent Gerard on a mission."

"What mission? Another rogue?" he asked.

"No, a Valkyrie." Nick said.

Dan could feel his blood boiling. "I'm sorry, what?! Where's Drew now?" He demanded.

Nicolai looked at the monitors flicking between screens, expanding and shrinking them as he searched the places he was likely to find their brother. He was quick. Drew was usually found in only a few places. The gym, the house, and sometimes down in the old watering hole. That was assuming he wasn't outside running or on patrol.

"He's at home in the conference room." Nicolai said.

"Thanks bro. I'll see ya later." Dan said.

"See ya Dan. Hey. I hope she is your mate. It'd be nice for one of us to get the ball rolling." Nicolai said shooting a look back at Dan.

Dan nodded at Nick. Of all his siblings. Except of course Drew, who was singularly focused on becoming Alpha, and had no time for females. Nick was the one who showed the least interest in finding a mate. Dan had always thought Nick either didn't care or wasn't interested. Apparently he'd been wrong about that. Nick did want to find his mate, he just wasn't much for talking about it.

"Thanks Nick." He said patting him on the shoulder as he walked out.

Nicolai smiled, waved, and turned back to his computer. Maybe he was after a techy girl?

Dan practically sprinted back to the housing wing. He didn't want to miss his brother. He needed to find out exactly where he'd sent Gerard, now. Had Drew sent him after a new Valkyrie? Or was he going after Jem? His Jem. His mate.

Dan didn't want to jump the gun, but if Drew had sent another male after his mate he couldn't guarantee he wouldn't rip him a new one. Literally.

Bursting into the conference room, Dan's breathing was hard, and sweat dripped off his forehead. He'd never realised how large the distance between their home and the communication centre was before today.

"What... the... hell... Drew." he puffed.

Drew rolled his eyes. "What's your problem now baby brother?"

"Did you send Gerard after Jem?" he demanded.

"What if I did?" Drew said flippantly.

"She's my mate." his words came out as a growl.

"So you've said." Drew said dismissively.

Drew's tone of voice sent something within Dan into an angry rampage. Before he knew what he was doing he had shifted and was standing on Drew's chest growling. The smug look washed instantly off of Drew's face and he was left staring up at Dan, eyes wide. An uncontrolled shift was dangerous, particularly to the people around the individual who had shifted. Which was probably why Dan's Father, who had been standing next to Drew, was preparing to restrain him. Dan peeled his lips further off his teeth growling at both his Dad and Drew. They both froze.

"You're actually serious about her being your mate aren't you?" Drew said, his voice surprised. "I didn't realise. I thought. I don't know what I thought. But she'll be here soon enough. Gerard will bring her in."

Another growl ripped up Dan's throat.

"Andrew. That's not helping. Gerard going to get her instead of Dan is the problem here." Dad said.

"How? He'll bring her in, problem solved." Drew said confused.

Dan was considering biting Drew's shoulder.

"If this Jem truly is Dan's mate then another male being near her isn't going to thrill your brother." Dad explained.

"Wasn't he planning on taking her on a double date though?" Drew questioned, still looking beyond confused.

"A date where he would be right next to her, and Gerard would have no reason to touch her." Thomas said.

"Stand down Dan." Dad said, the Alpha command rumbling in his voice.

Dan looked up at him curled his lip back and growled louder. He would not listen to this command. His mate was at risk.

Dad and his brothers looked shocked. No one could ignore an Alpha command. No one, and yet he was. He snapped his sharp teeth inches away from Drew's face, then without a second thought turned and ran from the house. He needed to get to his mate. He needed to get to Jem, and he needed to get there now. Running was the quickest way. He might be tired when he arrived back at Ivaldi, but his wolf form could outstrip a car any day of the week.

Members of the den parted before him like the red sea. No one was stupid enough to attempt to stop or slow him. It was likely his Dad or one of his brothers had called ahead to have doors and security allow him through. There was no controlling him in this state. He would get to her, before Gerard if possible, and anyone who got in his way would have to be prepared to lose a limb, or two.

THE DUNGEON

By the time Dan got to Jem's apartment there was screaming echoing down the stairs. Dan was exhausted, beyond exhausted in fact. His coat was slick with sweat, yet he found the energy to bound up the stairs and into the room. His one and only thought was to protect Jem. He knew he'd have to explain all this to her now and he had no idea how he was going to do that, but he'd try. He had to. As soon he got into the room he knocked Gerard, who was massive in his black wolf form, to the floor, only to come face to face with not only Jem but a large male member of the Aesir. Jem hid behind the incredibly tall man her small frame shaking like a leaf.

Dan shifted to his human form in an instant. "Jem get away from him! He's dangerous!" he announced frantically.

Gerard moaned on the floor in his wolf form. Jem's eyes shot wide open in shock as she took in the two of them.

"You're a. You.." She stuttered her eyes darting

between the three men in her lounge.

Tears welled up in her eyes. "He told me, but I didn't believe him. I didn't want to believe him, but I can't exactly deny it when you change right in front of my eyes. I wondered why a guy that looks like you would ever be interested in a girl like me. It was just a way for you to capture me so I couldn't join the Norse gods to fight against you. You never even liked me at all!" She said, her tears spilling over.

Dan watched as the tears overflowed and ran down her face. He thought his heart might break right there in his chest.

"No little dove. It's not like that." He pleaded with her.

"So you didn't come to Ivaldi to capture me?" She asked, disbelief written all over her face.

Dan was so focused on Jem he didn't notice what the Aesir was doing. "Initially yes, but then I met you. I would never hurt you." He said.

"Then what is he doing here?!" she screamed, pointing at Gerard.

Dan prepared to answer. Tried to explain, but the next thing he knew burning red threads had been wrapped around his wrists, ankles and neck, and he was writhing on the floor. The Aesir had managed to bind the burning threads on both him and Gerard while Dan had been focused on Jem. The Aesir must have been one of Freya's. Or had borrowed a spell from her, because in an instant he managed to transport himself,

Jem and both Dan and Gerard to what had to be Folkvang, Freya's hall, in Asgard. Dan felt as though his stomach had been turned inside out, though he wasn't sure if that was from the travel to Asgard, the bright red threads that bound him, the feeling of complete and utter failure that was overwhelming him, or simply because he was forced to watch as Ali led Jem away without giving him the chance to explain.

He stared down the wood-lined hallway for what felt like an eternity, the masterfully carved panelling unable to distract his attention from the pain that left him crippled on the floor for more than a few moments. Before long two burley Einherjar arrived, picking up the writhing forms of both Dan and Gerard, half carrying, half dragging them into the bowels of Freya's hall. Even in his pain-ridden semi-conscious state, Dan knew this was not a good place. This was a place people came to die. Guilt ate at him as they were chained to the dungeon wall. Thanks to Dan he and his best friend would likely spend the rest of their lives in this dark, dank, death shrouded place. Honestly, what more could go wrong today? His mate thought he'd betrayed her and was nowhere to be found, and the screaming agony of the red threads was so bad he had started retching. It was actually a relief when sweet nothingness finally took over and he blacked out.

"Dan. Dan! Daniel!" Gerard's voice reached Dan through the fog of unconsciousness.

Turning his aching head he saw his friend chained up on a wall. The red threads had been removed from his neck and ankles, and he hung naked in human form by his wrists, one of which was still bound by the painful thread.

Given the ache in his own shoulders, Dan surmised he was bound much the same way and had been suspended like this for quite some time.

"Man, are you okay?" Gerard asked, his voice sounded raw.

Dan looked over at him cringing at the purple and yellow bruises that coloured Gerard's side. Dan had rammed him hard when he had crashed into him in Jem's apartment.

He nodded. "I'm alive. You?"

"Great. And now that we've gotten that out of the way, do you want to explain to me what the hell is going on?" He asked, "Why did you take me out back there? Why didn't you just grab the girl when your Dad told you to?"

Gerard looked pissed, though truthfully that was actually a pretty common look for Gerard, at least when he was on a mission. When he was on a job he was all business. They both were.

"She's my mate." Dan sighed.

Gerard's eyes bugged out. "But she's Valkyrie!" He exclaimed.

"You think I don't know that!" Dan said in

frustration.

"Why didn't you just tell me? I wouldn't have taken the mission." Gerard sighed.

"I would have if Drew hadn't gone behind my back and sent you out! I've been looking for you since I got back to the den." Dan exclaimed in frustration.

Gerard's face shadowed. "Drew! What is it with that guy? Considering he's your brother he can be a real dick."

Dan sighed. "He thought it was some kind of spell or something. He was trying to protect me." Even as he said it, he knew it was true. Drew could be a jerk, but he loved his family. He had honestly thought he was protecting Dan. That sending Gerard out would help. That it was the right thing to do, and the most efficient way to get things done. Otherwise Dan knew he wouldn't have done it. Like Dan, Drew had never reacted to any of the females that had reached their heat. It was actually a bit of a running joke amongst his brothers. None of them had ever understood why the males around them acted like such idiots when the females came into heat. Heck, he'd felt the same way before he met Jem. But as soon as he met her it was like something shifted inside of him. From a logical perspective, he should have been fine with Gerard collecting Jemima and bringing her home to the den. But he hadn't been. He didn't want anybody, any male, to put their hands on her at all, and he hadn't wanted her to be just snatched up from her home. He hadn't wanted to scare her. He'd wanted to give her a chance to get to know him, to choose him. To give him a chance to share who he was with her. He'd wanted a chance to court her. But if he had just done what his Dad and brothers had wanted him to do in the first place and grabbed her, then she wouldn't have been home when the Aesir came to get her. If he'd done what he'd been told, he and Gerard wouldn't be in this mess and yet another Valkyrie wouldn't be in the hands of the Aesir. This whole situation was his fault, and now he didn't know what he could do to fix any of it.

Dan had spent his entire life in and out of caves. All Fenrir dens were made in caves, it was just the norm for his people, but the place he and Gerard were being kept was nothing like their well-maintained home. The dungeon was dark, dank, and despite the damp smell of mould it also somehow managed to be dry and dusty. The thing that worried Dan was that even though it was obvious there were no Fenrir in the dungeon with him and Gerard, the scents in the room were a clear sign that at some stage there had been. They weren't the first, nor were they likely be the last Fenrir to be held in this place, and going by the smell of sweat, blood, and other unpleasant odours, torture was definitely on the tables.

Dan had absolutely no idea how long the two of them hung from the rough stone walls of the Aesir dungeon, but it wasn't long before he realised that he would have happily hung there even with the physical exhaustion and the burning pain of the thin red band than answer to the Aesir.

The first sign they were coming was the smell. Dan had never met an Aesir up close. At least not before coming face to face with the one in Jem's apartment, and that Aesir had smelt reasonably pleasant, like the pages of books, sunlight, and rain on hot soil. The smell that came in with the Aesir who entered the dungeon was definitely not good. Perhaps it had been once, but now it was like something off, like sickly sweet apples, vinegar, and iron. He smelt dangerous, and that didn't bode well for either Dan or Gerard.

"Greetings gentlemen." A refined voice said from the doorway. "It's a pleasure to meet you."

Out of the darkness stepped a man with a grim smile and hair a startling blood red. He stood with confidence and grace. Simply put, the man was beautiful. Not handsome, but beautiful, in a severely menacing way.

"I can't say the same about you." Gerard coughed.

"Well now, that's not very polite." The man said, his grin ever-widening, exposing straight white teeth. "But not to worry. I'm sure we'll be sharing our innermost thoughts and feelings in no time. Now my name is Freyr." He said.

Dan's stomach dropped as he shot a look at Gerard for confirmation. Freyr was the goddess Freya's brother, and between the two of them, they ruled over the entire Aesir race. Usually with Freyr assisting his sister in whatever task she wanted done. Most of her tasks seemed to relate to tracking down and killing the Fenrir.

"What are your names?" Freyr asked.

Neither of them answered.

"I see." He tutted. "I guess I'll need to break the dominant first then. That seems to have been the most successful route in the past."

He looked back and forth between them.

"I can't imagine either of you will enjoy this." He

said, stripping off his high necked, long-sleeved, knee-length black jacket with gold embroidery.

He was wearing a pair of white slacks and a white shirt underneath. Perhaps to make a point. Dan had no doubt that his white clothes wouldn't stay that colour for long.

"You're the dominant then." Freyr said looking at Dan.

"I'm the dominant." Gerard growled.

Freyr laughed. "Further confirmation then." He said looking at Dan. "Your man not only defends you, he looks to you as though waiting for direction. That's a well-trained soldier you have there. But when I'm done with you, he'll wonder why he ever followed you." Freyr smiled.

Freyr pulled out what looked like a whip, only instead of thongs of leather, it had five long strips of the red ribbon that was burning its way into Dan's wrist.

"It doesn't look like much I know. But I think you'll be surprised at its effectiveness." Freyr said stretching his arm back and whipping the light ribbons forward.

It would have been comical, perhaps even a beautiful gesture. Like someone dancing with ribbons. But the sheer pain that lashed through Dan when the ribbons made contact with his flesh, and the way his skin split with each strike, carving out deep gouges before his Fenrir healing could take care of the wounds was monstrous.

He wanted to cry out, but he kept his teeth

firmly clenched and his lips tightly together. He wouldn't give Freyr the satisfaction of hearing him scream, grunt, or make any kind of noise, instead he glared over at Freyr.

Freyr's grin widened as blood ran down from his face onto his clothes. "This always was my favourite part." He said, his arm extending to strike another blow.

Gerard growled, and Dan continued to stare straight at Freyr.

Freyr laid lash upon lash on Dan's bare skin. Meanwhile, Gerard's wrists were coated in drying blood from where he fought against the restraints in an attempt to get to Dan. By the time Freyr stopped lashing Dan his face and clothes were completely red with blood, sweat plastered his body, and his smile had faltered only slightly.

"Well my friends." Freyr said cheerily, as though they had just sat down for a leisurely cup of tea rather than endured a half-hour whipping session, "We shall take this up again in the morning. For now, sleep well."

He snapped his fingers as he left and the chains around their wrists snapped open. Dan tumbled to the floor, unable to stand in his own strength. His wounds were oozing blood. At this point his accelerated Fenrir healing was completely useless. His body had been valiantly repairing itself for the last thirty minutes, and now he was so exhausted he'd be lucky if he didn't bleed out.

Gerard roared towards the closing door. But it closed before he could get there, so he turned and ran to Dan's side "Da…" Gerard started.

"No names." Dan said, his voice cracking.

Gerard nodded seriously. "Are you okay?"

"I've felt better." Dan laughed. "What's bothering me now is that except for our names he hasn't asked us anything. Which means either he's going to start with the questions tomorrow, or he doesn't actually care to ask us anything and is just getting pleasure from beating the tar out of me."

"We just need to take these things off and then we'll have no problems getting out of here." Gerard said.

Gerard took Dan's wrist in his hand and attempted to pull the thin red ribbon off. The moment he pulled on the cord agonising pain shot through Dan's entire body. Gerard released Dan's band as though it were on fire. Clearly trying to pull the band off had not only hurt Dan, but had shocked Gerard as well.

"I'm going to go with there being a spell to prevent us from removing these." Dan said on a painful exhale.

He pushed himself up into a sitting position and leaned against the wall, cringing when his raw back made contact with the jagged stone. Gerard stood up and spent a few moments shaking the door before collapsing down next to him.

"So what do we do now?" Gerard sighed.

"There's not much we can do as far as I can tell. We just have to wait it out." Dan said.

"How much of this can you take?" Gerard asked, indicating Dan's back.

"I'll take as much as I have to." Dan said, "In the meantime you keep strong. At this rate, you may need to carry me out." He laughed.

"I don't know how you managed not to cry out, just yanking that ribbon made me want to scream or shift. Wait. Shift." Gerard said.

"No. Don't." Dan said.

It was too late. Gerard was already in the middle of attempting a shift. He got partway through, dropped to the ground in agony and started retching before laying down on his back to take a few deep breaths.

"I tried to warn you." Dan said coughing, "I tried to shift when he was whipping me."

"You couldn't have warned me sooner?" Gerard asked.

Dan laughed. "Would you have listened?"

"Probably not." Gerard acknowledged with a laugh of his own. "I can't believe a tiny piece of ribbon managed all that."

"Me either. But it does." Dan said.

THEY WERE NEVER MYTHS

J em had been beyond excited to be going out with Dan. To be fair it was her first time actually being officially asked out on a date, ever. All the guys she'd 'gone out with' up until this point had been guys she'd only talked to on the phone. Or maybe hung out with at school or during youth events. She'd never actually been out anywhere with them. Come to think of it, in the time she'd been working in the cafe the only dates she'd gone on had been double dates with Jewel and whoever her flavour of the month was. There were never repeat requests on those dates, and there was something about someone only agreeing to go out with you as a favour to a friend that made you feel awful. It was like Jem had been cast as the loser friend in some terrible coming of age movie, only the director had failed to notice Jem was about ten years too old for the role.

Dan, however, had seemed very keen. Though

it shouldn't have mattered, having a guy look straight past your bubbly best friend, who happened to be one of the most physically beautiful people you'd ever known, and straight at you as though you were the piece missing from his puzzle. That couldn't help but make you feel kind of beautiful.

From the moment he'd asked Jem out everything had just seemed better, and the only one who hadn't been impressed with her newfound enthusiasm was Marty. He'd still insisted that Dan could just be some crazy serial killer or something. Jem had decided to ignore Marty. Boy had she been wrong to ignore him. She'd actually been considering that maybe Marty needed a date of his own on her walk home. Of course, if she were in Marty's position and her friends were trying to set her up it would be terrible. She couldn't have thought of anything worse. She hadn't enjoyed a single one of the dates Jewel had dragged her along on. Sometimes she enjoyed the meal. She enjoyed it when there was decent conversation. But most of the time the conversation seemed to centre around parties, girls, alcohol, and dirty jokes. It was like the guys hadn't aged past their late teens. Either that or they really were only interested in sex, alcohol, and money. Jem had hoped Dan had a few other interests, and that he was intelligent. As far as she was concerned there were few things worse than a guy who had no interest in anyone but himself and his needs or was as thick as a post. It was funny, as a teen she had always prayed for a guy who was a little bit athletic, someone who would challenge her to put down the book and go and do something outside. To help her to stop living in her head, and start doing the things she'd only imagined. She wasn't sure when she'd given up on that dream, on that prayer, and had decided she'd just be happy with a guy who was interested in her. Somehow Dan brought those long-buried dreams back to the surface, and Jem realised she still wanted a guy who would not only love her but would challenge her to grow as a person. A guy who she would happily spend the rest of her life with. Who she could be a help-meet to. A guy she could trust would honour her in that role. She'd been so excited that the day before their date she'd already picked out her outfit. Then she'd decided the outfit wasn't right, and had gone out and brought a new one. Then she'd wondered if her first choice had been better. In the end, she'd decided she needed to try on both dresses before the date then get Jewel to have a look and give her some advice. She'd been so nervous. So excited. She'd never felt this way. Which had made Jem wonder when the other shoe was going to drop. Everything felt so right, so good, right up until it wasn't. Even at the time, Jem had been trying to push aside the feeling that something would have to go wrong just to balance out how happy she was feeling. She shouldn't have had that kind of attitude, she knew that. But she couldn't seem to switch off the feeling of foreboding that was walking hand in hand with her excitement. Turns out that her foreboding feeling wasn't far off.

The entrance of Jem's apartment was something like a small, thin library combined with a sunroom. It had large sun catching windows, and bookshelves built into the walls. It even had her favourite comfy blue chair sitting in it. That way when she read one of her favourite books for the hundredth time she always had a nice spot in the sun where she could read.

After work, Jem had walked inside her home the same way she always did. Just like every other day her front door was locked and her books were all where she'd left them. Everything was exactly as it should be, until she'd walked into the room just past the entrance where her kitchen, dining, and lounge were. There, leaning against her kitchen bench, browsing through her most recent read was a frighteningly tall man with shoulder-length blonde hair, a coarse blonde beard and piercing hazel eyes. Despite his imposing height Jem managed to get halfway across the room before noticing him. When she finally did see him she'd gasped in shock, then very nearly tripped over her coffee table.

"Greetings. I am Ali." He said calmly, as though being in a random stranger's kitchen was normal.

Jem had prepared herself to scream. Prepared herself to run. She'd been preparing to do something, anything, when he disappeared from his spot by the kitchen bench and appeared at her side. He placed a supporting hand at her elbow to help her keep her balance.

"Careful." He said.

"Who are you!" Jem had exclaimed pulling out of his gentle grasp.

Her eyes darted between where he was standing at her side, and the bench where he had been standing.

"How did you do that!?" She'd screeched.

He frowned at her. "Humans." He said, shaking his head in exasperation. "I am Ali, son of Odin all father. I am of the Aesir."

The word Aesir triggered a memory in Jem. "You're talking about Norse Mythology." She said dumbfounded, taking careful steps away from the crazy man and towards the exit.

"Norse, yes. Mythology, not quite." He said.

"You're trying to tell me you think you're a god? Look I'm sorry sir, but you need help. That and to get out of my apartment. I'll call someone for you if you need me too. But you need to get out of my home."

Looking back Jem could safely say that she'd sounded a lot more confident than she really was. Especially given that he'd just travelled across her room without moving. She'd wondered if maybe she was having a breakdown, or had blacked out or something. She still wondered if something like that was going on now.

"Not a god. An Aesir." He said simply.

"Look, why are you here?" Jem asked, trying to keep the panic out of her voice.

"I'm here because we need you in Asgard. There's a war going on, and we need all the warriors we can get." He said.

"But I'm not any kind of warrior. I'm a cafe worker and a barista. But otherwise I'm a pretty ordinary kind of girl." She said.

"You may not be a warrior now. But you will be. You are a female descendant of one of the Valkyrie who returned to earth to live with the humans after Ragnarok. You were made for a time such as this." He said.

"A Valkyrie? Look. I'm sorry. But I'm about the most uncoordinated person you will ever meet. I don't know anything about war, and I don't know that I'm keen to find out." She said.

"Not every Valkyrie is a fighter. It's possible you are a healer." Ali said. "It really is important you come with me now. Not just because we need you, but because it isn't safe for you here." he'd said.

Jem hadn't believed him, right up until she didn't have a choice but to believe. Ali had just been saying how a group of wolf people called the Fenrir had sent someone to abduct her, and the next thing she knew a huge wolf burst into her living room, followed by yet another. Then to add to her fears of insanity the second overly large wolf to enter her home had morphed into Dan. She had watched in horror as the large wolf's jet black fur shimmered, seeming to retract into its body, its muscles lengthened and its skin paled, softening until it was clearly human. The process was quick, over in just a few breaths, and may have even been beautiful if Jem hadn't been so terrified. Her heartfelt as though it were breaking when she realised she recognised the now human wolf. It was Dan. There he was, clear as day, standing buck naked in her living room. He even admitted that he had been sent to get her, all while insisting that he was genuinely interested in her. Jem's whole body had gone numb at that point. Yet again she had the proof that no one could ever truly want her. How could she have been stupid enough to believe that anyone ever would, especially a guy as attractive as Dan.

Before Jem could really even talk to Dan. Before she could get to the bottom of what was going on, or even process any of it. Dan and his friend had pieces of what looked like red ribbon wrapped around their bodies and were screaming in pain. Ali said something she didn't understand, and the next thing Jem knew she wasn't in her apartment anymore. She was in a massive wooden hallway while Dan and his friend continued writhing on the ground, and even though she felt hurt by him, everything in her was desperate to get to Dan and help him. Only she couldn't. She was in shock. It was like her mind and her body were running in slow motion, and before she could get to him Ali was leading her away and had called over four enormous guys to escort Dan and his friend to the dungeon.

"Welcome to Folkvang Valkyrie." Ali said to her with a smile, "I am sorry about how abrupt our meeting was, and how quickly I brought you here. Usually one of your sister Valkyrie would come to meet you first, explain what is going on. But in your case, we received information that the Fenrir had found you, and we needed to do what we could to keep you safe."

"What are you doing with them now?" Jem asked, unable to stop herself from watching as Dan was carried away.

"They'll be taken to the dungeon for questioning." Ali said, "I know this is all a lot to take in. But we are in a war for the lives of our people Jemima, and those Fenrir, they are the enemy. I have no doubt that if I hadn't arrived when I had that Fenrir would have you in his clutches right now."

"So why if the Fenrir were planning on kidnapping me didn't they do it days ago? Dan's had plenty of opportunities." She admitted.

"He's had you alone?" Ali asked.

"Well, no. Not really." Jem said. "We were supposed to go on a date tomorrow." She admitted.

"Then it would seem he was just waiting for the right time." Ali said.

Despite how she'd lost it at Dan earlier a small part of Jem had been holding out hope that maybe he had genuinely liked her. After hearing what Ali had to say, she knew that wasn't the case. It made sense that all Dan was trying to do was capture her. Who would want her?

"I want to go home." Jem said.

Ali looked down at her. "I can understand that." He said.

"But you won't take me back will you." She said.

"I will. But not until you meet your sisters." He said leading her down a long hallway to a pair of enormous wooden doors.

"I don't have any sisters." She said.

"You do now." Ali replied throwing the enormous doors wide open.

Through the doors was the biggest room Jem had ever seen. It was almost like a church. Almost. The room was shaped like an A. It had a high ceiling with rafters crossing overhead. The entire far wall, as well as the length of the wall on her right, was floor to ceiling windows. The space was huge. Like a football field, maybe even as big as four football fields. More astounding than the sheer size of the room was the number of women inside of it. There were women everywhere. Women of every nationality you could think of. They were of varying ages, though most appeared under forty, and over fifteen. Some were big, others little. There was no rhyme or reason to why these specific women were chosen. Even when Jem noticed how they were gathered in clusters, as though they were all doing something specific together, there was no way to establish what exactly qualified them to be here, let alone to be placed in the group they were in. Of course, she had no idea why she was here. So knowing why any of the other women were here was a bit of a stretch. Ali was noticeably the only male in the room, and the deeper they made their way into the crowd the more noticeable his presence was.

As Ali led Jem into the room she noticed other women being led in, including to her surprise Jewel. Before she could run over to her friend a horn began blowing. The horns trumpeting seemed to be coming from everywhere at once and was almost deafening. As soon as the horn sounded, women throughout the room stopped what they were doing and flocked towards the end of the massive room. As soon as they started moving Jem's view of Jewel was blocked off and within moments she had been absorbed into the swath of women.

"It was lovely to meet you Jemima." Ali said placing a hand on her shoulder, "I can't stay for this. Folkvang is meant for women only, especially when Queen Freya addresses her Valkyrie."

"Um. Thank you?" Jem said, looking at him.

He smiled down at her. "It really was lovely to meet you Jemima. I'm sure we will meet again."

Jem smiled back at him as he left, then it suddenly occurred to her that she had no way to find him when she wanted to get home.

"Wow." A girl with super tight black curls and an English accent said looking at Ali's retreating form in awe. "Were you brought here by Ali?" she asked.

Jem shrugged. "I guess that's what he said his name was."

"Again, Wow." She said, "You know who he is right?" the girl asked as she led Jem with her to the far end of the room.

"Um. Ali?" Jem said.

The girl laughed. "He's one of Odin's sons, Freya's stepson. He's one of the Aesir gods." She explained.

Jem turned toward the door that she entered through and watched as it closed behind Ali.

"He's a God. Like you know GOD?" Jem asked.

The girl shook her head, sending her dark curls bouncing against her light brown skin. "Not like the big G.O.D. I mean they're super powerful and live a ridiculously long time, like they're thousands of years old and stuff, but they aren't God." The girl explained.

Jem looked at her blankly. How could they be Gods, but not God?

"It's kind of like God, but with a little g. I guess that humans thought they were gods the first time they encountered them, and for a while they played on that. You know Greek gods, Norse gods, all that stuff. They aren't God, but they're not humans either." She said.

"So like angels then?" Jem asked.

She shook her head again. "Nah. I don't know exactly how it works. I mean in some ways I think they're the same as humans. In others not so much."

"So they're like us? Like humans, but live longer." Jem asked.

"Oh, Hun. You're not human. None of us here are. Not entirely at least. You're a Valkyrie." She said.

"What exactly does that mean?" Jem asked.

"It kinda means you're awesome." A girl with porcelain skin, pitch-black hair and a fresh cut across her nose said.

"Heck yeah it does, Maisie." The curly-haired girl said.

Jem frowned and both girls laughed.

"Don't worry chick. It takes a while, but I swear, eventually it all starts making sense. In the meantime, I'm Lettie, descendant of Skuld, and this is Maisie, descendant of Gunnr." Lettie said.

"Oh. I'm Jem, Jemima, um. I have no clue who I'm the descendant of. I'm not entirely sure I should even be here." She admitted.

Maisie threw an arm over her shoulder. "You wouldn't be here if you weren't meant to be Jem."

"Yeah don't worry Jem. We'll take care of you." Lettie said.

"Thank you?" Jem said.

The girls laughed.

"We felt the same way when we first got here Jem. It's all a little bit overwhelming. But Freya will clear everything up." Maisie said.

"You're lucky you arrived before orientation." Lettie said.

"Whoa." Maisie said, and the three women looked to the front of the room.

On the stage stood one of, if not the most stunning woman Jem had ever seen. With creamy pale skin, hair an almost unnatural red, and wearing a dress that looked like a cross between spun gold and sunshine.

"Who's that?" Jem asked.

"That is Freya, Queen of the Aesir, and our leader." Lettie said, "Today must be special.

Usually we're addressed by Lady Gna on Queen Freya's behalf."

Maisie smiled broadly. "Something big is going on." She said excitedly.

Once the women, correction, the Valkyrie, were gathered at the far end of the room where they could all see Queen Freya, the Aesir goddess began to speak.

"Greetings Sisters." Freya said, and her voice wove through the crowd like perfume.

Jem watched as all around her the women sighed and smiled up at their Queen. Every single woman in the room was clearly in awe of Freya, and though Jem couldn't help but find the woman both charming and charismatic, she felt a niggle of unease deep within her. Like something wasn't right.

Freya smiled broadly showing off her beautifully white teeth. "I am so glad I could be here with each of you today." She said clasping her hands together. "You may not be aware of it ladies, but today is both the end and the beginning for us. Because today we found the last of your sisters in Midgard."

Freya nodded. "That's right. We have finally brought every single Valkyrie back to Asgard and for the first time in centuries we are all together again. The Valkyrie have finally returned to Folkvang."

A cheer rose up across the room with some women raising fists in the air in celebration and to Jem's surprise some shooting sparks of what had to be magic up toward the high roof.

"Congratulations to those of you who have helped us track down the gifted descendants of my original Valkyrie. You have served me well in this task. To those of you who have trained, and assisted in the training of our new sisters, thank you. Your hard work has not gone unnoticed, and your team leaders have given me glowing reports on each of you. And finally, to our newly found sisters. Welcome." Freya said looking around the room making eye contact with every one of the new Valkyrie, including Jem.

"Magic." Maisie said leaning closer to Jem.

"She's so amazing." Lettie said.

"Now many of you have heard before why after so many generations on Midgard, I have gathered you all together. But as we are entering into the next phase of our mission I feel it's worth reminding us all of why we are here. Of the important role each of you are playing, both for the Aesir of Asgard and for the humans living on Midgard." Freya smiled triumphantly.

Jem looked around the room, feeling a little as though she were missing something. All eyes were on the stage. On Freya, and each of the women in the room appeared to be hanging off of Freya's every word. Jem tried to focus. She wasn't sure she wanted to be here, but she didn't want to be rude either.

"My Valkyrie have always been the most talented, intelligent and strongest of all the warriors of Asgard. As the daughters of my original Valkyrie, you are no different. You are the best Midgard has to offer. Each one of you with your own gifts. Many of you are still unaware of just how gifted you truly are. You, we, are the protectors of the innocent. We stand in the gap between the monsters who would destroy the worlds and the people who live there. This age is no different. Sister Valkyrie, we again are called stand in the gap, shoulder to shoulder with our brothers the Einherjar protecting the worlds from its newest threat. The Fenrir." Freya said.

An angry murmur echoed through the room.

"The Fenrir are destined to try and destroy us." Freya said, tears welling in her eyes, "They want to hurt my people. Our people, and I just can't stand by while they try to hurt anyone else."

Freya scanned the crowd, as though confirming she had the attention of the room "Many of you have seen the damage the Fenrir have done. Some of you first hand, and to those of you I was too slow to get to, I am sorry." The tears dropped from Freya's eyes. "But I promise you, that together we will be the shield that protects the helpless from experiencing the same loss. We will be the weapon that breaks the Fenrir. We will be the voice that speaks reason into a world in chaos. We will be the healers who take the broken and make them whole."

Across the room cheers rose again.

Freya's tears glistened like gold, and Jem could even see the women closest to Freya reaching out to catch the tiny drops.

"Freya's tears are special." Lettie said, "Magic even. They don't stay water like ours. It's actually kind of amazing. Her tears turn into pieces of amber."

Jem stretched up on her tiptoes and watched as the women who had caught the tears gazed almost lovingly at the now hard pieces of amber stone that sat in their palms.

"For my new sisters, I must explain to you that we are at war. A war for our very existence. A war against the Fenrir. A race of people born from the beast who killed my husband Odin. A race who even now that my husband is gone seek to destroy anything and everything of beauty in this world." Freya said, her face becoming hard and angry, though still managing to be unbelievably beautiful.

"The Fenrir are a race of people with the ability to appear human. But can become wolves of the most destructive kind. Many years ago I received a prophecy. One that showed how the Fenrir would start with destroying the Aesir in revenge for the destruction of their sire the Fenrir beast, and after destroying the Aesir they would turn to the humans, destroying and enslaving them." Freya explained. "But do not be concerned my sisters. That is why you are here. A war is coming, but we are prepared. Every day we train is a day we build a defence against the Fenrir. Every day is a day we protect our human friends, and one day soon we will bring the battle to the

Fenrir. We will end them!" She declared.

Jem tried to hide the shudder that attempted to work its way up her spine. Freya's words seemed inspiring on the surface, but once again she had the feeling that something just wasn't right. All she could think of was how genocide had been tried before, and it had never been the answer. Not to mention the leaders who called for the eradication of a race of people tended to have more than a few screws loose, and ultimately drove their people to their own destruction. While the women around her cheered and nodded at each other Jem felt as though something oily and unpleasant was working its way through the women here. Even the noticeably friendly Lettie and Maisie were being drawn in, and Jem couldn't stop herself from wondering how bad these Fenrir could possibly be. She wanted to understand. But all she could see was Dan putting himself between her and Mrs. Grover. If he had wanted to hurt her, then why had he done that? Why had he spent time just talking to her? Getting to know her? Telling her about himself? Why would he do that? Why would he hurt his own friend in an attempt to protect her? But maybe that's just what Dan was like. What the Fenrir were like. Maybe they were the type of enemy that slipped beneath your defences and destroyed you from within.

"For those of you who have just arrived, once again I would like to welcome you. I can understand if you are confused, and even a bit scared. But I can assure you that you are in a safe place. You are with your sisters. With your friends, and we will help you to not only understand but to become the very best version of yourself." Freya said.

"War is coming." Freya continued. "But for now we are safe. For the moment at least the Fenrir are waiting. But very soon the day will be upon us. The prophecy did not give a time, but we can see it coming. The numbers of Fenrir are increasing, and so we will get stronger until we can bring the fight to them." she said.

Jem looked around the room and watched as the women nodded solemnly.

"Go well sisters." Freya said, "I look forward to seeing your progress with my own eyes today, and meeting the most recent Valkyrie to join us in this battle for the future."

Freya stepped off the stage, exiting into a room off to the side. Smiling at, but not verbally engaging with any of the women she called her sister Valkyrie. Even as Jem watched Freya walk regally away, she couldn't turn off the unsettling niggle that had settled in her stomach. Something was so off about this place, and it had nothing to do with the fact that only a few hours ago she would have sworn black and blue that Asgard and Norse Gods were only myths and legends, or the basis for some of her favourite Marvel movies.

Though Queen Freya had left the room, all the women stayed right where they were, a few chatted, but overall the room could be considered quiet. Especially given the number of people in the room.

"Oh, here's Lady Gna now." Lettie said.

A woman walked up to the stage, her long red hair curling down her back. Lady Gna's face was stern, and though she appeared reasonably young, there was something about her that made her seem old. She looked hardened in a way that few women in their late thirties or early forties did. She stared out over the room. Unlike Freya, there was no welcome smile. She didn't seem pleased to be there with them, if anything she seemed as though she were completing a necessary chore, one she disliked.

"Greetings Sister Valkyrie." She said, her voice carrying across the room in an emotionless monotone.

"Greetings Lady Gna." The room of women echoed back reminding Jem of a class of school children.

Lady Gna nodded in acknowledgement.

"As our Queen has said, the last intake of Valkyrie have finally been found and brought to Folkvang. Which means, not only will your training intensify from here on out, but I will expect each and every one of you to be performing your best. We have a responsibility to not only teach our new sisters how to fight but to show them exactly what it means to be a Valkyrie." She said.

There were nods and murmurs of agreement around the room.

"For now please return to your training." She said, "Unless of course you have been selected to partner with our new sisters. For those women, I would like you to come forward and join myself and the new Valkyrie at the front of the room. That will be all." Lady Gna said stepping down from the stage.

Lady Gna was clearly all efficiency, and Jem couldn't help but get the feeling that no matter what circumstances she met her under that Lady Gna would be prickly. Jem had always had an intuition about people, and up until recently she'd been spot on when it came to her feelings about people. Right up until she met Dan. She had been convinced that he was a good guy. That he had the potential to be something more to her.

But even if she put her positive feelings about him aside and assumed that she only thought positively about him because of how attractive he was, it still didn't mesh. Because the fact was, she wasn't scared of him. She didn't feel like he was bad news. Even when he'd been standing naked in her living room after transforming from a hulking great wolf she hadn't been afraid. If anything she had felt hurt and betrayed. Like he had tricked her. But never did she have the feeling that something was amiss around him. Of course, she'd clearly been wrong. Jem sighed, watching as the Valkyrie split off into their groups. Her perception was obviously miles off because from the moment she arrived here something just seemed off, and nothing had seemed more off than Freya and Lady Gna.

Lettie looked at Jem and smiled. "Come on Jem. Maisie and I will go up with you." She said.

"Thanks." Jem said.

"All good." Maisie said, "We were selected to join the new Valkyrie, so we've got to get over there anyway."

Jem walked up to the front with Lettie and Maisie. Meanwhile, the women returning to their training were watching Jem with interest. Most smiled, some seemed to be trying to size her up, and others barely even noticed her, or avoided looking at her at least. It was hard to say if those women were just nervous, or if they were avoiding looking at her for another reason entirely.

"How long have you been here?" Jem asked them.

"We both arrived with the previous intake." Lettie said.

Maisie nodded. "Yeah, so that was about what? Six months ago?" Maisie said.

"Maybe eight?" Lettie said.

"Sometimes it feels like time travels a little differently here." Maisie said, "Slower maybe."

"I don't know." Lettie said, "Some days it feels like it's going really fast."

"True." Maisie nodded. "The training is heaps of fun though. It's easy to lose track of time."

"What's the training?" Jem asked just as they reached the front of the room.

"There are four different Valkyrie factions." Lady Gna announced to the group, her loud monotone preventing either Lettie or Maisie from replying.

Lady Gna started pacing in front of their group. There were maybe forty women, and of those Jem would have wagered only twenty of them were new recruits like her and Jewel. The other women, the ones that looked confident rather than nervous, were wearing clothing you would struggle to see outside of a cosplay event. Many of the women who were wearing red or gold like Maisie had cuts and grazes of varying degrees on their bodies. Those were clearly the existing Valkyrie.

"Factions step forward." Lady Gna demanded.

Lettie gave Jem's arm a squeeze and moved to

the front of the group. Once the existing Valkyrie had moved to the front of the group it was easy to see the differences between the factions. Though it helped to have Lady Gna explain.

"Each of you ladies will be placed into one of these four factions. Before being placed in a faction you will be given a chance to learn the basic skills of each." Lady Gna said, moving across to the group of women in green, which included Lettie. "Most Valkyrie will find themselves in the faction founded by their Valkyrie matriarch. But we believe it is important for you to know about each faction. That way you will better understand the members of the squad you will join. We give you a chance to test your skills in each area of expertise. The Valkyrie in green are our healers." Lady Gna said.

She moved over to the next group of women. "In blue, we have our negotiators."

Jem did a scan around the room and noticed that this group was amongst the smallest in the Hall of Folkvang, even though there were hundreds, if not thousands of women in the room.

"In white, we have our magic wielders." Lady Gna said. "And in red and gold we have our warriors." Lady Gna looked at each one of the new Valkyrie, her gaze steely. "You will all be expected to learn how to fight. The Fenrir are ruthless, and if you do not train, then you will die."

"Can't we just go home?" One woman asked. "I

don't want to be a part of a war." She said.

Lady Gna's lips pursed in disgust. "Yes you may go home. But whether or not you stay here, you are part of a war. By sitting back and doing nothing you are allowing the world's greatest threat to freedom to survive so they can hurt all the people you love." She said.

The woman who had asked the question looked down at the ground, her cheeks red with embarrassment.

"For now all we ask is that you stay and get to know you sister Valkyrie. Find out what gift your matriarch passed down to you that makes you qualified to be here. Then make your decision about whether you want to stay." Lady Gna looked around the group. "Or if you would prefer to return home." She said, then she left in the same direction Queen Freya had.

An older woman, at least in comparison with the rest of the group, stepped forward, her pale green dress swaying beneath her cloak of darker green. She was one of the healers.

"My name is Erin Galen, though for many years I was known simply as the Eir mender of the gods." She said smiling at their group. "I would like to welcome you all to Asgard. Each of you is special in your own unique way. But many of you will find that you have very similar Aesir gifts, this is because you are descendants of the same Valkyrie. I have personally known many of your matriarchs as I am one of the few surviving

Valkyrie to have stayed here in Folkvang rather than marrying amongst either the humans or the Aesir after Ragnarok." Erin smiled and indicated for three other older women to join her at the centre of their group.

"I can see that many of you are confused, and likely a little frightened. But you have no reason to be. My sisters and I will be here to guide you every step of the way." Erin said, her voice soothing. "From each of the four original factions at least one of the matriarchs remains. From the healing sisters, I remain. From the magic-wielding sisters, remains Gondul." A woman with chest-length white hair in a long white dress stepped forward.

"From our negotiating sisters, remains Radgrid, now known as Reyna Trussler." Erin said and a dark-skinned woman in blue with curly greying hair and an easy smile stepped forward. Jem felt a kinship with the woman. There was something about her, a feeling that Jem instantly associated with honesty. She seemed trustworthy, the type of woman who would let you know if she was unhappy with you but would be equally likely to tell you when she was pleased with you.

"Last but not least. From our warrior sisters, remain both Geirskogul, known as Temira Garrett." Erin said, and an incredibly tall, dark-skinned woman stepped forward. Her mostly black curly hair framed her face like a halo, and her golden armour moved soundlessly over her red leather skirt and corset. She was intimidating, but still looked approachable. On the other hand, the woman standing nearby her with her grey hair pulled tightly at the nape of her neck and a permanent scowl looked like an individual Jem would rather avoid.

"And Sanngrior, known as Marthe Freis." Erin said.

"From this point onward, whether you stay in Asgard with your sister Valkyrie, or return to the life you knew before, I can guarantee you will never need fear being alone again. Personally, I hope each of you will choose to stay. I have no doubt now that you know you are Valkyrie, it will stay a part of you forever, and we will always be your sisters." Erin said. "Many of the women who have been brought to Asgard have considered themselves alone, only to find that they have a family right here." Erin said, indicating all the women in the room.

"There is so much to learn. But today is not the day for it. Today I want to invite each of you to look around Folkvang. To meet your sisters and see what each faction is capable of. To see what the squads are doing together. I suggest that you talk to your Valkyrie sisters and have them take you around this beautiful place. Explore to your heart's content. Then tomorrow when you have had a chance to process all of this we will begin introducing you to the skills of a Valkyrie, and help you learn not only who your matriarch is, but also what your own special abilities are."

UNSETTLED

J em leaned over to Lettie. "Why didn't the Valkyrie just keep their original names?" she asked.

Lettie shrugged. "I'm not sure to be honest. Maybe it just made it easier getting around Midgard."

"Or maybe it was because we got sick of having to repeat our names to the descendants of our sisters. None of whom appear to have the intelligence or ability to pronounce them to save their lives." Marthe said staring down her nose at them and walking away to join a group of red-clad women.

"Don't worry about Marthe." Reyna said with a smile, "She enjoys a little drama." She said with a wink, her eyes sparkling with laughter.

"I'd still avoid her if I were you." Maisie whispered leaning in close to Jem as Reyna made her way to the blue-clad Valkyrie.

"Jem?!" Jewel exclaimed, rushing over and launching herself into Jem's arms. "I can't believe you're here too. If you're here then I know I'm not going crazy. Right?" she asked looking around frantically.

"If anyone is going crazy it's me." Jem said.

"How so?" Maisie asked.

"You remember Dan." Jem asked, posing the question to Jewel.

Jewel smiled. "Hotty Mc Phone guy. How could I forget?" She said with a smile, fanning herself as though the room had suddenly heated up.

"Well before an Aesir god transported me here, I had Dan standing buck naked in my lounge." Jem said.

"You didn't!!" Jewel exclaimed interrupting her, her smile wide.

"After I watched him transform into a human from an enormous black wolf." Jem finished.

"You what?" Jewel said looking confused.

"You had a Fenrir. An actual Fenrir in your house?" Lettie asked.

"So it would seem." Jem said with a sigh.

Jewel's smile dropped. "Oh, Jem. I'm sorry." She said, likely realising Dan's invitation for Jem to go on a date with him was just a ploy to capture her. At least that's why Jem assumed she was saying sorry, both Freya and Lady Gna had been adamant about the danger of the Fenrir.

"I really thought. Or at least I hoped he was genuinely interested in me." Jem admitted. "Turns out I was wrong yet again." She said.

Jewel wrapped her arms around Jem pulling her

into another hug.

"So if anyone is going crazy it's me." Jem said.

"If he wasn't genuinely interested in you then the only crazy person around here is him." Jewel said firmly, then she looked around the massive room, "Okay, and maybe us. I can't believe any of this is real." She said.

"Wait till you see the girls using magic, you'll lose your mind." Lettie said her smile wide.

"Nah. Wait till you get to try it yourself." Maisie said, "It's all kinds of bizarre. But still so so cool."

"Some of the girls can even turn into swans." Lettie said.

"It's mostly the descendants of the swan sisters that can do that though." Maisie said, then sighed wistfully, "Anyway, how about we show you two around." She asked.

"I guess. I mean what choice do we really have?" Jem asked.

It seemed like for every new Valkyrie there was at least one seasoned Valkyrie who seemed to be buddying up with them, so presumably that was what Jem and Jewel were expected to be doing as well.

Lettie and Maisie laughed.

"You'll love it. We promise." Maisie said.

"That Lady Gna person said something about most Valkyrie ending up in the same faction as their Matriarch. What does that mean? I mean how do they have any idea who we're the descendants of?" Jewel asked. "And will they ever let us in on it?"

"Back when Freya and her remaining Valkyrie started searching for Valkyrie descendants they would find them with magic. But the spells were a lot of hard work. Like physically draining, and they could only find one woman at a time. From what we've been told it was really slow going they were only finding maybe one or two new Valkyrie every month. But once they found a few tech-savvy girls it got a lot easier. They were able to do genealogy searches, trace girls through their family lines, then test with magic to make sure they've got the Valkyrie gifts, that sort of stuff. Since then most intakes of Valkyrie have had anywhere between twenty and a hundred girls." Lettie said.

"How many Valkyrie are there exactly?" Jem asked.

"Originally, not many. But after Ragnarok lots of them went to Midgard, that's what they call Earth here, and chose to live a normal human lifetime. They had kids, their kids had kids and so on." Maisie said. "I think, now that you've arrived our numbers are sitting somewhere around five thousand women, maybe more." She said.

"It could be closer to ten thousand." Lettie said.

"Wow. That's a lot of women." Jewel said looking around the room again.

"If Queen Freya's been recruiting for a while, and taking as many as a hundred women each time, then how is it that nobody's noticed all these women disappearing all over the place?" Jem asked.

"You know what?" Lettie said. "I have no idea."

"Maybe they are being noticed?" Maisie said. "Although, the Valkyrie come from all over the world, so it might not be that noticeable?"

"I'm fairly certain Sarah's going to notice if neither Jewel or I turn up for work on Monday." Jem said, "Marty will probably call the cops. He wasn't too keen on either of us going on that date in the first place. He'll think we've been murdered or something."

"This is certainly something." Jewel said, indicating a young woman who was standing with a white feathery cloak around her shoulders and her face all scrunched up, focusing very hard on something. Either that or she was suffering from some severe abdominal pains.

Next to the woman with the scrunched, and now very red face, stood a second woman her own white cloak over her shoulders. Within moments her skin bleached to an unnatural white, she sprouted feathers, shrunk to about half her size, and then, standing in the exact spot the woman had just been, stood an unnaturally large swan with a pile of clothing around her.

Jewel and Jem both froze and stared.

"Whoa." Jewel said.

"And return please Leda." The instructor said.

"That's Leda Vlund, she's a descendant of Hladgudr Svanhvit." Lettie said as Leda swiftly changed back, though now the woman was standing there wearing only the cloak and a massive smile.

"She turned into a swan." Jewel said in disbelief.

Maisie laughed. "We did tell you some of the girls could do that." She said.

"Yeah, but I didn't believe anyone could actually do it. I figured it was some kind of metaphor for something else. Like they went from being ugly ducklings to swans. Or to being graceful from being clumsy. But she was an actual freaking swan. A terrifyingly large one, but still, she was a swan." Jewel said.

"Who knows, you might have that gift too. Do either of you know who you're a descendant of?" Maisie asked.

Both Jem and Jewel shook their heads.

"Don't worry. They'll give you an orientation booklet later. That's got all the info on your matriarch. You'll likely even have a whole bunch of cousins here." Lettie said. "Some of the girls have even got to meet their matriarch."

"Really? But wouldn't they be hundreds of years old?" Jewel said.

"Some of them are thousands of years old." Maisie said.

"I'm sorry what?" Jem said.

"How does that work?" Jewel asked at the same time.

"I always feel like time works differently here." Maisie answered, "But from what we've been taught it's something about the Aesir genes, or at least Aesir magic being activated in us. It slows down the ageing process."

"For the likes of Queen Freya, it's practically stopped altogether." Lettie said.

"Are you saying she can't die?" Jewel asked.

Lettie shook her head. "No. She can definitely die. She just ages even slower than the other Aesir."

"It could be because she has more magic than the others?" Maisie suggested, "Or maybe because she isn't really Aesir. She's from another race of people entirely. The Vanir. They were destroyed during Ragnarok. Queen Freya and her twin brother Freyr are the only Vanir left."

"Their Father came with them to Asgard after the Vanir lost a war to the Aesir. But he passed away during Ragnarok." Lettie said.

"That sounds kind of miserable. Living for so long, and seeing all the people you love die. Or at least knowing they're all dead." Jem said.

"If her people all died during Ragnarok and they lost the war against the Aesir, then how is it that's she's now Queen of the Aesir?" Jewel asked.

"Oh." Maisie said, "After the war, Queen Freya, her brother Freyr and their Father Njord were sent by the Vanir to live with the Aesir, while the Aesir sent Mimir, and Hoenir to live with the Vanir. It was like a peace trade or something. So anyway, when she got here she was apparently one of the most beautiful women, well ever, and so Lord Odin married her. Then when he was killed by Fenrir during Ragnarok she became the ruler, since she was his Queen." Maisie said.

"Is that why she hates these Fenrir people so much? Cause they killed her husband?" Jem asked.

She didn't want to admit it, but she could understand how someone killing the person you love would make you hate their entire race.

Lettie shook her head. "It wasn't the Fenrir people that killed Lord Odin." She said, "It was a massive wolf creature called the Fenrir beast. He was apparently part Aesir and part Jotun. They're another race that were destroyed after Ragnarok. Anyway, apparently the Fenrir are descendants of that Fenrir beast and for some reason they've been trying to destroy the Aesir ever since Ragnarok. There's even a prophecy about it. Personally, I think after Fenrir gobbled up Odin his people got a taste for Aesir blood." Lettie said.

"Oh gross Lettie." Maisie said.

"Hey it makes sense." Lettie said.

"So this prophecy says that the Fenrir will what, destroy the Aesir if we don't stop them?" Jem asked.

"More like the world. The prophecy says that if we don't stop them the Fenrir won't just destroy Asgard and the Aesir, they'll destroy the entire human race." Lettie said.

Jem found herself thinking of Dan. For someone who was apparently part of a race of people who were intent on destroying the world, he'd been awfully friendly. The more she thought about it, the more she questioned what was being said about him, and his people. Granted it could have all been an act. But he seemed so sincere. He'd really seemed to like her. He'd seemed excited to be seeing her again. If all he'd been planning on doing was kidnapping her, then he'd really gone way too far. The night before what would have been their date he had rang her, and they'd chatted into the wee hours. Not just about trivial things like the weather, or how her day had been either. They had talked about those things, of course, but more specifically they talked about which was their favourite season. Jem's favourite season was summer because it was sunny and warm. Dan, on the other hand, liked summer, but spring was his favourite. He'd said he liked it the best because it was full of promise. New animals were being born. New flowers were blooming. The air was full of the sweet scents of life, and it was still cool enough to enjoy being outside without being cooked. They'd also talked about their families. Like the fact that she had no siblings, while he had seven. Why would he share that kind of information with her if he was planning on hurting her all along? It made no sense. Maybe it was all lies? It was just, usually, she was so good at spotting a liar, and he'd seemed so authentic.

Jewel looked at Jem and frowned.

"So what would happen if a Fenrir were to meet a Valkyrie or just a normal human?" Jem asked.

"From what we've been told they're pretty hostile. Especially if you know what they are." Maisie said.

"So the likelihood of one of them protecting a human?" Jem asked. "Or transforming in front of one?"

"It's pretty low." Maisie said, then she looked at Jem, "Did he transform in front of you? That Fenrir Ali saved you from."

Jem had a sinking feeling. Something just didn't feel right in this place. She nodded.

"Before or after Ali attached the Gleipnir bonds?" Lettie asked.

"I'm sorry, the what?" Jem asked.

"The Gleipnir bonds. They kind of look like red ribbons, only they can't be broken by Fenrir. They're enchanted to prevent any Fenrir from breaking free from them, and they hurt them if they try." Lettie said.

"He transformed before." Jem said.

Lettie and Maisie looked between each other, their eyes wide.

"Are you sure? I mean, it must have all happened really quickly." Maisie said.

"I'm pretty sure." Jem said.

It was clear Maisie and Lettie had no idea what to say after Jem's little revelation, instead they went back to showing Jem and Jewel around Folkvang.

If Jem had thought the training hall was big, then the rest of the hall, palace really, was simply mind-boggling in its proportions. Folkvang was enormous. There was the training hall, the dining hall, the bathing rooms, classrooms and armour rooms. There were bedrooms and entertainment rooms. There were women everywhere, and that was just inside! Outside there were stables, training fields, walking tracks, mountains, and streams. In all likelihood, Jem still had plenty more to see. But from her small sampling, she knew that this was a whole other world. A vast one, and one where though some of the rules were the same, many were different.

Despite all the changes, Jewel, it seemed, was thoroughly enjoying herself. Of course, Jewel always seemed that way, right up until that moment when you knew she wasn't. Jem's best friend seemed airy-fairy and carefree, but once you got to know Jewel, really know her, you could see that she used her carefree, happy exterior as a mask. Sometimes when it seemed all was well with Jewel, deep down she was actually really unhappy, miserable even. Even having known Jewel most of her life, Jem often struggled to see the cues that let her know her friend was unhappy. For now, as far as Jem could tell, it seemed like she was genuinely happy, and when it came down to it Jem couldn't pretend that this place wasn't amazing. Because it was.

Jem doubted she could imagine a place half as wonderful, and she had quite an imagination. The women here were amazing too. Jem found herself not only liking most, if not all, of the women she met but feeling as though she had an instant connection with many of them. Jem enjoyed chatting with the other women as they ate, and the bunk room style accommodation, used specifically for Valkyrie who had been in Folkvang under a year, reminded her of camping trips with her youth group when she was younger. The women even stayed up chatting most of the first night which sparked a real feeling of nostalgia. As the new Valkyrie had chatted, Jem had noticed Jewel's ears perk up at the mention of the Einherjar. A group of male warriors, much like Valkyrie, that they would often train either with or against them in competitions. The Einherjar were apparently rather attractive, at least according to the woman who had worked alongside them, or in some cases had gone to collect their spirits from the battlefield. That was one of the special things about Valkyrie. They could go to a battlefield to collect the souls of worthy men, worthy warriors who had died, or were dying, and bring them to Valhalla to train and fight to protect Asgard from the threats that faced this world. The Einherjar's earthly lives ended, but they had another shot at life here in Asgard, while the women all chatted animatedly about the hot Einherjar, Jem couldn't stop her thoughts from detouring straight back to Dan. Every time she relaxed for even a second she found herself wondering where they had taken him. Obviously to the dungeon, but she couldn't stop herself from wanting to know exactly where. Jem wanted to see him. To talk to him. She wanted to understand why he had really come for her because for better or worse she had liked him. She possibly still liked him. Even the fact that he was sometimes a huge wolf didn't bother her. Not really. Sure she'd been shocked when he'd transformed right in front of her. But the more she thought about it, the more she found that she didn't really care. It actually kind of made sense, in a strange way. The way he moved. The way his eyes changed colour. The way her heart raced around him. Well. Maybe that was more to do with how he looked in his human form. The fact that he was a wolf, a Fenrir, it just fit. Jem just couldn't wrap her head around the fact that he was gone now. That he was a prisoner of the Aesir, or that he was the bad guy. At least she kept being told he was the bad guy. Over and over again she heard it repeated that the Fenrir were dangerous, aggressive, evil. But no matter how hard she tried to listen to what the women were saying, women who had been in battle with the Fenrir for thousands of years, there just never seemed to be any solid proof that the Fenrir had ever done anything that could even be considered bad. At least if you didn't include the Fenrir beast killing Odin. When it came down to it, no matter what anyone had to say about the Fenrir, Jem still couldn't stop herself from thinking of Dan, and every time she did her heart ached. It ached much in the same way it had when she had lost her Mum, which was crazy because she had loved her Mum her entire life, and had only known Dan a few days, most of which she hadn't even seen him over.

Jem's shoes padded softly against the pressed dirt path as she walked the tree-lined walkways surrounding the Hall of Folkvang. She'd tried to avoid wandering inside the bustling walls of Folkvang, instead opting to walk outside. That way she could avoid most of the women. In the evenings when the bulk of the training had ended for the day you could find women everywhere. Sitting together around campfires, sharing meals indoors, and though Jem had joined the social groups more than once over the two weeks since she arrived. More often than not she found herself needing time on her own. It was the only way she could decompress from the day of learning. So far she'd done training under all four of the Valkyrie factions and had found herself able to complete the tasks set by each. She'd also found that she was the descendant of the Valkyrie Pogn, a negotiator Valkyrie, which suited her because she found herself enjoying the company of the blue-clad women. Even though she was disappointed to find Jewel was the descendant of Hildr, a warrior Valkyrie, and that they wouldn't be training together. At least not much. In particular, Jem was drawn to Reyna. She reminded Jem of her Gran. Although she looked much younger and had latte coloured skin, rather than her Gran's porcelain. It was something about her manner. Something about her nature. It radiated from the negotiator Valkyrie and made Jem feel safe and secure, just as she did with her Gran. Both Reyna and her Gran were calming. They listened and really heard you. They weighed carefully what they were going to say before opening their mouths, and when they did open them, the people around them left feeling empowered and cared for, even when the conversation hadn't ended where they had wanted it too. Jem had no doubt that she was meant to be a negotiator Valkyrie. That knowledge was only trumped by her desire to walk the halls. With each step she tried to convince herself that she wasn't searching for Dan. But she was. It didn't matter if she was inside or out. Training. Studying. Eating. Or well anything else. He was never far from her mind. Two weeks. It'd been two weeks, and now she was waking up at night. She couldn't shut off the feeling that he was calling her, asking for her help. Which was why she found herself at one o'clock in the morning walking around the forest, before making her way back into

Folkvang where she would no doubt wander the now familiar halls 'not searching' for Dan. Some nights she would swear that beyond the gentle snoring and the occasional flush of a toilet she could hear screaming, and her heart would wrench deep inside her chest, afraid that it was Dan, and that she'd never see him again.

The screams were louder tonight, or were they more strangled, as though the owner of the scream was losing their fight to take another breath. Whatever they were, Jem's heart was racing in panic. A bone-deep fear gripped her. The anxiety was so overwhelming that when she heard the heavy footfalls of someone else walking the halls she ducked around the corner, out of view. When she came back out she saw a tall thin man with blood-red hair, much like Queen Freya's, disappear around the corner. except for of Ali, who she had seen only once or twice since he brought her to Folkvang, this red-haired man was one of the only males Jem had seen, and there was something about him that made her skin crawl. Which was strange, because the more she thought about it, the more she realised he looked very much like a masculine version of Freya. Jem's heart rate amped up, and before she realised what she was doing she found herself halfway down a stained glass-lined hallway, the one the red-haired man had just come from. Once she was sure she wouldn't be seen she descended the stairs to who knows where. The further down she went the faster her heart seemed to race, and the more determined her footsteps. It was as though something deep within her had taken over, her brain had been circumvented and some primal part of her was in control. The air became damper and mustier, as though both dust and mould had found its way into this place and were fighting for dominance. She continued walking forward not even glancing left or right. Almost as though she knew exactly where she was going. Only she had no idea, and maybe, just maybe it was fear that kept her from looking to the sides, because no matter how much she tried to deny it, this place that she'd found seemed more and more like a dungeon, and from what she could tell a dungeon was a lot more like an abattoir than it was like the jail cells in Midgard police stations. Surely they wouldn't be keeping Dan and his wolf friend here? It had been two weeks, what could they possibly gain from keeping them here. Besides, the Aesir were supposed to be the good guys, and the good guys didn't torture people. Did they?

A husky voice croaked from a cell at the end of the hall. "Dan. Dan?! Are you alright?"

She heard a cough and thump, and her heart skipped a beat.

"No names, remember." Dan's voice said.

"He already knows our names Dan." The first voice said in exasperation.

"He thinks he does. But he's not sure." Dan said.

Jem reached the huge wooden door and looked past the bars that formed a small window at the top. Jem couldn't prevent the gasp when she looked inside and saw Dan, naked, his hair matted, and the floor around him covered in blood, some old, some clearly new. His eyes shot up to meet hers, at first shocked, but then softening.

"Hello little dove." He said, forcing a smile.

Dan's friend looked between the two of them and growled, his lip rolling back to expose his teeth. Dan shot him a look, shaking his head, and his friend went silent, though he glared at Jem as though she were evil incarnate.

"Dan…" she started, but there were no words. How did you say sorry? He was supposed to be evil. This was apparently how criminals were treated in this world. But no matter how she tried to justify it, seeing him sitting on the ground, his friend crouched beside him looking completely unharmed, with the exception of deep wounds around his wrists, while Dan's flesh was red raw, torn into strips that hung from his thinning frame and still bleeding, made her feel like vomiting. She felt like a monster. There was no way, not in any world that this was right. She felt a tear run down her cheek and Dan frowned.

"What's wrong Jemima?" he asked, completely ignoring the condition of his broken body, focusing instead on her.

She shook her head in disbelief, hoping against hope that if she shook her head hard enough all of this would disappear.

"What happened to you?" she asked dumbly, as though she couldn't figure it out. As though it wasn't her fault that he was here.

Gerard growled. "I don't care if you do think she's

your mate Dan. This stupid girl. This Valkyrie is the reason I'm watching Freyr beat you to death." He said to Dan, then he turned to her. "You want to know what's happening?" he growled.

"Gerard." Dan said, warning in his voice.

Gerard shook his head. "Dan came to save you, from me. To stop me from capturing you and bringing you back to the den, and in return you got him captured by the Aesir, and now they're making me watch while they torture him to get information about our den so they can kill all our people."

"You were trying to capture me then?" she asked. Dan nodded and though he looked ashamed he refused to look away from her.

"So you never really liked me?" she asked, her voice full of hurt.

"I fell in love with you from the moment I saw you Jemima. You're my mate." Dan said.

"I don't believe you." She said, and then she turned and ran, tears streaming down her face, while Dan called out her name. No, while Dan said, as loudly as he could manage in his condition. "I'm sorry Jemima. I love you."

Dan couldn't believe he'd seen her. Jemima. His little dove. She'd been right outside the door of the cell. He would have done almost anything to be able to get up and walk over to her. But the fact was, it had taken every ounce of his strength to just lift his head up and look at her rather than collapsing to the ground, allowing his body to rest and heal before Freyr returned to give him his next beating. Just seeing her gave him hope. He'd been praying that the Creator would let him see her again, and clearly, He had been listening. Dan might not see her again, though he hoped he would. But even if he didn't, seeing her gave him hope that he could hold out through the next beating. She reminded him why he was keeping his mouth closed. She reminded him of all the people he was protecting. He knew that as long as he and Gerard were down here there would be another beating. He just didn't know when it would be. There was no rhyme or reason to when Freyr would come. The beatings were never at the same time. Sometimes Freyr waited for what seemed like a few days before he beat Dan, other times it seemed as if he'd only been gone a few hours. The only constant in the dungeon was that Freyr was always on his own. That, and that Dan and Gerard were only given food after a beating. Food that Freyr provided. In fact, anything they were given came via Freyr. Things like water or bandages, and except for seeing Jemima, Dan and Gerard hadn't seen a single soul aside from Freyr. It made Dan wonder how, and why Jemima had come down here. At least he knew she was okay. It broke his heart to see her crying. To have her think that he was only trying to capture her. To have her doubting that he cared for her. If anything his time in the dungeon with Freyr had solidified how Dan felt about her. Because every time Freyr beat him Dan had been able to find a place of calm deep within himself, and Jemima was always there. She had become his place of peace.

Gerard was still raging even after Jemima was gone. All the while Dan found himself breathing in her scent, thankful to have just a moment with her. She was alive. She was safe, and no amount of torture would change that.

"I should have killed her." Gerard raged.

At those words, Dan's attention snapped to Gerard. He growled at his friend, and Gerard glared at him.

"I can't believe you're still insisting that woman is your mate." Gerard yelled "She's the reason we're stuck here! She's the reason you're getting tortured everyday! If it weren't for the fact that you're Fenrir you'd have been dead a week ago, but as it is I'm going to be watching you be beaten for weeks, if not years!" Gerard yelled, his face getting redder and redder.

Dan glared right back. "She. Is. My. Mate." He said, his voice low with warning.

"She's a filthy Valkyrie!" Gerard yelled at him.

"If you call her that again I'll make you regret it."
Dan said.

"It's what she is! A Valkyrie! She's not one of us. She's not Fenrir. She. Is. A. FILTHY. Valkyrie!"
Gerard raged.

Dan turned to Gerard, whipped back his fist and let fly. His fist finding Gerard's nose with a crunch.

Gerard looked at him in shock, cradling his nose.

"If she's your mate, then why did she leave?"
Gerard said, though the anger seemed to have seeped away.

"She may be my mate." Dan said, "But until she accepts me, I'm not hers."

Gerard sighed. "How much more of this can you take?" he asked.

Dan shifted his position, and his raw skin protested the movement "I'll take whatever I need to." He said, "I'll die before I sell out our people."

Gerard nodded. "I know you will. That's what worries me." He said.

THE TRUTH
COMES OUT

J em had no idea what had come over her. She'd been thinking about Dan for days. No. Not days. Weeks. She'd been thinking about Dan non-stop ever since she first met him. Even after she'd been told over and over again how the Fenrir were evil she couldn't get him out of her mind. Even now, when he admitted to planning on kidnapping her, she couldn't stop thinking about him. Jem wanted to be mad at Dan, and yet all she'd felt when she'd looked at him was hurt and rejection. She felt like a part of her was crumbling because it had all been a lie, and he didn't actually want her.

Her heart ached as she thought about him. Some of the pain was her own feelings of rejection, but the rest of it was shame. She hadn't been raised to see someone bloody and broken and just leave them to suffer. What the hell was wrong with her? Why did she just leave him there? She'd managed to get all the way to the top of the stairs when she heard his friend shouting at him, and despite her best intentions, despite knowing that she should leave him there, that he was the enemy, she couldn't stop herself from turning around and going back to him. As she walked back down to his cell she took a deep breath for courage and looked from side to side, terrified the entire time that the cells would be filled with half-dead people. People like Dan and his friend. Her fears were unfounded, mostly, because each of the cells were empty. She'd stopped and peered inside the other cells through the small barred windows, and tried to only notice the fact that there were no other prisoners, rather than seeing the stains on the walls and floor that hinted at blood. She had no idea what she was thinking. What she was planning. But she walked back to his cell and seeing a board of keys she reached out and took the only one that looked as though it had been recently used, a large metal key that coated her fingers in fresh blood as she lifted it from its peg. She slotted the key into the door, turned it till she heard a distinctive click, threw the door open and stepped inside.

Dan looked up at her, actually, both men were looking at her. Dan's friend with his mouth open in shock, and Dan his eyes wide and his lips turning up in a slight smile. Once Jem was through the doorway she found herself just standing there, staring at Dan. No words came out of her mouth. She couldn't seem to move her feet any further. She just stood there in the doorway and stared at them as though she had gone completely catatonic. Dan, who was sitting awkwardly on the ground, pushed himself first onto his knees, then using the wall, pulled himself onto his feet. The red ribbon at his wrist glowed as though it was wrapped around a glow stick and lit with glitter, illuminating the dimly lit room. He ignored it, even though with each intensification of the glow it appeared to tighten and dig deeper into his skin until blood dripped off of his fingers. He walked towards her, and then with his clean, or at least cleaner, hand he reached up and cupped her cheek, running his thumb across her cheekbone.

"Are you okay little dove?" He asked.

This whole trip to the dungeon felt like a dream. A strange, slightly scary, ridiculous dream. One where Jem's body and even her mind were acting completely independently of her. She was completely out of control. Or maybe she was out of her mind?

She looked up into his concerned eyes, reached up with both hands to touch the stubble on his chin, and the next thing she knew she'd stepped into his arms and was kissing him. Kissing him as though she were drowning and he was her only source of oxygen. Kissing him in a way she had never kissed anyone before. Not ever. It was a full-on desperate kiss. One that made her heart race and her brain quiet, and when they finally pulled apart, both of them were panting as they attempted to catch their breath. Jem's hands had slid down to rest on his bare chest, and Dan's hand slid down to her hips, pulling her as close as he could. She could feel her body moulding against his, as though they were two pieces of the same puzzle rather than two individuals. It was about that point, when her body was heating in response to his and he started to sway with the effort of standing, that she felt his body shift against hers and her mind caught up. Before she remembered that he was not only still naked, but more than a little aroused by her. Her heart skipped a beat and heat invaded her cheeks as embarrassment flooded her. Dan lifted his hand back to her face, tilting her head up, forcing her to look him in the eye. He placed one more sweet kiss on her lips before saying.

"I couldn't have asked the Creator for a better mate than you. You are already everything I ever wanted and more, and as long as you are safe and happy, I'm happy." He said.

"They told me you're evil." She said, stepping away from him, her eyes darting between Dan, Gerard, and the door. "They said the Fenrir are out to destroy the Aesir and then the rest of the world. That you're trying to finish the job started by the Fenrir Beast."

Dan just stood and listened, swaying every now

and then as he tried to stay on his feet.

"It's not true. The Aesir came after us. They've been hunting us into extinction for as long as our histories have been written." Gerard said.

Dan stepped closer to her, reached out and ran his hand down her hair, his fingers slipping between the loose strands and tickling her neck. She trembled beneath his touch, and she felt goosebumps come up all over her body.

"I can't believe I finally found my mate." He said with a smile, placing yet another kiss on her lips. She kissed him back automatically, leaning into him, wrapping her arms around his neck and gripping his hair between her fingers. The stickiness of the wet blood, combined with the dry flaky texture of the blood that had already dried on Dan's skin brought Jem back to herself. There would likely be blood on her clothes, just like it now coated her hands.

She pulled away. She shouldn't be here. His eyes had shifted to an unnatural gold sending her heart into a panicked sprint. She stepped away from him, backing up till she was standing outside the door.

"I shouldn't be here." She said absently, her fingers hovering over her kiss swollen lips. "I. You. I need to go."

"Jemima." Dan said.

She stopped in her tracks. She didn't know what she was expecting him to say. But whatever it was, she hadn't been expecting him to say "You need to lock the door my love, and put back the key. Otherwise Freyr will know you were here, and I don't know what he'll do to you. Keep yourself safe Jemima. These Aesir, they can't be trusted." He said.

Jem locked the door, placed the key back on its hook with shaking hands, glanced one last time at Dan then turned and sprinted from the room.

Gerard was looking at Dan with wide eyes, disbelief written all over his face.

"She really is your mate, isn't she?" He said.

Dan nodded.

"Dan. She could have gotten us out of here." Gerard said in frustration.

Dan attempted to lower himself to the floor gently, but at the last minute collapsed, landing painfully on his tail bone with an audible grunt.

He took a deep breath against the pain, looked across at his friend and sighed. "She could have Gerard. But there's no guarantee we could have escaped, and it would have put her in danger." He said.

"But if she's your mate then surely she'd want to keep you alive." Gerard said.

"I have no doubt that she is my mate. But clearly she's fighting it. She's been dragged into our world. She's being told that Fenrir are evil, and it's not as though we've given her any reason to dispute that. We were there to kidnap her after all." Dan said.

Gerard frowned. "Dan, if she doesn't come around soon we're both going to die down here."

"Without some kind of escape plan all three of us would die anyway." Dan said.

"You could have asked." He said.

"If she were your mate, could you have asked when it might have meant her dying too?" Dan asked.

Gerard's head dropped. "I guess not." He said,

then looking up asked. "What's it like?"

"What's what like?" Dan asked.

"Finding your mate?" Gerard clarified.

Dan smiled. "It's like coming home, and finding the best part of yourself all at once."

"I hope I have a chance to find that." Gerard sighed.

"I know it sounds stupid given our situation, but finding her makes the likelihood of dying easier. It's like she's proof that all those times I prayed to the Creator he was listening. Because only he would know that she is exactly what I need. From the moment I met her I could just tell that she was made for me. That I'm made for her, and if the Creator listened to me when it came to my mate, then I have no doubt that his other promises are true too. So even if we do die here, this isn't the end." Dan said.

"I'm glad you found her then." Gerard said, "But I still hope she'll find a way to get us out of here."

"Me too." Dan agreed.

The last thing he wanted was to be responsible for his best friend dying, and if they died here he would be. Dan not snatching Jem the moment he met her was the only reason his friend was stuck in this place.

"I'm sorry about all of this." Dan said.

Gerard looked over at him. "It isn't your fault Dan."

"It kind of is. If I'd just grabbed her neither of us would be here." Dan said.

Gerard shook his head. "This was just like any of our other missions. There's no way you could have predicted this." He said.

Dan nodded. He wanted to disagree with his friend, but the odds of an Aesir god being there, waiting for them at Jem's had been impossibly low. They had been unlucky. It was as simple as that.

Jem walked back to her room in a daze. She scrubbed her face and clothes, desperate to erase any evidence that she had been in the dungeons. Once clean she got dressed, slipped into bed quietly, and somehow managed not to wake up any of the other women, even though her blood was pounding so loudly in her ears that she was sure everyone would be able to hear it. Despite her anxiety and confusion, sleep came almost instantly. But every moment seemed to be overwhelmed by dreams. Dreams that filled her night hours with visions of Dan. Some had her wrapped in his arms, kissing him, and feeling more at home than she had ever felt before. Others had her watching as he was beaten in front of her. When she finally woke up she was exhausted and confused. There was no doubt that she was attracted to Dan. Even beaten, bruised and covered in blood he was the most attractive man she'd ever had the opportunity to meet. Even his voice made her pulse kick up a notch and her toes curl. Even knowing the Valkyrie's assertion that the Fenrir were not only dangerous and vicious, but evil, didn't change her feelings for him. Now that she'd found him down in the dungeon her feelings for him seemed only to have increased. All through lessons she thought of him. She just couldn't help but think that there was some kind of misunderstanding between the Aesir and the Fenrir. That they really weren't that bad, and the thing was, knowing they were beating him down there just didn't sit right with her. The Aesir were meant to be the good guys, and the good guys weren't meant to torture anyone. Not even the bad guys. But they were. Dan had looked really bad. How much longer could he possibly last down there, and if he was so strong how was it that they were managing to keep him and his friend down there. From what she'd learnt, the Fenrir were impossibly strong. If that were true then surely together the two Fenrir would have been able to break the door down. Only they seemed to be struggling to simply sit upright.

Jem felt as though she only fumbled through the drills, but her teachers seemed impressed with how quickly she was catching on. She ducked, jumped, spun, punched, and kicked, weaving in and out of each of her opponents. Her mind was on Dan, but her body had almost taken on a life of its own. The trainers tried a range of different fighting styles with each of the new Valkyrie, trying to find their perfect fit. Some of the girls focused primarily on boxing, others were almost magic with swords, guns, bows, throwing stars, and a range of mixed martial arts. The teachers seemed to give the girls basic defence moves for hand to hand and then just let them have at it, assuring them that as they engaged in battle their Valkyrie senses would rise to the foreground. That they would naturally find their fighting style. Jem had scoffed. It sounded ridiculous. The extent of her fighting ability involved all of two karate lessons as a child, a few unsuccessful attempts at that computer game Tekken, and an embarrassing battle with a sweater while in a changing room. She had as much fighting ability as a... well she didn't know... a marshmallow perhaps? She just wasn't a fighter. She wasn't even a lover! She was just Jem. Nothing out of the ordinary. Not that she wasn't special in her own way. But she was hardly going to be the next American Ninja Warrior, and yet, within a few moments of her opponents first attack she felt as though something slipped into place. Dan was still in her mind, but a feeling akin to breathing in the cleansing scent of spearmint washed over her. Her breath came out as a gentle sigh and she felt her body drop into what could only be compared to a squat. She moved like she never had before, her arms deflecting punches, her legs swiping and taking out the legs of her opponents. Jem's movements were fluid but strong, she felt more powerful than she ever had before, and she seemed to have gained flexibility unlike anything she'd had since childhood.

"Well done Jemima." Reyna said with a wide smile as she clapped her hands together.

"How is she a negotiator when she moves like that?" one of the red garbed warrior Valkyrie asked.

"Just because one of our sister's primary gifts

is negotiating doesn't mean she doesn't have abilities in the other disciplines. In fact, once our Valkyrie heritage is unlocked some of the women here find that they have enough talent to belong to any one of the factions. When that happens they choose based not on their ability, but on their passion." One of the older Valkyrie stated.

The warrior Valkyrie who'd asked the question nodded, but she still didn't look as though she really understood.

It was hard to explain. Or maybe it wasn't? Jem hated fighting. What she was doing now, she liked it, whatever it was that she was doing. It made her feel centred, peaceful. But she didn't want to hit anyone. She was happy to swipe the feet out from someone. But when it came to actually fighting to hurt someone. That made her skin crawl. She felt such an aversion to it that she would rather she was the one taking the beating than the one handing it out. As far as she was concerned the best way to win a fight was to put a stop to it before it even got to the point of being physical. At that thought, her brain was drawn back to Dan. The woman she was fighting thrust her arm forward towards Jem's centre. The moment she had fully extended her arm Jem caught it, pulling her forward and spinning her around so the woman's arms were behind her, pulled out on a funny angle so that she would experience sharp pain if she tried to pull away.

Essentially Jem had hogged tied her.

Then seemingly out of the blue she looked up and Reyna and asked. "Do Fenrir get married?"

Reyna's eyes opened wide for a second, in shock. "I'm sorry Jemima, what do you mean?"

"I keep hearing that they're evil, but how do their communities work? Why do they attack the Aesir? Are they just like wild wolves? They presumably have children. So do they marry, or have a single partner? Or do they just have children with whoever?" Jem asked.

The corner of Reyna's lips turned up in a small smile.

"This is what you were thinking of while you were fighting?" She asked.

Jem nodded and waited for Reyna to answer the question.

"Well from what we can tell the Fenrir only ever have one partner that they refer to as their mate." Reyna said.

"How do they choose their mates?" Jem asked, thinking about what Dan had said.

"It seems to be a mix of an attraction and a biological response. To a point it seems as though they don't have a choice. They're bodies tell them which member of the opposite gender is biologically compatible with them and from there they seem to decide based on who the person is. Though from what I've seen all their pairings are successful." She replied.

"Would they ever make a claim that someone

was their mate to manipulate them?" Jem asked.
Could Dan have been doing that to her?

Reyna frowned but shook her head.

"That's not something the Fenrir joke about.
Ever." A blonde-haired woman with one brown
eye and one blue eye said. "It's just not acceptable
in their culture." She said.

"Oh! Lady Elena, Welcome!" Reyna said, bowing
to the woman.

The blonde woman nodded but continued to
look at Jem with intrigue.

Jem released the woman who had started
making pained noises.

"What about torture?" Jem said.

"I wouldn't have a clue, they're yet to catch any of
our people." Elena said.

"And what about the Aesir?" Jem probed.

Reyna and Elena both shook their heads.

"No." Reyna said, "Absolutely not."

"The Fenrir that the Aesir encounter are either
killed or on occasion, if they are willing, become
servants." Elena said.

Jem's gut churned. Going by how Dan and his
friend were being treated, either these women
were lying to her, or they were being lied to.

"If they're evil how could you ever trust them as
servants?" Jem asked.

A handsome man with long, fine, blonde hair,
walked up behind Elena, wrapping his arms
around her waist and kissed her on the cheek.
Elena's cheeks flushed as she looked at the young

man and smiled shyly.

"Oh my! Lord Hod!" Reyna said in surprise. "Does your mother know you're here?" she asked.

Hod laughed, a rich deep sound. "No Reyna. It's a surprise. Elena and I are both getting sick of the trials of court. Especially while they're doing this ridiculous courting ritual stuff. It's completely unnecessary for us. We've known who our other halves were for a long time, and growing up with Mother I hardly need more etiquette lessons." He looked over at Jem, assessing. "The Fenrir taken on as servants are expected to wear a Gleipnir bond. It prevents them from being able to hurt any of the Aesir. Or anyone else for that matter. If they even think about it they experience crippling pain." He explained.

"I thought you said you didn't torture." Jem said to Elena.

"Gleipnir only causes pain if the Fenrir wearing it intends harm." Hod explained.

"How?" Jem asked.

Hod smiled then looked at Reyna. "I like this one. She doesn't just accept. She wants to know why." He said, then returned his attention to Jem, "Gleipnir is an enchanted bond. It looks like a red ribbon, but has been treated with special spells specifically to control and dampen the gifts of the Fenrir."

Dan, his arm bleeding as he stood in front of her, the red ribbon glowing and biting into his skin flashed to the forefront of Jem's mind. There was no way Dan had been planning on attacking her. Not after he admitted that he believed she was his mate. Assuming that part of what Jem had just been told was true. Dan hadn't even tried to escape. Instead of going out the door right behind Jem, he'd simply kissed her. So if this red ribbon, that only hurt them if they planned on harming someone, was working how Hod said it was, then why had it been digging into Dan skin as though it were a razor blade?

Jem nodded. But now she questioned everything else she had been told, at least about the Fenrir.

"Hod?" Queen Freya's voice came across the room.

Hod and Elena looked up and smiled as Freya approached.

"Greetings Mother." Hod said

Queen Freya was Hod's mother?

"And Lady Elena." Queen Freya frowned. "How exactly have you left the ladies training halls?"

Hod laughed. "You think a few wards would stop me from getting her out?" he said. "Besides all the other Aesir Lords are meeting the Ladies and I refuse to share even one moment of my Elena's time with them."

Queen Freya frowned, but a smile broke through. "Oh, you terrible child." She said with a laugh, "Just like your Father. Forever getting into mischief."

"Of course." Hod said with a smile, pulling Elena against his side, "What's life without a little adventure?"

Queen Freya smiled at her son indulgently, although Jem noticed she only just barely acknowledged Elena. Which seemed strange.

"So. You're over here meeting some of my Valkyrie?" Freya asked.

"Actually." Hod said, "We were on our way to find you when Elena became mesmerised with.." He looked at Jem.

"Oh Jemima." Jem gave her name.

"Jemima's impressive interpretation of Wushu, and then I became entranced with her thirst to understand the Fenrir culture." He said.

Freya's expression darkened. "They are not fluffy pets for you to fall in love, or become enamoured with." She said, her tone cool. "They are a dangerous, violent people. No, not people. Animals who would sooner kill you than look at you. Their culture is little more than a mask for their true device, destroying our people out of petty revenge." She said.

"But Mother, Fenrir and Father died so long ago. These Fenrir, they wouldn't have anyone alive who would even remember receiving the history second hand." Hod disagreed.

"I received a prophecy about them the moment they entered this world." Queen Freya said with a curl of the lip. "My prophecies are never wrong."

"Of course Queen Freya." Elena said, elbowing Hod none too gently.

Queen Freya completely ignored Elena, tears

welling up in her eyes. "I'm just trying to keep you and my people safe." She said.

A feeling of nausea settled in the bottom of Jem's stomach. Something about what Queen Freya was saying just wasn't sitting well with her. Actually, everything about the woman felt false. As though it was somehow manufactured, or like a mask. Something altogether different was going on in Asgard than what they were all being told. She needed to get Dan and his scary friend out of this place. The more she stayed here the more she felt she needed to leave. Jem loved the idea of the Valkyrie. She even thought most of the Valkyrie were amazing. But this place. Queen Freya, and even the entourage she had trailing after her. They gave Jem a horrid oppressive feeling and made her heart do a terrified tap dance. The only time her heart ever did that was when the person was beyond dicey or was full-on dangerous. She'd been trying to ignore it for days. But standing here right next to the Aesir Queen, Jem felt like she'd been given a warning that screamed nothing short of 'The Apocalypse is coming' and she wasn't one to ignore it. Jem was getting the heck out of here, and she was taking Dan with her.

Jem finished out the day of training before making her way back down to the dungeon as stealthily as she could manage. Not that any of the women were particularly bothered by her comings and goings. After the last few weeks, they were used to her going for her walks. Even Jewel would just wave and keep on chatting with her new friends. Jewel had taken to Folkvang and the whole Valkyrie thing like a duck to water. Jem, on the other hand, felt as though she was floundering. She seemed to be doing well in each of the Valkyrie disciplines, but when it came to the women... She liked them. They were friendly. But it just didn't quite fit. No matter what happened from here, things just weren't quite right. Jem felt completely out of sorts, and all she knew was she had to see Dan. Had to talk to him. She had to come up with some way to help him. Something was going on with the Aesir. But not something she understood. All she knew was that the Fenrir weren't what the Aesir were saying they were, and everything in her was screaming to get Dan out of this place.

Jem padded softly through the hallways. She didn't know why, but her instincts said that this time she needed to make absolutely certain she wasn't seen. She'd stripped down to her tight, but soft linen workout gear, and she'd slipped her shoes off. She felt almost as though she were wandering around naked. Of course she wasn't. But it didn't stop the fact that she felt impossibly exposed. Of course, that might have been more to do with the fact that she was thinking about doing something that was guaranteed to mean the Valkyrie would never accept her. It wasn't long before she realised her instinct to stay hidden was a good idea. Because the moment she stepped into the hallway housing all the cells screaming filled the air around her. Dan's screaming. As she listened to his pained cries she felt as though a part of her was being torn asunder. It took everything in her not to just rush in and try to save him. Instead, she slowly moved forward and slipped into the empty cell closest to the one Dan and his friend were in.

"Well Fenrir."

Jem heard a smooth masculine voice say through the wall.

"I don't know how much more of this your dominant can take." The voice tutted. "All I'm asking for at the moment is your names, and then once I have those we can start getting down to the important things. Things like where your den is so we can put an end to all you filthy Fenrir."

The screaming stopped abruptly, though evidently, the beating hadn't slowed at all. For what seemed like forever Jem listened to the slap of a whip and the occasional grunt from Dan. A low growl echoed through the wall the entire time. It was an angry sound, and yet the man who had clearly been whipping Dan continued to chat. At first it was just inane things. He spoke about the weather. He spoke about the Valkyrie his sister was training to destroy the Fenrir. At which point Jem had no doubt that the torturer was none other than Freyr, Freya's brother, and then he said something that cemented Jem's resolve to get Dan out of here.

"When Freya told me about the prophecy she'd received I was worried. We knew that your people would try and stop us from achieving our goal. But you know what? Revenge is so much more fun when I can trick an entire race of people, and I get to destroy another as a bonus. Now. Don't get me wrong. Your forefather, the Fenrir Beast, did us a favour killing Odin. But when it comes down to it I've never been partial to dogs. I'm more of a boar person myself, and Freya tends to prefer cats. So really, you are just collateral damage. Of course, if you promised to step out of the way and just let us do what we need to do, it would be fine. But we both know that will never happen, don't we." Freyr said, then he went quiet, and all Jem could hear was the low growling, Dan's pained grunts, and the rhythmic snap of the whip.

"Well Fenrir, I shall see you." Pause, "Soon." Freyr said.

Jem's skin crawled. There was no way that psycho would be seeing Dan if she had anything to say about it.

She waited until she heard him close and lock the cell door. Heard the jingle of the keys as they were put back up on the hook, and held her breath, freezing in her corner as Freyr made his way past the cell she was hiding in.

Once she was certain he was gone Jem stood cautiously. She may have been certain he was gone. But an unmistakable terror filled her at the thought of him returning, so she wasn't going to be anything but cautious. There was no possible way that being found down here would be a good thing. She pushed the door open slowly, doing her best to stop it from creaking. Then padded softly over to the hooks and lifted the key silently from its spot.

"Dan." She whispered as she opened the door.

The low growl from behind the door intensified for a moment, stopping abruptly when she stepped in. Dan was laying in a heap on the ground, and his back looked like it was made of minced meat rather than flesh.

Jem rushed to Dan's side lifting his head into her lap.

"Dan are you okay!?" she exclaimed.

He looked up at her and managed a weak smile. "Better now." He said.

A few tears dripped down her cheeks and dropped onto Dan's face below her.

What was she going to do? She needed to get him out of here.

He raised his hand to her cheek. "Don't cry little

dove, I'll heal up in no time."

Gerard made a huffing noise. "Yeah, just soon enough for Freyr to do it again."

"I need to get the two of you out of here." She said.

"Too dangerous." Dan said lowering his hand so it sat next to his face on Jem's thigh.

Jem ran her fingers through his hair. "Did you mean it?" she asked him, drawing his attention back to her face. "That I'm your mate."

He nodded his head. "I knew from the first moment I saw you, the first moment I scented you." Dan said.

"He's too weak to get out of here." His friend said, "And I won't leave him here to be tortured."

"Gerard." Dan said, a slight warning in his voice.

"We could carry him together maybe?" Jem suggested.

Gerard looked at her and sighed. "You might be strong enough. But with this thing on I won't be much help." Gerard said lifting his wrist to show the thin red band.

"Is it Gleipnir?" Jem asked.

"What do you know about Gleipnir?" Gerard asked.

"Mainly that it's made to stop Fenrir from hurting the Aesir." Jem said.

Jem felt Dan chuckle, then cringe at how the movement shook his scarred body.

"It stops us alright. It stops us from doing anything they don't want us to do by cutting and burning the skin it's up against and sending an electric current strong enough to make your hair smoke right through your body." Gerard said. He didn't seem to find it as amusing as Dan had.

"Maybe I can break it off. It shouldn't affect me right?" Jem said.

Gerard held his arm out to her.

"Try it on me first." He said, "I can handle the shock if it doesn't work. But Dan, well. It might not be very good for him to try it at the moment."

She reached forward, but Gerard pulled his hand away. Dan seemed as though he may have fallen asleep.

"It could hurt." Gerard said.

"You said that." Jem said.

Gerard shook his head and looked at her more seriously. "No Jemima. It might hurt you."

Jem pursed her lips together and nodded at him. He put his arm back out to her again.

"If you're sure." He said.

Jem put her fingers tentatively on the red cord, ribbon really. It was smooth like silk but felt strong like wire, and nothing. Not even a tingle. She pulled on the cord, pausing only to look at Gerard. He shook his head. She pulled harder. Clearly there was no shock for either of them. But the cord didn't budge either. Gerard sighed, but Jem refused to let go, even when he made to pull his arm away.

"I can do this." She said, and for the first time, Gerard smiled.

"I can see why he likes you. You would have been a good mate for him." He said.

Jem looked him in the eye. "I am a good mate for him." She said, though she had no idea where the assertion came from.

"You won't ever give up will you." Gerard said with a smile.

She shook her head. "Not until I'm tied up here next to you both." She said.

Gerard chuckled.

"I'm not going to stop until all the people here know the truth. I heard what Freyr said, and there's something more going on here than what they are letting on. They aren't just trying to destroy the Fenrir. They want to destroy everyone else as well. I just don't understand why. I mean, aren't the Aesir supposed to be their people. Freya is the Queen for goodness sake." Jem said. "Maybe if we could get hold of that prophecy Freyr was going on about."

She was certain she could feel the cord loosening.

"Freya and Freyr aren't Aesir though." Gerard said.

Jem frowned. "What do you mean they're not Aesir."

"Freya and Freyr are from a race of people called the Vanir. Their people were defeated in one of the Aesir wars, and they were kind of traded across as a type of treaty between the Vanir and Aesir." Gerard explained.

"One of the Valkyrie told me that when I got here.

But all of them are so enamoured with Freya, and constantly calling her the Aesir Queen that I forgot." Jem admitted, giving the cord one last pull, snapping it between her fingers.

"Ha!" She exclaimed.

She turned instantly to Dan's wrist and started working on the red ribbon wrapped there. After a little bit of a struggle, the ribbon there snapped. Dan sighed, and it seemed like his bleeding had slowed down. Which surely couldn't happen, but Jem was sure it had.

"We can't just leave." Gerard said, "We need a plan. Besides." He lifted up his other arm.

"They're on both our ankles too." He said.

Jem nodded. "I know the best and least populated routes for getting out of this place." She said, "It's just. Once we get out of here I have no idea where to go. I mean we're essentially on an entirely different planet or something. I don't know where we are, or how we go about getting from Asgard to Earth."

"There's a portal from Asgard to Midgard." Gerard said, "Do you have any idea where we are at the moment?"

"We're in Folkvang." Jem said.

Gerard nodded. "From what I understand, after Ragnarok, the Aesir resettled in the same places. Kept the same place names and such. So if I paid attention in school like I was meant to, then we're already in Southern Asgard. All we need to do is travel further south to the Himinbjord

Mountains and find Heimdell's Palace. Then it's just a hop skip and a jump to the bridge and home." He said.

Dan stirred and looked up at Jem. He coughed

"Of course he was always too busy egging me into doing something we weren't supposed to be doing. So it's just as likely the bridge is in the complete opposite direction." Dan said with a chuckle.

Gerard laughed. "Whatever man. Everyone knows I was the innocent being taken along for the ride, and you were the evil mastermind."

"Freyr kept talking about some prophecy." Jem said.

Dan coughed again. "He's been going on about it for days."

Jem stopped and thought about it. "He's scared of you." She said.

Gerard chuckled. "And how do you figure that?" He asked.

"From what I briefly heard, the reason they're trying to kill your people is because they think you'll stop them from doing whatever it is they are trying to do." She said, "They're scared of what you can do. What they think you will do. We need to see that prophecy." She announced.

After a few moments of discussion. A discussion that centred primarily around Dan and Gerard reluctantly agreeing that they should try and get a look at the prophecy. As well as Jem insisting she needed to try and get Jewel out of here as well. She was on her way back up to her room. Jem had tried to convince Dan and Gerard to come with her, and just hide so they could leave straight away but they'd been adamantly against it. Freyr didn't stick to any kind of schedule when it came to the beatings he gave Dan. Beatings he gave exclusively to Dan so that he could physically break him while trying to break Gerard mentally. Freyr was making both of the Fenrir males feel helpless, and he was managing it quite successfully. It had been a few weeks. A few short weeks for her. But a few impossibly long ones for the men. Jem could see the cracks appearing in their resolve. She strongly doubted either of them would give away anything about their people. She would be shocked if Freyr would even be able to get their names. But that didn't mean the torture wouldn't erode their minds eventually. Fenrir may not be as fragile as humans. But even they had to have a breaking point, and from what Jem had seen, neither men were far from reaching that point.

It wasn't as late as Jem had first thought it was when she went down to see Dan. She'd completely forgotten about eating, walking straight to the cells. Which was why there were masses of women making their way to dinner, or to their rooms from dinner. The scent of roasted meat and vegetables flowed to her from the open doors at the end of the hall and she felt her stomach grumble in response. When was the last time Dan and Gerard had eaten? She breathed in deeply and released it. Going in there looking panicked wasn't going to help anyone. Not her, and certainly not Dan and Gerard. If she didn't find her calm then she was going to blow this thing before she even got started. Jem only had three things she needed to do. Find the prophecy. Get Jewel to leave with her. And get Dan and Gerard the heck out of here. That and possibly packing some supplies would be a good idea. She had no idea how long it would take them to get to the Himinbjord Mountains. But given that she could barely even see the mountains from Folkvang she couldn't imagine it was going to be one of those weekend walks. For all she knew, it was going to take them weeks to get there, and that wasn't taking into consideration the fact that they'd probably have to carry Dan most of the way. No. It was fine. She could do this. She scanned the rows of tables. The same ones that reminded her of a cross between Hogwarts and some kind of high school coming of age movie. Or you know, one of those women's prison TV series, and searched for Jewel. She was at a table filled with smiling women, chatting animatedly. Even in a place like Folkvang where there were talented, beautiful, and intelligent women to spare, Jewel remained one of the most radiant and charismatic people Jem had ever known. She even seemed to have captured the attention of Hod and Elena, who had abandoned the head table and sat listening and laughing at something Jewel had said. As soon as Jewel saw Jem making her way over to the table she raised her hand high and waved, a massive smile on her face. She was so happy here. Potentially happier than Jem had ever seen her before, and what she was going to say to her friend was more than likely going to shatter all of that.

"Hey babe." Jewel exclaimed happily, "I've been wondering where you were. I thought maybe a Fenrir got you." She giggled, along with the rest of the table.

She had no idea how close she was to the truth. But she would soon. Jem forced a smile. She was aiming for normal, casual. She was fairly certain she didn't manage anything close. Jewel, of course, saw it immediately.

Her face went serious. "Jem is everything okay?" she asked.

Jem looked around the group. But they had gone back to discussing whatever it was that they had been laughing about earlier, except Hod and Elena, who though they had joined the discussion, Jem could have sworn had directed their bodies so they could hear her better. Jem sat down at the very end of the long bench seat, a couple of spaces away from Jewel. Jewel slid down the seat so they were closer. She put a hand on Jem's arm.

"What's going on Jem?" Jewel asked, her voice quiet so they were less likely to be heard. Jewel had always been good at knowing when to keep things on the down-low.

"It's this place." Jem said.

Jewel looked at her in confusion. "What do you mean? It's great here." Jewel said.

"Some things just aren't adding up Jewel. Especially the things involving the Fenrir. I.. I really think we need to get out of this place." She said.

Jewel looked at her in disbelief. "Leave. Why?"

Jem watched as her best friend got that stubborn look she had when she either didn't believe or didn't want to believe something. It was rare, but when it happened Jewel could be more stubborn than even Jem.

Jewel rolled her eyes. "This is because of Dan, isn't it? You liked him, and now you're coming up with excuses for him. Making him the good guy, and Queen Freya and the Valkyrie the bad guys. Well it's not true Jem. The Fenrir are evil."

Jem straightened her spine. "No. They're not. They aren't anything like what Freya is saying."

Jewel was shaking her head. "The Valkyrie and Queen Freya are the good guys, and you're being stupid." She said.

Jem felt something inside her shatter. Her heart maybe. Or possibly just her control.

"Good guys don't torture people Jewel!" She said a little too loudly.

Jewel's eyes opened wide, and behind her Hod and Elena were watching Jem with interest.

"What are you talking about?" Jewel asked.

"I went down to the dungeons. I heard Freyr beating Dan, taunting him. Going on about some prophecy. I've seen Dan, Jewel. Freyr has whipped him until all the flesh has torn off his back." Tears started to well up in Jem's eyes as she told Jewel.

Somehow the others at the table seemed as though they hadn't even noticed the, now loud, discussion going on between Jem and Jewel.

"Jem." Jewel started, her voice softer. "I don't know what you've seen. What he told you, but…"

"I'm his mate." Jem said helplessly, "And I can't leave him down there for Freyr and Freya to kill."

Jewel shook her head. "He's lying to you Jem. Manipulating you so you'll set him free." She said.

"Fenrir don't lie about their mates." Jem said.

They didn't lie, and he couldn't fake the way she felt about him.

Hod and Elena moved closer.

"She's right." Elena said, looking at Jewel, "Fenrir don't lie about their mates. They would never claim that someone was their mate unless they actually were. Especially not to the individual they were claiming."

"What were you saying about a prophecy?" Hod said.

Jem clamped her lips tightly closed. This was Freya's son. There was no way she could trust him.

He sighed. "I promise, I won't say anything to Mother." He said, "I have a friend, one who was banished."

"Vidar." Elena said, her eyes wide.

"He was sent to Midgard many years ago. Every now and then Elena and I will visit him, and he has always insisted he saw Mother receiving a vision. A prophecy, and that then she thrust him out of Asgard. Maybe there's a little bit more truth to what he was saying than we thought." Hod said.

"Do you think you could get it for me? At least let me see it. Can you help me get Dan and Gerard out of here?" Jem asked.

She was desperate. Asking these two Aesir for help was probably the stupidest thing she could ever do. But the more help she had the better, at least if she wanted any shot at getting the Fenrir out of here alive.

"I can't believe you're even listening to this rubbish!" Jewel said.

"I'm not lying to you!" Jem exclaimed.

"Oh, I have no doubt you think that what you're saying is true. But for once Jem I think your intuition is completely wrong. I'm not going to help you with this, I'm not leaving, and neither should you." Jewel said.

"But Jewel. This place. It isn't safe here. They're lying to us." Jem said.

"I don't want to hear anymore. You need to forget about this. We've got a good thing here Jem. I finally have a good thing, and I'm not about to let it go for some feeling you had. Or even some conversation you heard." Jewel said, and then she walked away.

Elena and Hod still watched Jem.

"Come with us. I think I might know where Mother keeps the prophecy." Hod said.

Jem stared at him. How could she trust him? What choice did she really have?

"We won't let anything happen to you." Elena said, "I promise."

There was something about Elena. Something pure, honest, and transparent. Jem wondered if the young woman would have been able to lie even if she wanted to, and so, even though it could be a terrible mistake if the two Aesir ended up being liars, Jem followed them. The three of them walked across the mess hall, into the training room Jem had been brought into that very first day, and across to the door Freya had walked through after her big speech.

"It'll be in here somewhere. I can almost guarantee it." Hod said, crossing the lush red carpet to a large desk made almost entirely of what looked like gold and amber.

"You don't think she'd keep it in her main palace?" Elena asked, making her way to the bookshelf that lined the wall behind the desk and rifling through books, papers, and pushing aside the ornaments that decorated the shelves.

"With all the guests she constantly has there?" Hod said. "I highly doubt it. She's able to control who comes and goes here more easily. Not to mention there are no Fenrir here."

"There are Fenrir here, in Asgard?" Jem asked.

Hod nodded, but his face was solemn. "That's what makes me wonder if what Mother has been telling us all these years is true. The Fenrir in Asgard are used as palace staff. You know, the Fenrir who 'choose' to serve. Very few people know they are Fenrir, and when I enquired once Mother told me they all chose to serve her. But I got the distinct impression that they had very little choice in the matter."

"Were they wearing Gleipnir?" Jem asked.

"That was the only way they would be accepted to serve in the palace." Hod said.

Jem looked at him. "Then they had no choice." She said, "The Gleipnir bonds don't just stop the Fenrir from hurting the Aesir. They've been spelled so that they have to do anything the Aesir say. Or at least anything certain Aesir say, or they experience agonising, even crippling pain." Jem said, thinking of the blood running down both Dan and Gerard's wrists and ankles.

Hod nodded. "I see." He said.

"Found it!" Elena announced scanning a thick scroll.

Hod took it from her hands, reading quickly, his frown deepening. Jem peered over his shoulder at it but couldn't read a word.

Hod had just opened his mouth to say something when he froze.

"Jemima. Hide. Now." He said, his voice low, quiet, urgent.

Jem slid behind a cabinet near the door. There was no way anyone could see her there.

"You'll have to travel south." Elena whispered, "If you can get them out make your way to Lofntyr Manor. Lady Lofn will help you."

The door across the room swung open, and going by the sweet scent of apples that wafted in Freya had entered, not that Jem could see from her hiding spot.

"Oh my!" Freya's voice gasped. "Hod, Elena. What in the heavens are you doing in my office?" she asked.

Jem could hear the flap of paper as Hod spoke.

"What is this Mother?" Hod asked, his voice not entirely concealing his anger.

"It's a prophecy of course." Freya said, ignoring his tone entirely.

"You told us the Fenrir were trying to destroy us." Hod said.

"And they are." Freya replied

"That's not what this says." Hod said, flapping

the scroll in front of his mother's face.

There was a pause so silent Jem was terrified they would all be able to hear her breathing.

"Oh my dear. You read it. Both of you read it." Freya's voice said, half sounding sad, though mostly sounding annoyed.

"We did, and you need to tell the people the truth." Hod said.

"Or we will." Elena's sweet warm voice announced.

Freya's voice turned hard. "You silly girl." She spat, "You never were good enough for my Hod. But as he is so enamoured with you I had considered allowing you to live once my plan was finally achieved. I have the power to allow more than a few of the Aesir to live. Though only the ones of my choosing. I had hoped to keep each of my children in the dark until the last moment. But you stupid girl. You've filled his head with all kinds of ideas. Right from the beginning I knew you'd be trouble, and now I have no choice but to take you out of the equation."

"What are you saying Mother?" Hod asked.

"Oh, my sweet stupid boy." Freya said, "She knows too much. You both do."

Jem's heart thumped. Was this woman. This Queen. Going to kill her son and his girlfriend?

As if reading her mind Freya continued speaking, answering Jem's question.

"Don't worry. I won't kill her. That's much too light a punishment. She's stolen you away from me my boy. I've already lost you once. I won't lose you again. But for now, I will have to send you away." Freya said.

"That won't stop us from telling the people what's going on." Elena said.

"Oh, but it will my dear. Because neither of you will remember. You won't remember any of this, or even who you are, and you never will. At least not until I'm ready for you to." Freya said.

"You can't just make me forget Elena mother." Hod said, "She's my soulmate."

"And I will turn her into your fiercest opponent. You'll never even want to be around each other you'll hate each other so much. More than that, you'll never have the chance." Freya said. "Don't worry son. You'll be well taken care of."

Jem heard two distinct thumps, and through a small gap, she could see the tip of Elena's slippered foot. What exactly had Freya done to them? Clearly it was nothing good.

The door across the room creaked and a second person stepped in.

"Ah Lady Fulla, impeccable timing as always." Freya said, "We have a little situation here."

"I can see that My Queen. What would you have me do?" Lady Fulla asked.

"First things first. Throw the prophecy into the fire." Freya said, "I never should have kept it."

A GREAT ESCAPE

J em didn't know how long she stood behind the cabinet. All she knew was that her legs had started to ache and that Freya and Fulla had worked together, casting a spell that would strip away all the memories of Hod and Elena. The entire spell was spoken in old Norse, so Jem didn't understand a word, well, not a word except for Elena and Hod's names. Once the two women had cast their spell they had discussed where they would send them, but they moved them from the room before Jem could hear exactly where they were going to be taking them. Guilt ate at Jem. This was her fault. She got Elena and Hod into this, whatever this thing was. They'd been the good guys after all. Even when they were faced with Freya they didn't turn Jem over. They helped her hide, and they told her what she needed to do to help Dan and Gerard survive. Head South. Find Lofntyr Manor. Jem felt guilty. But she wasn't going to let that paralyse her. They gave her a chance. They'd chosen to give her a chance, and she was going to take it. Even if it meant she was doing it without Jewel at her side. It hurt her heart leaving her friend. It hurt her even more deeply that Jewel hadn't believed her. Hadn't wanted to believe her. But her responsibility now was to help Dan and Gerard, and that was exactly what she was going to do.

Jem slipped from her hiding spot, easing her body carefully into the room. The last thing she needed was for Freya or Fulla to catch her. The supposed Queen of the Aesir had just stripped the memories of her son and his girlfriend and was banishing them to, well the Creator only knew where. If Freya could do that to her child, then there was absolutely no doubt in Jem's mind that she would have no problems making Jem disappear. Jem needed to get out of here. She needed to get Dan and Gerard out of here, and quick. Stepping out into the centre of the room Jem was about to race out of the room when she saw what was left of the prophecy scroll sitting on the hearth in front of the fireplace. Most of the delicate paper had burnt away, but portions of it were still legible. Or at least they would have been if she could read the language. Looking around the room she spotted a beautiful gold scarf. No doubt Freya would be spitting mad once she saw it was gone, and she'd be even less impressed when she realised it had been used to wrap the charred prophecy. Jem didn't bother to unravel the scroll, partially because it was still pretty darn hot, but also because she didn't want to damage it anymore than she already had. She placed the prophecy carefully in the scarf, wrapped the scarf tightly around it and went quickly back to her room. Most of the girls were asleep. Well, all of them except Jewel who gave her a funny look, paused as though she might say something before pursing her lips together and rolling over in her bed. Jem didn't want to leave Jewel behind. But really, what choice did she have? If she tried to convince Jewel to come it would likely end in another fight. One that was guaranteed to wake up the rest of the girls. One that would be a death sentence for Dan and Gerard, and possibly even her. Jem shoved the wrapped scroll into the bottom of her bag. Shoved some clothes inside, and pulled on her battle gear, plus a warm cloak. Then she raced to the kitchen and took as much of the dried meat, cheeses, bread and flagons of water as she thought she would be able to carry. She was tempted to take a weapon, she even stopped by the training room to grab one, but she knew it would just weigh her down, and as it was she would need to help carry Dan. Instead, she grabbed some of the bandaging and healing implements from the healers' table. She had no doubt she could use them. She just wasn't certain it would actually be any help to Dan or Gerard. Maybe Fenrir and Valkyrie magic wouldn't mix. Still, she had to try. As she raced back toward the dungeon she found two large cloaks hanging from pegs where they kept the spare armour. Men's ones. She spied around the room. Men had been here. They must have been visiting or preparing to train with the woman. Clearly, the Valkyrie were due for their first introduction to the Einherjar the next day. Jem would have to be extra careful she wasn't spotted now. Although the addition of the men may help her get the Fenrir out. She actually felt kind of bad stealing the guys' jackets, whoever they were. At least Jewel would be happy to see the guys wandering around all buff in their Einherjar armour. She'd been talking about it for days, looking forward to them finally coming. Jem pushed away the pain that came with the thought of Jewel. Jewel would be fine without her. Probably even better than fine, and Jem had a job to do. She rolled the heavy cloaks and shoved them under her arms. She needed the clothes. Partially to keep Dan and Gerard warm and dry outside, but mostly to stop them from being noticed or recognised, and she could guarantee that two men as attractive as them, even when they were covered in blood, were going to get noticed if they started wandering around naked. She'd certainly notice.

The route down to the dungeon had become familiar, despite only having travelled it a few times. It was as if Jem were drawn to wherever Dan was, rather than remembering the path.

Whatever it was Jem just went with it, moving with a speed and agility she was completely unaware she had. She was in the cell door quicker than she thought possible.

"I'm back." She whispered.

"Did you get the prophecy?" Gerard asked.

She cringed. "Sort of. I'll tell you later. For now we need to get the heck out of here." She said reaching forward and snapping the three remaining Gleipnir bonds on Gerard's wrist and ankles. She chucked him the cloak and turned to do the same for Dan.

"Are you okay?" He asked.

"Peachy." She said in frustration, then sighed. "I'm not going to be fine until we get the two of you out of here and you're on the mend."

"I'm sorry about all of this" Dan said.

Jem chuckled, shaking her head. "I can't imagine you planned for any of this to happen. It's not your fault. If it's anyone's fault then it's mine. If I hadn't been Valkyrie and your mate, you wouldn't even be in this position." She said.

He frowned and went to protest.

She interrupted. "I know you want to blame yourself a little more, and we can talk about it later if we live through this. For now, can we just say it was out of either of our control and get out of here?" she asked, throwing the cloak around his shoulders.

Gerard laughed. "You know what Dan? I actually think I like her." He said coming over, slinging one arm around Dan and hoisting him up.

Jem got in on the other side of him.

Jem looked at Gerard. "Your strength seems to be coming back fast." She acknowledged.

Gerard nodded. "It was only the Gleipnir slowing me down. Once my body has had time to heal a little more, and flush the poison that was leaching into me I'll be fine. Might take a day till I'm back to full strength."

"What about Dan?" She asked, he'd passed out when they hoisted him to his feet.

"Longer." Gerard said, "So where do we go from here?"

Jem led them cautiously from the cell, only stopping to lock the door and rehang the key. Hopefully that would make it take longer to notice Dan and Gerard were gone. She wove from hall to hall, taking the path she knew had the least traffic. It was late. Unlikely that anyone would be up and about. But with the Valkyrie, and with Freya, you never knew. Some of the Valkyrie leaders liked to run night drills. Some of the women were more night owls than day, or were very early morning people, and there were even a few who seemed to have insomnia, or at least really limited sleep needs. Luckily Gerard was able to warn her before each of those. Every now and then his face would turn to her and he'd shake his head. She could only assume he'd either heard or smelt the women coming. So far they had been lucky, the women had turned into a room, or they'd been able to duck into a doorway or around a corner. Jem didn't hold out hope that their luck would last much longer. The night was swiftly becoming morning and they really needed to get as far away from Folkvang as they could before the Valkyrie woke and discovered she was gone, or worse, before Freyr realised his Fenrir captives had escaped.

"Can we take horses?" Jem suggested as the neared the exit.

Gerard shook his head. "I'd like to say yes. But we Fenrir tend to spook horses. We must smell more like wolves to them than human."

"Right. Okay. Well, Elena said we needed to travel South, and find a place called Lofntyr Manor." Jem said.

Gerard froze. "You told someone what you were doing?" He asked.

Jem gave him a stern look. "I did. Elena and Hod."

His eyes went wide. "Did you say Hod."

"I did." She said.

He opened his mouth to protest.

"Before you say anything, they are the only reason we have any of the prophecy or know where to go. They protected me, hid me from Freya, and for their trouble they got caught. Freya knocked them out, stripped them of their memories, and is banishing them. Even when they got caught they didn't hint at me being there." She said, and tears welled up in her eyes.

Gerard sighed. "Look I think I've got him." He

said carrying Dan himself.

They made it to the woods, out of sight of Folkvang. Thankfully before the sun was high enough to make them noticeable. Gerard heaved Dan onto his back in a fireman carry.

"Are you sure you can carry him? We've got a long way to go." Jem said.

"I'll be fine." Gerard said, and then he started to run.

Jem ran beside him, keeping pace.

"You're not what I expected you know." He said.

"What do you mean?" Jem asked.

"That first day I saw you. You seemed fragile." He said.

"You mean the day when you broke down my front door as an enormous black wolf. What were you expecting? Xena Warrior Princess?" She said with a chuckle.

She couldn't believe how much fitter she'd become in just a few weeks. Some of it must have been to do with being Valkyrie. But exercise, running in particular, had never seemed so easy before she came to Folkvang and found out who, and what she was.

He shrugged, a feat that should have been impossible given Dan was slung across his shoulders, and they were running.

"Pretty much. The Valkyrie are like the bogeyman to a lot of Fenrir. They come in and kill us, steal away our people. They're dangerous, and then there was you. Standing next to that

Aesir, shaking like a leaf. You just seemed so small. Like a child almost. Someone who needed to be protected, not someone we should be scared of." Gerard said.

"And then Dan came charging in to protect me and your worst nightmare came true." She sighed.

"That wasn't your fault you know." He said.

Jem ignored the comment. It felt like her fault, even if she had no control over any of it.

"So what about now? Do I still seem fragile?" She asked.

He looked her up and down. "Yes and no." He said.

She frowned. "What do you mean, 'yes and no'?" she asked.

"There's still a gentleness to you, but I can see now that it's wrapped around a core of steel. If it wasn't you wouldn't be here now." Gerard said. "You wouldn't be helping us escape, and giving up all of that for an unknown future."

"What's the point of a future if you know that it's wrong. Freya could promise me the world. She has essentially promised those women in there whatever they want, as long as they do what she says. Even when what she says is wrong. I don't want the world if I forfeit my soul in the process. Besides. Dan's my mate. If the creator made him for me and then went so far as to put him in my path, well, I'm not one to look a gift horse in the mouth." She said.

Gerard chuckled again. "I can see you'll be good for Dan. He needs someone steadfast, and you seem to be the kind of woman who once she makes up her mind will follow the path to the bitter end."

"It's not always a good thing." Jem said, "Sometimes it's important to be flexible." She said.

"And sometimes it's just as important to stick to your guns. Some things in this world weren't meant to be fleeting. The simple fact is that at times Dan and I can, and have been reckless. We haven't thought about things, we've rushed in half-cocked without getting all the information. We've made spur of the moment decisions and changed our minds at the last minute and it led to no end of trouble. You don't seem the type to do that." Gerard said. "You seem to be thoughtful. Even the escape. You didn't just rush at it. You slowed down. Thought about it."

"Only cause you both agreed." She said.

"And that's another thing. Even though you make a decision you're willing to hear what other people have to say, even when you don't like it." He said.

"I don't know how. But you're managing to make it sound like I'm inflexible and flexible all at the same time. I don't see how that's possible." Jem said.

"It's possible because you look for the truth." Gerard said, "You accepted that Dan was your mate right?" he asked.

Jem nodded.

"But you didn't just take it as gospel did you? You tested it. You asked someone what it meant. You were attracted to him. You liked him. You thought it was true. But you didn't let your emotions rule you completely. You found out the truth and then once you knew, you made your decision and followed through." Gerard said. "Even once you knew, you could have left us. You could have done what would have been best for you. You could have convinced yourself you would eventually find another mate here in Asgard and left us to our fate. But you're steadfast in what you believe is right and wrong, and once you knew the truth you couldn't have left us there even if it put your own life at risk." He said.

Jem didn't know what to say.

"He deserves someone like you. A mate who will stick by him, who will help him to slow down and think rather than just rushing in. A mate he can trust to look out for the right path, rather than the easy one." Gerard said. "I just hope I can find someone like that someday too."

Dan's entire body ached. Even with the Gleipnir bonds gone he could tell his healing was going to be slow. The fact that he was slung over Gerard's shoulders like a sack of potatoes certainly didn't help. Especially when the movement from Gerard running had Dan slamming against his friend's shoulders every few seconds. He'd heard Gerard talking to someone earlier. No not just someone, Jem. Her sweet scent was all around him, accentuated by the fact that she, like Gerard, was sweating from all the running. Dan had no idea how long they had been running, but at this point, both Jem and Gerard had stopped talking. The only sound filling the air was the rustle of leaves, animals in the woods around them, the rhythmic sound of their feet hitting the ground, and their laboured breathing. Clearly a fair amount of time had passed because the sky had made the transition from pitch dark to bright morning light.

"You two need a break." He said.

In the distance Dan suddenly heard the sound of a horn. Jem gasped and Gerard's pace increased impossibly.

"They've discovered we're gone." Jem said, "They know I've got you out of there."

Her voice sounded panicked.

"We need to get as far from here as possible." Gerard said, "Did Elena say how far it was to this Lofntyr Manor?" he asked.

"No." Jem puffed.

"Put me down." Dan croaked.

"You won't be fast enough." Gerard said ignoring him.

"I think I can shift." Dan said, and he hoped it was true.

Gerard stopped. "If you can't I'm going back to carrying you." He said.

"If I can, you shift too." Dan said, he looked at Jem, "You'll have to let her ride you." He said to Gerard.

"Are you sure?" Gerard asked.

Touching another males mate, especially when they were as early into the mating process as Dan and Jem were could be a volatile situation. Most males were very protective of the females that were made to be theirs. Dan couldn't say seeing another male that close to his mate really appealed to him. Even if it was his best friend. But what choice did he have? It was that or get caught, and he wouldn't allow Jemima to be hurt because of his pride.

"I might be able to shift and run. But I doubt I'll be able to carry more than my own weight." He admitted.

Gerard nodded.

"Did you say ride?" Jem asked looking nervous.

Gerard nodded. "You saw me in wolf form, I'm plenty big enough to carry you."

She looked nervous.

"It's just like riding a horse. Well kind of." Gerard said.

"I know I suggested it back there. But I've only ridden a horse twice, and one of those times I fell off. I'm not sure it's a good idea." She said.

"It's our only choice if we want to get out of here alive." Dan said.

"Let's just hold out on that and see if you can shift first." Gerard said.

Dan sighed, called the change, and it came. It rushed up to greet him just as it always did. The cloak around his shoulders tightened as his neck grew in size. Jemima rushed over, slipping the clasp undone so he wouldn't choke.

Gerard nodded.

"Right." He said, unbuckling the clasp of his cloak.

Jem spun around to face the other way, her cheeks flushing red. He always forgot how humans were so unused to nudity. Although he couldn't say he wasn't glad she'd avoided looking at Gerard. It was hard enough knowing she would be riding Gerard rather than him, and Dan didn't want his territorial instincts to take over.

"Use the cloaks as a saddle as much as you can. I can't imagine the ride will be all that comfortable." Gerard said.

Jemima nodded and Gerard shifted.

Dan walked alongside her, nudging her so she would know it was safe to turn around. She looked nervous. More than a little nervous even. But she took a deep breath and walked to Gerard, her fingers dropping to Dan's fur and digging in until they touched his hard flesh beneath.

"Umm. How do I get up?" she asked.

Gerard dropped to his belly and Jemima approached. She struggled to get onto Gerard's back, and despite the real danger they were facing, both he and Gerard found themselves laughing.

"I know you think I can't tell you are laughing, but I can." Jemima grumbled, "And this is not funny." She said as Dan gave her a gentle push to get her the rest of the way up. They both laughed a little more.

Dan watched as Jemima gripped her hands tightly in the fur at Gerard's ruff and clenched her legs around his sides. A jealous growl escaped before he could stop it. Gerard looked at him, and Dan sighed.

"I'm sorry. Can't help it." Dan yapped in the wolf language only Fenrir, and the occasional true wolf could understand.

Gerard nodded. "I get it." He paused. "She really is something." He said and launched into a run. Jem let out a panicked shriek that had them both laughing again.

"Not funny." She said, her voice muffling in Gerard's fur.

Dan ran beside him. Running in wolf form was definitely faster. It also made it easier to smell dog, a scent that was not unlike wolf to a Fenrir. They'd been running for hours, and Creator be praised no one from Folkvang had caught up to them as of yet. But it was only a matter of time if they didn't find somewhere to hide, and soon.

LADY LOFN

The further south Jem travelled with Dan and Gerard the more exposed the landscape became. If Jem hadn't spent the entire time gripping onto Gerard for dear life and praying that they found a place to hide, she may have found the fields full of wildflowers beautiful. But the thing was, they were on the run, and if Freya or any of her people were close on their heels they would have no problems spotting them running in the distance. As soon as they raced out of the dense woods the land seemed to roll out into fields. Fields that were as flat as a pancake. Which was bad for them. Every now and then Jem would hear the horn sound back at Folkvang. Possibly closer. She knew that Freya, that her sister Valkyrie, her new friends, were out searching for them. Jem knew that Jewel was searching for her and that if any of the Valkyrie found her, if they found them, then all three of them would be dead, or at the least, would wish they were.

Gerard and Dan should have been showing signs of slowing, they'd been running for hours.

Jem's backside hurt so much. She would have considered telling them she was saddle sore, except for the fact that it was clear both Fenrir were exhausted themselves. They had each gathered a layer of sweat on their coats, and now, as they forced their bodies to travel even harder and faster, foam was starting to gather at the corner of their mouths. There was no way they could last much longer. But Jem had the feeling that they wouldn't stop until they had been caught, or they collapsed. Then right when Jem was beginning to think they had no chance, a cottage came into view.

"Please Creator, let this be a safe place." She prayed out loud.

The three of them tore towards the flower strangled wooden garden gate, slowing as they came closer. Both Fenrir sniffed the air and started talking to each other. Or at least doing what Jem assumed was talking for a Fenrir in wolf form. Once they reached the gate Gerard lowered down so Jem could hop off. She tried to climb down, but her legs were aching and had about as much strength in them as jelly. As soon as her feet touched the ground her legs collapsed beneath her, her knees jarring as they impacted against the pebbled path beneath her. Dan rushed over, helping her up with his muzzle.

"I'm fine." She said looking him in the eye.

She was fine. Achy. But fine. On the other hand, after all that running, not to mention carrying her, there was no way Dan or Gerard were okay. Jem watched their sides heave in and out as their exhausted bodies worked desperately to get the air they needed. It at least seemed as though Dan had stopped bleeding, although with him standing so close she could clearly see the deep gashes that covered his back, and that was beneath a thick layer of fur. She hated to think what his back was going to look like in human form.

"We need to get you help." She said, steeling herself to approach the front door of the house.

Dan attempted to block her way. She glared at him, but he moved more resolutely in front of her.

"I'm going in no matter what." She said, "You might be the big bad wolf Dan, but you've been running for hours and I've got energy to spare. You couldn't catch me if you tried at the moment."

Gerard released a wolfy chuckle, and Dan growled at him.

"You can either come with me or stay here. Either way, I'm going." Jem said pushing softly past him.

He moved. Though clearly, he wasn't happy about it. Jem pushed the gate open and her senses were assaulted with a range of beautiful scents. Some familiar. Roses, lavender, rosemary, mint, basil. Some unusual. Floral, yet somehow spicy. Plants were growing together that never should have been able to bloom at the same time and yet were. There was a magnetism to the garden. Something that made you feel as though you were coming home. Jem would have happily stayed here forever. It was a place that reminded her of her Gran. Sweet, and beautiful. But strong. Able to weather any change and come out the better for it. Jem followed the white pebbled path to the front door. The large wooden door swung out on its massive metal hinges. For a moment Jem and both men froze, and then a tiny fluffy ball of white dog sped out at them yipping and yapping merrily bouncing around Dan and Gerard as though they were long lost brothers.

"My my my." A beautiful voice practically sang from the doorway. "It's been a long time since Beth has greeted anyone other than my Sarah like that." The short red-haired woman said, "And even longer since I have seen a Fenrir."

Gerard growled, and Jem felt Dan sway beside her. If he fell there was no way she could keep him upright. Not in wolf form at least.

The woman laughed. "Don't get your tail in a bunch wolf. I'm no danger to you."

Jem couldn't imagine her being a threat to anyone. She was almost the smallest woman Jem had ever seen. Shorter even than her Gran who had shrunk to five-foot as she had aged and osteoporosis took its toll. This woman stood confidently at her full height. She was perfectly regal. Standing more surely than even Freya had when she addressed the Valkyrie. But where Freya was well over six foot, this woman was no more than four foot five.

The woman smiled as she scanned their group. "A Valkyrie and two Fenrir. How interesting. My name is Lady Lofn. Welcome to Lofntyr Manor." She said, and they all released a sigh of relief.

Dan swayed again and a horn sounded in the distance. It was definitely getting closer, which didn't bode well for them. Not in the slightest. Lofn looked out into the distance, then across the horizon.

"I think that coming inside might be prudent at this point. Don't you?" She asked. Then looking at the men frowned and said, "I don't know how we'll get you inside though. You're both so big."

Gerard grunted and began to shift.

"Oh my." Lofn said going a little red in the cheeks. "Well, you are different from your ancestor after all."

Dan changed as well, though his transition was slower, and where Gerard had managed to move into a crouched position, and end up standing before his shift was complete, Dan was on his hands and knees gasping, and his wounds appeared to be opening up again.

"Henry!!!" Lofn screamed. "Ingrid! We need help, quickly!"

Gerard looked worried for a second, like he was about to shift back.

An older looking man and woman came round

the corner, their eyes were wide with fear. They took one look at Dan's now sinking body and gasped.

"Oh dear Creator!" the woman, Ingrid exclaimed.

"Get my herbs." Lofn instructed and Ingrid ran off again, moving faster than Jem thought possible.

"Help me get them inside." Lofn instructed Henry.

"I've got him." Gerard grunted moving to Dan's side.

Henry gave Gerard a look. "Young man you are struggling to stay upright yourself. This young woman and I have him. You just get inside and out of sight before we have the entire Valkyrie army on the doorstep."

"Hurry up Gerard." Jem said giving him a gentle push and ducking under Dan's other arm, very conscious that at this point she had seen Dan without clothes more than she'd seen him in clothes.

Gerard sighed and stepped across the threshold of the cottage. Which on closer inspection was much larger than it looked from the other side of the gate. The little dog, Beth, happily yapped at Gerard's feet until the hulking guy picked her up and she was able to lick his face affectionately.

"This way, this way." Lofn said leading them down a long hallway and into a large dining room. It was an open space, bright with white stone and sunlight, the beams of the room exposed. Somehow the room exuded the size of a small castle, while providing the warmth of a cottage, and the glorious scents from outside. Lofntyr Manor smelt of plants and life seemed to fill every space inside just as it had outside.

"Get him on the table." Lofn said.

"I have some medicines." Jem said pulling the pack from her back and tipping everything she had not so delicately onto the floor.

Beth wiggled in Gerard's arms till he let go and she could inspect the contents of the pack. Eventually she snatched up a few pieces of jerky and returned to Gerard, dropping a piece at his feet before yapping at him to pick her back up again.

Gerard sighed. "Thank you little one." He said.

Apparently, Gerard was more of a gentle giant than Jem had at first thought.

Dan groaned, drawing Jem's attention back to him, while Lofn looked through what Jem had grabbed.

"Some of this might be useful." Lofn said picking a few pieces from the pile. "Do you know how to use them…"

"Oh, Jemima. Uh, Jem." Jem introduced herself, "A little bit. Not much. I was accepted as a negotiator Valkyrie." Jem said, hoping that explained at least a little bit.

Lofn nodded. "Well that explains it. The negotiator Valkyrie are the most likely to search for, and see the truth." She smiled at Jem, "And so

Jemima, what has happened to your mate."

"My." Jem started. How did this woman know that?

"Your mate. That's the only reason I could see why a Valkyrie would ever even question the lies Freya feeds you up in that place." She nodded in the direction of Folkvang. "Besides, I have a gift when it comes to knowing which couples are meant to be, and the two of you... Well if it hasn't happened yet it's not far off. So what happened?" she asked again.

"Freyr happened." Gerard said.

Lofn nodded.

"Sir, if you wouldn't mind." Henry said picking up and passing the discarded cloak to Gerard,"Let's make this situation just a little easier for the ladies shall we. I imagine you want their focus on your friend rather than, well, you know."

Gerard chuckled, tied the cloak around his waist rather than his neck, and sat down on one of the free seats. Beth instantly leapt into Gerard's lap.

Ingrid rushed back into the room carrying a tray loaded up with metal instruments, bottles, bowls of liquid, and some clothes.

"Do your people heal like your ancestor? Like the Fenrir beast?" Lofn asked.

Gerard looked at her strangely. "From what I've been taught we don't heal quite as quickly, but it is still fast in comparison with others." He said.

Lofn frowned. "They used Gleipnir?" she asked.

Gerard nodded.

Lofn turned to Henry. "We need a fire. We need to be able to dispose of any bloody rags quickly." Then she turned to Ingrid. "Sweep the path. Check for blood. Erase anything that would let the Valkyrie know that the three of them are here."

"Shall I prepare the room for them as well?" Henry asked.

"I think you'll need to. There's no way they won't want to search the house. Anyway, Sarah would be devastated if they found Beth." Lofn said.

Both Ingrid and Henry started rushing around.

"You'll both have to help I'm afraid. He's been beaten too severely and his body can't heal him quickly enough. He needs a little help, so I'm going to need to stitch him up. That way if the Valkyrie arrive before he's fully healed he won't bleed out on us." She explained.

"Lofn. Lofntyr." Gerard said, his eyes wide. "I know who you are." He said.

Lofn looked up at him. "You'll need to hold your friend down. This is going to hurt."

"You're the Dwarven Princess who was married to Tyr. The Aesir who kept Fenrir locked up until Ragnarok." Gerard said.

"I am. But I'll have you know that Tyr treated Fenrir like a part of our family. It was Odin who had him locked up. Even then my husband refused to abandon Fenrir. He chose to give up his arm and get Fenrir into the cage rather than allowing Odin to murder him. It broke his heart. Both of our hearts to see what was done to that child." Lofn said, and the pain of the loss showed in her eyes, ceasing even Gerard's objections.

"You're a Dwarf?" Jem asked, handing Lofn a cloth she had just rung out at the woman's instruction.

Lofn smiled. "The last, except for my daughter Sarah, who is part Aesir."

Gerard looked to the side, as though he had something to say, but didn't actually want to share.

"Is she here too?" Jem asked, looking around. Wondering if she should cover Dan up a little. She was getting used to seeing his body. But she wasn't sure how happy she was about the other women seeing him. Particularly Lofn's daughter. If the girl looked anything like her mother, she would be beautiful and she found herself feeling quite proprietary about Dan's attention.

Lofn shook her head. "No. Sarah is at Freya's palace with all the other Aesir maidens." She said, "I didn't want her to go. But what choice do I have? She has to find a place in this world, and the only way to do that is to let her meet the people and learn the culture. No matter how convoluted it might be. All I can do is what I have already done. Teach her the truth, and pray that she holds on to it no matter what she is faced with."

Beth barked at the mention of Lofn's daughter's

name.

"Why do you need to hide Beth?" Gerard asked, looking down at the small dog.

"Freya banned Fenrir after Ragnarok." Lofn explained as she threaded the needle with its fine silk through Dan's skin. He moaned a little but didn't move. "Once that edict had been made she banned any creature with any similarity to a Fenrir from Asgard, including wolves and dogs. There may be the occasional fox, but most animals with any type of canine features have been completely hunted into extinction."

"So how did you get Beth then?" Jem asked.

Lofn smiled. "Beth was a gift from my husband to Sarah on the day she was born. She is a very special dog. She and Sarah have a type of magical bond. It allows her to live as long as Sarah does. Sarah's companion forever, and her only real friend for most of her life. As long as Beth isn't killed, she will never age, she will only die if Sarah does."

Jem looked at the little dog. "How old is Beth?"

"Well over two thousand years old." Lofn said.

Ingrid raced back into the room. "I can see them approaching my Lady Lofn." She said.

"How far Ingrid?" Lofn asked, tying off a knot and snipping the end tidily.

"Ten minutes, maybe less at the pace they're travelling." Ingrid said.

"Right." Lofn said pursing her lips together, threading the needle with new cotton and sliding it smoothly through Dan's flesh as though it were a shirt she was working on rather than a person "Put on the kettle. Get out the cakes. We'll move…"

"Dan." Jem offered.

Lofn gave her a smile. "We'll move Dan as soon as I'm done and you set the table."

"You're setting the table?" Gerard asked.

Lofn looked at him. "What would you suggest I do? Perhaps I should act suspicious and try and kick them out. I need to make today seem like any other day, and on any other day, I would insist they stay for tea. I'm meant to be a devoted subject of Freya, and devoted subjects do whatever their Queen wants." She explained stitching yet another deep gash closed.

"This is too slow." Jem said, "You're never going to finish in time."

Lofn nodded. "We'll need to wrap him for now." She announced. "You four lift, I'll wrap." She said motioning Ingrid and Henry over.

They lifted Dan's body up and Lofn deftly wrapped his torso.

"We need to get them hidden now Lady Lofn." Ingrid said urgently, surveying the mess in the room.

Lofn nodded. "Henry."

Henry rushed to the fireplace and proceeded to push and slide a number of stones. The fireplace slid to the side and exposed a set of stairs.

"Quickly inside." Lofn said.

Jem's mind was instantly brought back to the dungeon. From the way Gerard froze he was thinking much the same.

"I know it looks foreboding. But I swear to you, you'll all be safe down there." Lofn said.

A feeling of calm washed over Jem. "Come on Gerard. I know it sounds dumb. But I trust her. Besides we don't have a lot of choice."

Once again Henry took one side of Dan, but Gerard shook his head and handed Beth to Jem. "I've got him." He said lifting his friend over his shoulders once again. This time Henry didn't argue. Just ushered them in and turned to the mess on the table.

As they descended the stairs Jem heard them bustling around above.

"You must change Lady Lofn." Ingrid said, "You're covered in blood."

Then there was a knock on the door.

Lofn's hideaway was nothing like Jem had been expecting. She'd been waiting for the stone encased stairwell to give way to a hideous dank dungeon-like area. Basically, she was expecting a space like where she found Dan and Gerard. Instead, at the base of the stairs, it opened up into a wide circular room. It almost looked like a cave except there were cozy fireplaces with fires burning within them all, heavy couches and warm rugs. The room was inviting, beautiful even.

"Wow." Jem said.

"Huh." Said Gerard.

"What?" Jem asked.

Gerard lowered Dan carefully onto one of the couches.

"It kind of reminds me of home." Gerard said.

"Really?" She asked.

"Yeah." Gerard said with a slight smile, "The Fenrir live in caves. So this is pretty similar."

"You live underground?" Jem asked.

Gerard nodded, and Dan stirred. Dan sat himself up with a slight cringe, and Jem found herself right next to him checking to see if he was okay. He smiled.

"You'll like our den." He said.

Jem sighed and shook her head. "Dan. I don't know if that's a good idea."

He looked at her, his expression so confused it was almost laughable.

"I might have helped you and Gerard get out of

Folkvang. But even if we get out of Asgard I'm still Valkyrie, and from what I've learnt over the last few weeks, Valkyrie and Fenrir aren't exactly friendly." She said.

"You're my mate." Dan said raising his hand to her face and sending tingles radiating from the point where he made contact right down to the tips of her toes, "They'll accept you."

"I don't see how." Jem said.

Dan chuckled, then cringed again as the movement stretched the stitches on his back.

"You don't now. But you will. The thing you have to know about Fenrir is that we take our mates, and finding them pretty seriously. No one will reject you." Dan said.

"They'll be too scared to." Gerard laughed from his seat in a single chair beside their couch.

"Why's that?" Jem asked.

"Other than the fact Dan and I would eat them alive." Gerard said, "There's also the fact that Dan is the pack Alpha's son. The youngest male of seven, with just one sibling younger than him, his sister Peta, and he's the first of all of them to find a mate."

Jem opened her mouth to say something.

"Finding a mate is a lot harder than you might think." Dan said, "Any Fenrir finding their true mate is rare, and the fact is. Our family isn't the only one struggling. None of the children of the Alphas in any of the packs have found their mate yet. None except me." He smiled at her.

"You're all of what twenty-three, twenty-four? I'm pretty sure you've got time." Jem said with a laugh. Although her heartfelt heavy just saying it. She was twenty-eight. She at least felt as though she was on some kind of clock. But twenty three? Dan had plenty of time to find the right person for him. He'd met her for all of two minutes, and he was convinced she was his mate. It just didn't seem real.

Now both Gerard and Dan laughed.

"Why are you laughing?" Jem asked in frustration.

"Jemima." Dan said with a smile, shaking his head, "I'm not twenty-three, or twenty-four."

"So what you're twenty-five?" Jem asked. This conversation was making her feel older by the minute.

"I'm ninety-three Jemima." Dan said.

"I'm sorry what?" Jem asked.

She had to have misheard him.

"Fenrir don't age the way humans do Jemima. It's something like a quarter of the rate." Dan said, although it sounded like more of a question than an answer.

"Yeah approximately." Gerard agreed.

"You're ninety-three?" She stammered.

Gerard laughed. "You're scaring her off brother." He said.

Dan slung his arm across the back of the seat so it lay right behind Jem's shoulders.

"Surely you don't scare that easily?" Dan said

pulling her into his side.

"Dan, I'm twenty-eight. I definitely age like a human." She said.

"You used to." Dan said.

Jem frowned. "What do you mean?"

"He means my dear, that once your Valkyrie birthright was unlocked that all changed for you." Lofn's voice said from the stairwell.

"What do you mean?" Jem asked.

"Valkyrie live much the same lifespan as Fenrir, often longer in fact. Though I have a feeling that by the way the two of you are linked your life spans will be much the same. You're a good match." Lofn said with a wink at Dan.

Dan squeezed Jem's shoulder, pulling her closer to his side and smiling at Lofn. Jem felt her face flush. She was really REALLY glad he had thrown the cloak over his lap. Apparently, Fenrir had no shame when it came to being naked. Something that couldn't be said of humans. Or at least it couldn't be said of Jem. Actually, she was feeling more than a little bit embarrassed. Partially because she was so attracted to Dan and it was a struggle not to check him out. Which inevitably led to her cheeks flushing bright red, and partially because he kept looking at her in a way that made her feel both sexy and self-conscious all at the same time. Which also managed to leave her hot, flustered, and blushing bright red. At this point, Jem was beginning to think that she'd be permanently stuck looking like a tomato.

"They left quickly." Gerard said, his face carefully neutral.

Lofn's expression lost its teasing smile. "They did. Though I don't doubt they'll return within the next day or so. I think it will be best for you all to stay awhile. At least until Dan heals." Lofn said.

Gerard shook his head. "We need to get out of here." He said.

"I don't dispute that." Lofn agreed. "But if you leave now you are guaranteed to be captured and end up right back where you started. Then Jem's sacrifice, and don't you doubt that it was a sacrifice, will have been for nothing. Not to mention, I see no point in healing your Alpha if you plan on getting him killed before I even have a chance to gain my strength back." She said.

Gerard glared at her.

"I'm not his Alpha." Dan said, his thumb tracing lazy circles on Jem's exposed shoulder.

Lofn raised an eyebrow.

"We're equals. Always have been. Always will be. We're like brothers." Dan said, he looked at Gerard.

Lofn continued to give Dan a disapproving look.

Dan sighed. "But if you want to be technical about it, I'm his dominant."

Lofn looked at Dan, her eyes assessing. "You're not his Alpha?" She asked.

"That would be my Father." Dan said.

"Ah. That would explain it." Lofn said, her gentle air returning.

Clearly, Lofn didn't suffer fools or liars.

"Explain what?" Dan asked.

"The air of command about you." Lofn said indicating the air around him. "Son of an Alpha. Destined to be an Alpha." She said.

Dan laughed, gripping his sides as his chuckles

pulled his stitches.

"I'll have to wait in line." He chuckled. "I'm the seventh child born of eight to the Alpha male and female of the Lovell pack. I'm the youngest male, and the least likely to ever take the mantle of Alpha."

"I wouldn't be so sure about that." Lofn said. "Come now, let's see to healing your wounds. Then maybe we can get you fed and watered, and formulate an actual plan for getting you out of Asgard." She looked pointedly at Gerard. "Going off without a plan given all of Freya's people are after you would be stupidity of the highest degree." She said.

Gerard growled, but Dan sighed.

"At this stage, she's right Gerard." Dan said, "I'm not even certain I could get myself back up the stairs on my own at the moment, let alone to the Bifrost."

"The what?" Jem asked.

She was feeling so out of her depth. She'd been chucked into a world she knew nothing about, and it seemed like in every conversation she was lacking some important piece of information that everybody else instinctively knew.

"The Bifrost." Lofn said, her smile gentle, understanding. "It's the name of the bridge that will return you to Midgard. Though why they insist on calling it a bridge is beyond me. It's more like a staircase of pure rainbow light if anything."

"If that's how we get home, then how come when Ali came to get me we didn't use it?" Jem asked, "I mean one minute I was in my house, and the next I was in the passage outside of the great hall." Jem said.

"He must have been given permission to use one of the Bifrost gems. They're a kind of crystal used for travelling. There are very few of them in circulation. They're only owned by a select few, and can only be used twice before they need to be returned to the Bifrost and recharged. A duty that may only be performed by Heimdell or one of his trainees." Lofn said. "No one uses the Bifrost or one of the gems without Heimdell knowing about it."

"So it's safe to say that there will be guards at the Bifrost." Gerard said.

Lofn nodded. "And I would wager that Freya will be quick to add her own guards to the existing number until you are captured."

"Wonderful." Dan sighed.

Though it was shaking, Jem placed her hand on Dan's leg, just above the knee and squeezed gently in an attempt to comfort him. This was an impossible situation, but he, they, were not alone. He looked down at her and placed his free hand on hers, returning her squeeze.

"Don't worry." Lofn said. "The Aesir aren't half as clever as they think they are. I've been sidestepping their laws for years."

Beth chose that moment to bark as though

agreeing with Lofn, and it seemed as though the tiny teacup dogs mere presence in a world that banned any manner of canine spoke to the truth of Lofn's comment.

"But how does dodging a few laws get us past dozens of trained soldiers?" Gerard asked.

Lofn's smile widened. "Now you don't think all that lawbreaking was just for myself, do you?" she asked. "I'm the goddess of forbidden marriages. I've rubbed shoulders with some of the lowest, and some of the highest. There are plenty who would happily do a favour for me. Even if it infuriated Freya. Some of them would do it for that reason alone. You'll have plenty of help when you need it." She said.

"But we'll owe you." Gerard said, looking at the beautiful woman as though she had grown a second head.

Lofn looked genuinely shocked. "Absolutely not!" She exclaimed.

"I'm sorry Lady Lofn. But if you don't expect anything in exchange, then why would you help us?" Dan asked.

"I am the last of my people." Lofn said. "Do you think I would allow another race to be wiped from existence if I could stop it?" she asked. "Besides, despite the histories that Freya allowed to be spread, Fenrir was not the monster he was said to be. The Aesir were cruel to him, and he, for better or worse, during his captivity became a member of our family. Had we been able to free him, to return him to his people in Jotunheim, without the rest of the Aesir taking it out on our newborn child, then we would have. But Fenrir would never have allowed it. Sarah was his sister as much as he was our son." Lofn said, her eyes misting. "The Aesir's pointless, greedy war destroyed Fenrir's home, along with all the Jotun who lived there. Including Fenrir's birth family. That was the thing that broke him in the end. That was why Fenrir killed Odin. To avenge his family. It was grief and pain that destroyed that poor boy, and I will regret to my dying day not protecting him." She said.

Lofn wiped her eyes, then put on a smile. "Now. Enough of that talk. Let's get you healed." She said walking to the couch where Jem and Dan sat. After removing the bandages she'd wrapped around Dan earlier and arranging him so he lay chest down on the couch, his head resting on Jem's lap, Lofn covered his lower half and set to work. First, with Gerard and Jem's help, she finished up the stitching. Then she coated Dan's back in a white cream that smelt of a mix of familiar herbs and oils and repeated the process on his chest. Dan managed to stay surprisingly still through the entire procedure. Something Jem doubted she would have been able to do had she been in the same position. He spent the entire time laying on his back looking at Jem, asking her questions, and sharing stories with her. Somehow he even managed to make the stoic Gerard laugh, even though his friend clearly still wasn't convinced he could trust Lofn.

The beatings Freyr had inflicted on Dan had been, well, severe was putting it mildly. Interestingly Freyr had almost exclusively focused on Dan's torso and back when he had whipped him, with only the odd lash reaching any other area of his body. It meant that Dan's face, arms, legs and pelvis had remained practically untouched. But that his chest and back were almost unrecognisable as flesh in some spots. It actually made Jem wonder how Dan could stand to have her, or anyone for that matter, touching him, the pain had to have been excruciating.

"And now that we've done that, the healing can begin." Lofn announced.

Jem thought she meant that it was time for Dan to relax and let his body do its job. Like someone sent to a human hospital, the next step would effectively be time. Time to heal. Instead, Lofn raised her hands and began to sing. Her voice wrapped around the four of them and the air seemed to warm and glow. Lofn's voice was just how Jem imagined angels would sound if she were ever given the pleasure to hear them. Before long a low masculine voice joined Lofn's. Jem looked up and saw Gerard, his face open rather than guarded. She couldn't understand a single word, and yet it was clear as day what he was saying. He sang of Dan's character, of their friendship. Of who Dan was, and what he meant to Gerard. It was enough to make tears well up in her eyes. Especially when she realised that Lofn's words were doing the same thing. Saying the same kinds of things. Though she had only met them that day she sang of courage, of strength, of loyalty. She sang of the Creator and how he was present in every thread of Dan's life. Jem closed her eyes. Ashamed that she had no words of truth to share with him. Where Gerard and Lofn knew the words required to heal him she had no idea, she didn't know him. Had only just met him. The two voices rose and fell, twining together, singing of peace and restoration, and then Dan reached up a swiped a tear from Jem's cheek leaving his hand resting there by her closed eyes. Jem went to open her eyes, wanting to look at him. Instead, her lips parted and words spilt out. Words that were in no language she had ever learnt, yet were as clear as day. Her voice rose to meet Lofn and Gerard's. It wove between their voices, stronger and more passionate than either of theirs. She sang of hope and faith, of sacrifice and love. She sang about the possibility of tomorrow and of a future they had been promised. A future filled with love, laughter, and family. A family they would build and grow together. She would have felt embarrassed. If she could have she might have stopped singing. But her song wasn't over, and even while the words she said terrified her she could feel the truth in every one. The song rose to a crescendo as she sang along with the others of healing and completion, and then each of their voices softened until none of them were singing, just kneeling with their hands on Dan who was looking at Jem in wonder.

Gerard smiled at her. "After hearing that there's no way anyone will be able to doubt that you're Dan's mate." He said.

"None at all." Lady Lofn said. "The Creator can only use those who are willing to be used, and when he truly uses you, you can only speak truth. You, my dear, didn't just sing a song of love and healing. You sang words of prophecy. You spoke into your future and with the Creator's blessing carved out a path for not only you but everyone who will come after you. Amazing." She said.

Dan shifted his body, pulling himself up into a seated position. His eyes were glued on Jem. Then he kissed her, and she kissed him back, despite their audience.

Lofn continued on. As though seeing them kiss was something that just happened every day, even though Jem felt as though her pounding heart might just burst out of her chest.

"We've definitely healed all the internal damage." She said, "But the freshly healed skin will be prone to tear, which is why the stitches were necessary. Your body needs to have an opportunity to help with the healing. Luckily the thread I used dissolves once the magic senses the healing is complete."

"The Creator couldn't just completely heal him?" Jem asked in confusion.

Lofn smiled. "Of course he can. But sometimes we must have some pain so that we take the time to rest, and sometimes we need to have scars so we remember not only where we've been, but also why we keep pressing forward." She said.

Gerard looked at Lofn and nodded in thanks, while Dan and Jem actually said thank you. After a moment or two, in which time Lofn announced that it was probably safe for them to go upstairs, Dan nodded to Gerard as though they had been having some kind of deep, but silent conversation.

Dan cleared his throat. "Lady Lofn." He said.

She smiled at him.

"I wonder why you keep saying you are the last of the Dwarves." He asked.

Lofn frowned. "Because all my people were wiped out during Ragnarok. No Aesir or any other creature I have heard of has encountered one since." She said, her expression pained.

Dan and Gerard both shook their heads. "I don't think that's true. The Fenrir legends often talk about how Hati met the Dwarves while he searched for his mate, and how they became friends. The Dwarves were the ones who placed the protection spells on the dens that prevent Freya from finding us." Dan said.

Lofn looked at him, though very little if any hope filled her eyes. "And you have seen my people yourself?" she asked.

They both shook their heads.

"No. I haven't." Dan said. "But Lady Lofn they have to be true." He said.

She sighed. "And why do you say that."

"Because Fenrir have no magic to speak of, aside from our ability to shift. We couldn't have placed the wards ourselves, and the Aesir would never have done it for us." He explained.

Lofn looked hopeful. "That's true."

"Not to mention this room." Gerard said.

She frowned. "What do you mean?"

"Our dens look just like this. Identical in some areas. I would wager that your people were the ones who taught the Fenrir how to build our homes, otherwise, we might still be living in the caves that nature provided rather than building entire cities beneath the earth." Gerard said.

Lofn's smile was wide. "I'm not alone."

Jem smiled and took Lofn's hand in hers. "Neither you or Sarah will ever be alone. You both have a family with us." Jem said.

There was no way Dan and Gerard could promise that Lofn's people were still alive. But Jem could promise herself. If they ever found their way to safety Lofn and Sarah, even Henry and Ingrid would have a safe place to stay if they ever wanted to escape Asgard and Freya.

Lofn squeezed Jem's hand. "Thank you Jem.

Given the prophecy the Creator just gave you, inviting me to be a part of your family is one of the most generous things you could have ever done for my family." She said.

TRAVELLING

Staying with Lofn was easy. Even with Valkyrie dropping in unannounced regularly and being rushed down to the hideaway at the last moment, Jem hadn't felt so relaxed in what felt like forever. Even Dan seemed quite comfortable, and Jem couldn't pretend she hadn't enjoyed getting to spend time with him. The only person who seemed to be struggling was Gerard, and even he didn't seem to completely hate it. At least not when Beth was around. The little dog had taken a particular liking to him. Still. He was antsy. He paced a lot. After about a week at Lofntyr Manor Dan was well and truly healed. The stitches had dissolved, and somehow even the scars that should have covered his chest and back were gone. A fact that Jem couldn't help but notice given that Dan and Gerard sparred shirtless every single day. For the first day or two, Jem had watched them or spent time discussing things with Lofn. It was pretty clear Lofn's perception of magic outstripped everything that the Valkyrie knew, and just discussing things with Lofn was enlightening. But that couldn't stop Jem from wanting to try her hand at sparring with the guys. When Jem had suggested it initially Gerard had raised an eyebrow at her, looking her up and down as though a single gust of wind would blow her away, and then Jem proceeded to show him just what she'd learnt during her time with the Valkyrie. She hadn't beaten him. But she had definitely held her own.

"You're getting really good." Dan said dodging Jem's punch, and very nearly landing one of his own. Nearly, but not quite. It had taken a while before Dan had felt comfortable throwing a punch Jem's way. It took even longer before he was willing to use his full strength when attacking. That wasn't an issue Gerard had struggled with at all, and Jem actually kind of appreciated that he didn't go easy on her. He insisted that an Alpha male, especially one who happened to be his best friend, not only deserved a strong mate but needed one.

Jem laughed at Dan as she dodged yet another attack. "Thanks. You're not doing so bad yourself."

Dan laughed, and Jem wondered if he would be much harder to fight in his wolf form. So far both men had insisted on training in human form. Which no doubt was a valuable exercise for Jem. But probably offered very little challenge for them. The more Jem watched them, the more obvious it became that the two of them fought quite differently. Both from each other, and from the Valkyrie Jem had faced off against back in Folkvang. Gerard was a unit. Solid. Muscular. He was the type of guy who looked immovable. Not the type of fighter you went at head-on. Jem had learnt that with Gerard she had to be quick, avoid his punches. Because if he landed one she most definitely felt it. But Gerard's bulk made him slower than her, and so she knew now that she could use that to her advantage. Dan on the other hand, though muscular in his own way, was long and lean, and he was fast. In some ways fighting against him was more of a challenge because she had to move that much faster, so she was worn out a lot quicker. On the other hand, Dan didn't have the same force behind his punches as Gerard did. Not even when he stopped holding back. Jem enjoyed the sparring more than a little bit. It made her feel as though Dan mating her, a reality she still hadn't fully accepted yet, wasn't completely without its merits. For him, not her. From what she could tell Dan was her whole package kind of guy. He was protective, but not domineering. He was intelligent but never had to prove it by attacking the intelligence of the people around him. He was clearly a guy who loved sports and ALL things outdoors. But he also loved books and had even sat down with her on more than one occasion an arm wrapped around her while they each read. It was one of those sweet things that Jem had never even thought to imagine having someone to do with. She'd hoped her future spouse would occasionally cook with her. She'd hoped for a partner who would want kids and have a loving and supportive family that would welcome her. But she'd never even considered if he would just want to be with her. Reading. Not talking. Just being together with his arm around her while they did their own things. She had never considered another person would care about her happiness the way he did. More than anything he just wanted to see her smile. He was forever telling her funny stories. Or singing to her. Or just being generally goofy, just so he could see her smile. The only thing she worried about was that she wasn't sure she could ever do the same thing for him. Jewel was the bubbly funny one, and Jem, well she was just Jem. She was a people pleaser through and through. Not always a good thing. But when it came down to it, she was one of the most boring people she knew, even after finding out she was a Valkyrie. Once you boiled it all down Jem knew that all she was, was a girl who was okay to look at. But not beautiful. She was intelligent. But not super smart. She was a bit of a geek. She loved to read and watch fantasy and science fiction. She thought Jane Austen was brilliant. But would still prefer to watch the BBC movie over reading the book. She had never travelled. She had never really done anything of note, and yet this man. This mythical creature.

This Fenrir. Looked at her with stars in his eyes, and she couldn't help but wonder when that look would fade and this incredibly beautiful, sexy man, would realise that she was... nothing... and he could have so much better.

"You're thinking very hard." Dan said catching her arm as she reached forward in a punch, "I can almost see smoke coming out of your ears."

Jem twisted her arms and slipped from his grasp. "Maybe we should be trying this with you in wolf form." She said, avoiding the real dilemma she was trying to work through.

His eyes shifted to a wolfy yellow. "You will never have to fight one of our kind. You're my mate. They would never try and hurt you." He said, his voice angry. Though not at her, it was more of a protective anger than anything else.

"You don't know that." Jem said, "I need to be able to hold my own. Besides. Elena and Hod. They told me Freya had Fenrir as slaves. If they're loyal to her. I, we, may have no choice but to fight Fenrir in their wolf form."

He frowned. "Slaves?"

Jem nodded.

He pursed his lips together and shook his head. "Still no. You're not ready for that. Besides, I don't want you to have any reason to feel frightened of me."

Now she frowned. "Why would I be frightened of you?" She said, then surprised both of them by darting forwards and kissing him lightly on the back of the neck.

Dan spun around catching Jem by the wrist and pulling her up against him. She felt her whole body flush. She'd never been attracted to anyone the way she was attracted to Dan. It almost felt unnatural how much she wanted to not only be around him. But to be touching him. The way he seemed to always find a reason to touch her, was amazing, and frustrating. Because she couldn't push away the feeling that maybe she was the teenage girl with a crush on the hottest guy in school, and any moment now it was going to fall apart and she'd find she was the victim of some kind of cruel joke.

"You're frowning again." He said pausing his attack to rub the creases that were no doubt appearing between her eyes.

"Am I?" She said, trying to brush it off.

"Little dove. What's wrong?" he asked again.

She tried to smile, but it just wouldn't come. She sighed.

"Dan just because I helped you get out of Folkvang doesn't mean you have to force yourself to be with me." She couldn't look him in the eyes. "I mean. There must be plenty of women. Fenrir. Who would chop off their right arm to be with you, and I'm just. This. I'm nothing special." There. She'd managed to say it. Now he'd realise how stupid his assertion that she was his mate was. He'd agree with her, and he'd be kind. But he would leave, and he would find someone. Some Fenrir female who was amazing and Jem would fade into the distant recesses of his memory. She would be that girl who helped him get out of a sticky situation once, and nothing more.

"Sometimes you are ridiculous little dove." He said raising his hand to her face and forcing her to look him in the eye. "I don't feel forced to be with you in the slightest, and I've had plenty of opportunities to accept a Fenrir female as my mate. But the fact is, none of them were you. None of them will ever be you."

Jem closed her eyes feeling tears squeeze out of the corners.

"Dan I'm nothing special. I mean look at me. I'm boring and selfish, and I'm not exactly the most stunning woman on the planet..." She said drifting off. It was so embarrassing. She hated that she had to point out all these things, these flaws to him.

He wiped one of her tears away with his thumb. "I have no idea who told you all of that. But it's complete and utter nonsense." He said.

She opened her eyes and looked at him. She just couldn't wrap her head around what he was saying. Sure she heard him, and clearly, he believed it. But it just didn't seem true. It never had. She'd always known that she was the least attractive. The least exciting of all her friends. She was always the friend, never the girlfriend when it came to guys. She had just never been...

important. She'd always just been that girl who was so and so's friend.

"You are beautiful Jemima. You have a smile that lights up the room. You put people at ease with your friendliness. You make people feel welcome, loved, and cared for. You are the person I not only want to come home to, but you're also the person I want to go out with. You are a safe place for anyone who meets you. You're my safe place." He said.

"Exactly." She said, looking at him in despair. "I'm safe. Not fun. Not sexy. Not exciting. I'm safe. Like a pair of boring old shoes."

"You. A pair of shoes?" he laughed. "Oh no. I don't think so my love. Personally, I wouldn't compare you to clothes at all. You're more like springtime. You're sunshine and new life, and you are definitely sexy." He pulled her closer and she felt herself blushing. "You are exactly who I need, and now that I've found you, I'm never letting you go. So you are just going to have to deal with having me around." He said, and then he kissed her.

"Oh come on now!" Gerard groaned. "I thought you two were sparring. But every time I turn around you're kissing." He rolled his eyes, though if anything he looked amused. "If I'd known getting the two of us caught by the Aesir was just an excuse to spend more time with Jem I never would have gone to get her. I would have left you to it." He said with a grin.

"You'll be next brother, and then I'll get to tease you." Dan said with a smile, dropping one arm and tucking Jem under the other, her hand up against his bare chest.

"Never going to happen." Gerard said smugly.

"Of course it will. I'm sure some poor girl will eventually get past that face of yours and accept you as her mate." Dan teased.

"Dan!" Jem said smacking him on the chest. He looked down at her, his lips quirking and a low playful growl rumbling in his chest. Jem's heart started thumping hard in her chest. Would she ever stop blushing around him?

"No you idiot. You'll never get the chance to tease me because I'm not going to go all goo-goo eyed over some woman." Gerard announced.

Now Dan was laughing in earnest, his chest shaking hard, and tears forming in the corners of his eyes.

"I can't wait to see how your mate wraps you around her finger." Dan laughed wiping his eyes with the back of his hand.

"Never. Going. To. Happen." Gerard said.

"You just wait." Dan said, still laughing.

"We'll need to get home first." Said Gerard.

That sobered Dan just a little.

He wasn't wrong. Things were going well enough staying with Lofn. But they couldn't stay here forever. They needed to get back home.

The visits from the Valkyrie at Lofntyr Manor had reduced considerably. But Lofn, Henry and Ingrid were always on their guard. So were Dan and Gerard for that matter. Jem just kept waiting for the other shoe to drop. Dan was healed now. As good as new. In saying that Jem had thought he was pretty good even damaged. But that had nothing to do with his ability to move around without being in pain, and everything to do with the fact that he was gorgeous even when he was injured. Lofntyr Manor really was a beautiful place. The gardens were like something out of a dream. Much like Jem had always imagined heaven would look like. But the longer they stayed, the more they realised that they weren't meant to stay here. If they did stay they would definitely live. They would probably even be happy. But they agreed the Creator had a lot more planned for them than simply being happy and free. Jem was convinced that she was meant to help get that same thing for others as well. Others like the Fenrir who spent their entire lives hiding from people who were trying to kill them. Or like the Valkyrie who were being lied to and used as weapons in Freya's war. Lofn agreed that they had more to do. That they needed to share what Freya was up to, and she didn't hide the fact that she hoped they would find her people. That they would let the Dwarves know that she was alive. Lofn clearly loved Lofntyr Manor. She had made this place her home. But admitted that the only things keeping her in Asgard were Sarah, Beth, Henry and Ingrid. Henry and Ingrid had made it clear that if Lofn ever chose to leave, they would go with her. The older couple weren't just Lofn's staff, they had become her family. They clearly loved her like a daughter and Sarah as their own grandchild. They just needed to know that they had somewhere else to go. Lofn had them all seated around a table, maps out in front of them as she explained the best path for them to travel to get to the mountains. The best. But not the safest. It was a route that avoided the main roads the Aesir travelled but didn't guarantee no interference from wild animals, or Freya's search parties. The men weren't concerned about the animals. If anything the idea of hunting creatures that had no knowledge of wolves or Fenrir intrigued them both. But it was a long way to travel. Lofn suggested it would take the three of them at least a week to get there, and during that time they would need to make stops. She knew a few people who would take them in if they were desperate. There was one area at the base of the mountain that looked like it would create issues. It was the pathway to Heimdell's castle. The castle they would have to enter if they wanted to get to the bridge. That final part of their journey would be the riskiest. It would leave them in an area more exposed than even the fields had been. They would have to disguise themselves if they wanted to have any hope of making it to safety.

"Couldn't we just climb up the side?" Gerard asked, pointing to an area of the mountains that led straight off of the woods they'd planned to travel.

Lofn shook her head. "It's much steeper than you would think. The maps all suggest that the Himinbjord Mountains are simply mountains. But I've seen them first hand, and they're more like a range of jagged cliff faces.

"We've rock climbed before." Gerard said.

"Without gear?" Lofn asked.

Gerard and Dan nodded. Dan extended his hands and showed Lofn how he could release his claws even in human form.

"That might work. But what about Jemima?" she asked.

They looked at Jem and she had no doubt she was as white as a sheet. She was feeling nauseated just thinking about climbing a cliff. Well, not the climbing so much as the possibility of falling.

"I went abseiling once as a kid. Or I should say I tried to go abseiling. They couldn't even convince me to get my body over the edge I was so petrified." She said.

"I could carry you on my back." Dan said.

Jem steeled herself. "I. Okay. I mean, It's the safest option for us isn't it?" She said, "So I'll try. I just might have to keep my eyes closed."

"It's too bad we don't have one of the swan cloaks, then you could just fly up." Lofn said.

"Perhaps I could help with that." A soft voice said from the door.

They all spun around, both Dan and Gerard growling and their teeth elongating as they prepared to make the change.

"Reyna?" Jem said, as Dan put his body between her and the Valkyrie.

Reyna smiled, her straight white teeth lighting up her face. "I knew you were special from the first moment I saw you." She said, ignoring the others and speaking directly to Jem.

Jem looked at Reyna, and just like when she first met the older Valkyrie a feeling of comfort enveloped her.

"How did you get in here without us scenting you?" Gerard demanded, sniffing the air.

Reyna looked at him. "I flew of course." She said pulling her cloak across her body so she could show them the white feathers that covered it.

"What do you mean special?" Jem asked.

"Did you know you're the first Valkyrie descended from Pogn to arrive at Folkvang since Freya started her quest to destroy the Fenrir?" Reyna said.

"No, I didn't." Jem said.

"You remind me of her you know." Reyna said with a smile, "You look similar. But it's more about the feel of you. Pogn was talented in all of the Valkyrie disciplines just like you, and instead of choosing one of the flashier roles, she chose to be a negotiator, just like you did. During

Ragnarok, she was on the front line trying to broker peace. Trying to end the fighting." Reyna came further into the room, closing the door behind her.

"Pogn was my friend, and when she left I didn't understand. She told everyone else she wanted to start a family on Midgard. To live and to die. To have a human life. Especially now that the war was over. But in confidence, she told me that Freya was set on throwing our world into another war." Reyna frowned. "I didn't believe her at first. I didn't want to. I trusted Freya. She wasn't just my Queen. My leader. She was everything in Asgard that represented maternal love."

Reyna looked around their group. "It didn't take long. A few hundred years at most before I finally saw what my friend had been trying to show me, and by that point, I couldn't dispute it. Freya is trying to start another war. She's trying to start another Ragnarok. I don't know why. But she's hell-bent on it."

Lofn's eyes went wide. "Another Ragnarok?" she asked, her face pale.

Reyna nodded. "She's been lying to my girls for years. Only a few Valkyrie, like myself and Jem, could see the truth. Could sense the lie. The girls that could, were always from the negotiator discipline. I've had to teach the ones who haven't fallen under Freya's spell how to hide in plain sight because up until now there was nowhere in this world or on Midgard that I could hide them. Not until I saw you escaping with these two." Reyna said.

"You saw us escaping?" Jem asked.

Reyna nodded.

"She's lying." Gerard said.

"Then where do you think Jemima got those Einherjar cloaks from?" Reyna asked, "You don't really think men trained by Freyr would be undisciplined enough to leave their gear just lying around do you?"

Dan and Gerard looked at each other uncertainly.

"I've been watching you ever since you arrived Jemima. Watching how you questioned things. How you tested all the information you were given while the women around you just accepted what they were being told. I watched you go on your walks. I saw you go to the dungeon, and then you asked about Fenrir mates and I knew." Reyna said, smiling again. "If a Valkyrie could be the mate of a Fenrir, then there is definitely hope for me to get my girls out of here. There's hope if you'll help me convince them of the truth."

"She's not staying in this place." Dan growled, his face becoming less and less human by the second.

Jem placed a hand on his arm and she felt his body relax a little.

"Absolutely not!" Reyna said, "She can't stay here. None of you can. I hoped that once you got back to Midgard you could help me smuggle some of the girls out. Teach them the truth. Give them somewhere safe to stay." Reyna said.

"We have to protect our packs first." Gerard said.

"Dan. Gerard. These are my people. Sort of. Just like the Fenrir are yours." Jem said.

"The Fenrir are your people now too." Dan said.

Jem smiled. "I know. But these women. They don't have a pack to protect them. To fight with them. To fight for them. They don't have anyone. Except me."

Dan nodded.

"We couldn't bring them to the den." Gerard said.

"I don't think that would be a good idea anyway." Reyna said, "Most of these girls have been fed nothing but lies about the Fenrir for years. They've been taught to fight and kill you. But more than that, they've been taught to be afraid of you. They would need to be exposed to the truth slowly. Shown that you aren't mindless savages. That you won't just try and kill them. They have to see that you're people first." Reyna said.

"Of course we're people." Gerard said angrily.

"I know that." Reyna said, "But they don't. Think of it like this. Your entire life you've been taught that the Valkyrie are evil correct?"

Gerard and Dan both nodded.

"You were taught that they will always try and kill you." She continued. "And then you encountered Jemima." She said.

"But she's just one Valkyrie." Gerard said, "She's

an exception."

"Maybe that's true. But I'd like you to consider that she might not be the only exception." Reyna said. "There are other girls back at Folkvang who aren't accepting everything Freya says as gospel. There are Valkyrie who don't want to be at war. There are good people."

"Like Jewel." Jem said.

"Like Jewel." Reyna agreed.

Jem stepped out from behind Dan, but he took her hand, allowing her to step past him, but refusing to leave her side.

"Is she okay?" Jem asked.

"She's upset. Confused. Worried about you. Some of the girls are saying you were tricked. Clearly that's not the case though." Reyna said, looking at Jem and Dan's joined hands.

"Does she believe them?" Jem asked, feeling her heart sink.

"I don't think so." Reyna said, "She keeps saying 'Jem's never lied to me before' I assume you asked her to come with you first. That you tried to tell her what was going on."

Jem nodded.

Reyna moved forward and put a hand on Jem's shoulder. "She misses you. I know that much."

"If I write her a letter can you give it to her?" she asked.

Reyna nodded. "As long as you keep me and the other Valkyrie in mind when you get to Midgard, I would be happy to. I just ask that you at least think about a safe place for me to send the Valkyrie brave enough to break away from Freya."

Jem nodded.

"Lovely. Well then Jemima Pogn's daughter, I have something for you." Reyna said, shrugging off the swan feather cloak and handing it to her.

"I... Thank you." Jem said.

Dan still stood close to Jem, and Gerard was still glaring at Reyna, but after the offer of the cloak neither of them were growling.

Reyna smiled and looked at the two Fenrir. " I know it's hard to wrap your head around there being Valkyrie who don't want to be a part of Freya's war. Valkyrie that don't hate Fenrir. But it's true. As true as the fact that I will stay at Folkvang as long as I have to if it means getting my sisters out of there, and protecting them from the lies that they are being fed."

"If we find a place how can we get ahold of you?" Jem asked, and she really wanted to know. If she could help the Valkyrie, then she wanted to.

Reyna shrugged. "I have no idea, and at the moment it doesn't really matter. For now, you need to focus on getting out of this place." She said.

They spent the first leg of their journey travelling in their respective animal forms. Running. Or in Jem's case flying. As fast as possible to the forest where they would at least have some cover from prying eyes, and Valkyrie scouts.

After almost a full day of flying in swan form, it was clear to Jem that she couldn't travel that way all the time. Dan and Gerard, though coated in sweat and sides heaving seemed as though they could keep going if necessary. But Jem practically passed out when they finally stopped. Being in swan form for so long not only used her physical energy, it clearly drained her magic as well. There was no way she could travel like that for a while. Not till her energy built back up again, and even then, she needed to save her energy for the ascent up the mountain. Lofn had given them instructions for places where they could stay. For people they could stay with, and places they should avoid. But for now, all they could think of was avoiding coming into contact with anyone. Even people Lofn said they could trust.

That first night was miserable. They took turns sleeping. Or at least they would have if Jem hadn't been so tired. There was no way to hide how exhausted she was from her day travelling in swan form. She probably wouldn't have been so tired if she'd flown high in the air. But in the interest of staying under the radar, she had flown low. Which meant no access to the air currents that would have made gliding possible for her. She'd been flapping her wings all day long, and even now that she was in human form her entire body ached. She had offered to take the first shift. But she had been so tired she'd fallen asleep only moments after they had said no. The next thing she knew Dan was gently shaking her awake and her stomach was feeling more than a little hollow from not eating since Lofn had given her breakfast the previous morning.

"Rise and shine little dove." Dan said.

Jem shot to her feet, her body still aching from the previous days flying.

"What's wrong?" she gasped.

"Other than your snoring, nothing." Gerard smirked.

"I don't snore." Jem said, then looked at Dan, "Do I?"

Dan chuckled. "You do, and it's just a little bit adorable."

Jem sighed. "You should have woken me up." She said.

"Your snoring wasn't that bad." Gerard said.

"No. I mean." She sighed, "You should have woken me so that you could get some sleep." She said.

Both men laughed.

"And miss out on all the 'adorable' snoring." Gerard said with a grin.

"Not a chance." Dan said, still chuckling.

"I'll take the first watch tonight then." Jem said.

"Whatever you want." Dan said.

"I don't want to slow you down." Jem said.

"You're not." Dan said giving her arm a rub.

"I didn't yesterday. But there's no way I can fly the whole way." She looked at both men, "It took too much out of me. I'm not even certain I could shift today." She said.

They nodded.

"Don't worry about it." Dan said, "Gerard or I will carry you."

Jem shook her head. "I can walk, or run."

"I know you can. But it'll be quicker if you let one of us carry you." Dan said.

"I'm heavy." Jem said, feeling embarrassed.

Gerard snorted. "You're not heavy at all. Especially after carrying this Heffalump." He said indicating Dan.

"We aren't going to be travelling as hard here in the forest as we did out on the plains." Dan said.

"We can't." Gerard said.

"Not unless we want to kill ourselves running headlong into a tree or something." Dan agreed "Besides." He said moving closer and lifting her into his arms. "You're light, and you'll only seem lighter when I'm in wolf form." Then he gave her a quick kiss.

"Okay." She said, but she still felt unsure.

"We'll need to hunt." Gerard said.

"Isn't there enough food in the pack from Lofn?" Jem asked.

"Possibly. But we'll need our energy, and for

Fenrir that tends to mean meat." Dan said.

"How will we cook it?" Jem asked.

"If we eat it in our wolf forms we won't need to." Gerard said with a shrug.

"That's not going to work for Jem though dude. She's hardly going to eat it raw." Dan said.

"True." Gerard said with a frown.

"I don't need to have meat." Jem said.

"It must seem kind of gross." Dan said, looking embarrassed.

"I can't imagine it's much worse than when a vegetarian sees someone eating a steak." Jem said.

Dan gave her a look.

"Okay, it's kind of different. But only because you're catching them and eating them raw, and my meat tends to arrive wrapped in plastic, and I cook it." Jem said.

Dan laughed. "So I take it you're not a blue steak kind of girl?"

Jem shook her head. "I don't like it cremated either. But I'd rather it weren't mooing." She laughed.

"Fair enough." Dan said, smiling at her, "I wouldn't eat it raw in human form either, but when you're in wolf form it doesn't really even cross your mind. You need food for energy, and so you eat."

"I get it." Jem said, and she did, she just couldn't see herself joining in on eating raw rabbit, or whatever they caught.

"Once we're further in we could maybe look at having a fire." Dan suggested.

Both Jem and Gerard shook their heads.

"It's too dangerous." Jem said, "A fire will just attract attention."

Gerard nodded along with her.

"It'll draw the Valkyrie straight to us if they're searching nearby." Gerard said.

"It's going to get cold." Dan said.

It was already getting cold, but Jem could hardly wuss out now. They were only five days away from freedom.

"You'll just have to keep me warm then." Jem said, sending Dan a smile, "Besides. Every time you two shift you seem to be standing around naked and you're fine. So I'll be fine wrapped up in all my clothes. I'll even keep the swan cloak on and just not shift."

"We'll play it by ear." Dan said, "Fenrir run hotter than humans, so we don't have to worry about getting cold like you do."

He moved closer, wrapping his arms around her.

"In the meantime, I'll keep you warm." Dan said.

"We'll take turns hunting so that one of us can be here keeping Jem warm." Gerard said.

Dan growled at his friend, his eyes turning a wolfish yellow.

Gerard raised his hands in surrender, but it was Jem who put her hand on Dan's face and said.

"Dan you know it's not like that."

Dan shook his head from side to side, as though

he were shaking away the instinctively hostile reaction.

"I know." He said, then he looked at Gerard. "I'm sorry man."

Gerard shrugged. "Until you two are officially mated I get that you're going to be overprotective. But you know I'd never do anything to hurt Jem, or you." He said.

"I know." Dan said with a sigh, though Jem noticed he pulled her in closer.

"How about you both go and hunt tonight? It's not cold yet." Jem suggested.

"I'd rather you weren't on your own." Dan said.

"You can't keep an eye on me all the time." Jem said, pulling gently out of Dan's arms, "And I don't want you to either."

Dan frowned.

"Dan I like you. A lot. But. I'm not a child, and I don't want to be treated like one. I've been looking after myself for a long time, and I don't need a babysitter. More than that, I'm a Valkyrie, and I can look after myself." She said.

"I know you can little dove." Dan said, "It's not that I think you can't. It's just that when Fenrir find their mates they get a little protective."

"Do the females get protective too?" Jem asked.

Gerard snorted back a laugh.

"Not as protective as our males. But yes." Dan admitted.

"So why would you think I'd be any less protective of you?" She asked.

Dan just looked at her, lost for words.

"I may not be Fenrir. But now that I know you're meant for me I can't imagine letting anything happen to you. The thing is, we can't be with each other all the time, and we shouldn't be. It's important for us to be together, but I think it's just as important that we're able to be apart. Have our own interests." Jem said.

Dan pulled her back into his arms and gave her a kiss on the forehead. "Alright. We'll hunt. But you be careful."

Jem kissed him on the lips. "You be careful too." She said.

Every day they got up early, ate the provisions Lofn had provided them with and ran until dinner time. At which point the boys would hunt, and Jem would have a repeat meal of what she'd eaten for breakfast. The boys were trying to hunt enough that they didn't need to eat any of the food Lofn had sent with them. Especially as it was all Jem could eat. As soon as they had hunted they came back to the campsite. Usually they found a small cave of some kind or built a small structure out of branches. For the first six days of their journey they followed that same routine, with Jem riding Dan as though he were a horse rather than an enormous wolf. Every night Jem climbed down from his back, her muscles aching and her skin sore from riding bareback. He was gentle. Moving quickly but carefully. But that didn't change the fact that her body was sore each night, or that she was so tired she had usually passed out with exhaustion by the time Dan and Gerard returned to the campsite. Usually, she woke up with the morning light wrapped in Dan's arms. Often he was already awake and Gerard had gone to scout ahead or hunt again. By the end of day seven, what would hopefully be their last night in Asgard, it had become abundantly clear that they would need to find one of Lofn's friends. There was no way they could stay out in the open, and the men definitely couldn't travel in their Fenrir forms. They'd been travelling for half a day when people started appearing on the road, and though up until that point they'd been taking a path of their own making in the forest, the thinning trees would no doubt expose them if any of the travellers ducked off the path to make a pit stop. Or if they happened to glance into the trees at an inopportune moment, and so they decided it would be best to join the other travellers. To do whatever it took to try not to stand out. Which, given Dan and Gerard's size, could be harder than they hoped.

AT THE BASE OF
THE MOUNTAIN

Jem had never been more thankful that Reyna had left the Einherjar cloaks for her to find. Dan and Gerard were massive hulking figures even while walking through a sea of tall thin Aesir. But thanks to wearing the cloaks they only garnered a fleeting acknowledgement from the other travellers. For all intents and purposes, the three of them looked like a patrol, or some such thing sent out by Freya. They got the occasional nod, or wave. But overall they were ignored. Being ignored aside though, all three of them made sure to keep their hoods up. The last thing they needed was for someone to be able to describe them to any of the Valkyrie who were searching for them. They may have looked cool and calm to outside eyes, but Jem was walking on a knife's edge with anxiety, and going by the golden gleam coming from beneath both men's hoods, Dan and Gerard were feeling the strain of travelling in public as much as Jem was.

"Where did Lofn say her friend lived?" Gerard

asked, his head darting from side to side anxiously, watching the Aesir moving between the houses and stores that filled the small village that wound its way along the base of the mountains.

Jem looked up and down the street, searching for a moon hanging over a doorway. The one thing Lofn had told her to look out for. Lofn's friend was an Aesir woman named Nott. She was apparently the goddess who pulled the moon across the sky. Other than that, all Lofn had given them to go by was that Nott looked like a clear night with all the stars on display.

Jem scanned every building until finally, she saw an image of a crescent moon with a single star hanging from it. It had to be the place. It was literally the only building with any kind of moon on it. The only thing was, it was clearly an Inn of some description. Hardly somewhere they could stay if they wanted to go unnoticed. Surely there would be other guests in the building. Then, of course, a woman stepped out, and there was no doubt that this was the place.

Nott had skin so dark it was almost pitch black. She wore a dress that was pure black with a golden underlay, reaching down to her gold shoes, her fingers, and up to her neck. A tulle layer lifted the dress out from her body and golden stars were scattered all over it. Hanging from a chain at her ears were crescent moons. Her hair was an intricate arrangement of tight black corkscrew curls piled high on her head, and wrapped in a crown-like band were stars that wove their way through her hair. She didn't smile, and yet she had a serenity about her. Her dark eyes took in everything, including, it would seem, them. She took one look at their group, nodded, then turned and walked back inside the Inn without a backward glance. Nott left the Inn door wide open behind her. Jem was tempted to grab Dan's hand. An action she'd been tempted to do more than once throughout the day. Something she couldn't do without drawing attention to them. There was no way a Valkyrie and an Einherjar would be walking around holding hands. At least it was unlikely they would. Especially if they were out on official business, and for now it was best for the Aesir around them to think that was exactly what they were doing. Instead of taking his hand, Jem nudged Dan to get his attention.

"I saw her." Jem said, her voice only just loud enough for Dan and Gerard to hear her with their sensitive Fenrir hearing, "This way." She said louder, indicating the Inn.

Jem led the way with Dan and Gerard following close behind. They must have looked at least mildly intimidating because the Aesir in their path moved quickly out of their way. Either that or it wasn't uncommon for Einherjar and Valkyrie to be a little aggressive while out on tasks for Freya or her people.

"Welcome Jemima. Daniel. Gerard." Nott said, acknowledging them each in turn.

Nott's Inn was like something out of a medieval movie with its high ceilings, stonework, and open balustrade that exposed the doors to the Inn rooms. Yet despite its medieval feel, it was the furthest thing from old. The floor was in impressive mosaic made up of varying shades of blue and white depicting the night sky. The ceilings themselves were a dusky blue with golden stars painted on them, and the lights that hung from the ceiling were three-dimensional stars with what looked like enormous diamonds glowing within them. The fireplace was lit, and its warmth filled the room, as did the scent of something positively sinful cooking in a kitchen somewhere nearby. It was beautiful and homey. Much like Lofn's home. But every inch was clearly the work of Nott's skilled eye.

"Nott?" Jem asked nervously.

Nott smiled flashing perfectly straight white teeth. She seemed to shine, as though she were a night light.

"The one and only." She said, "My dear friend Lofn told me you'd be on your way to see me. I have a room prepared for you, and food ready to serve."

Jem almost collapsed with relief. "Oh thank the Creator." She said.

"Indeed." Nott said, still smiling.

"How do we know this is actually her?" Gerard said.

At least he was consistent in his mistrust of the Aesir. Jem couldn't help but wonder if he trusted anyone. Or at least anyone aside from Dan.

Nott laughed. "Oh, I like you." She said, "You remind me of my son. Ever the optimist."

"Even if she isn't Nott, what other options do we have?" Jem asked.

"We can leave." Gerard said.

Nott's smile dropped. "I wouldn't suggest it." She said, "Freya has been sending teams of her people through regularly ever since you escaped. I never know when one is going to turn up. Which is why I've given you my suite. They may have reason to check the other rooms. But absolutely no excuse to search my home. After all." She smiled. "I am an upstanding member of the Aesir community. I would never hide anything from one of the witch twins." She said with a wink.

"I hear what you're saying." Dan said looking at Gerard, "But I think we can trust Nott, and although it may not seem like it. I think this is the safest place for us to be for now. Besides. A hot meal and a decent night's sleep is exactly what we need tonight. We're going to need all the energy we can get to make the trip tomorrow."

"And on that note, I'd better show you to the room before my regulars start turning up." Nott said.

Rather than taking them up the stairs to the

landing that accessed the public rooms, Nott led them into the kitchen where she gave a woman wrapped in a white apron a nod. The woman returned Nott's nod and acknowledged their trio with a shaky smile.

"That's Greta." Nott said, "Don't worry. She's on our side. Believe it or not, there are plenty of Aesir who aren't happy with what's been going on under Freya's rule." She said, leading them to a doorway, and up a stone staircase.

The staircase wound its way upwards, opened out into a large room with a glass ceiling and a wide-open balcony that looked out across the small township.

"I like to see the stars at night." Nott explained with a shrug.

"Norse goddess of the night." Jem said, though mostly to herself.

Nott chuckled. "Exactly."

"You have a lovely home." Jem said.

"Thank you." Nott said with a smile, "I like it."

Jem sighed. "Is it safe for you to be helping us like this?" she asked.

Nott lay a hand on Jem's shoulder, which Dan growled at. Nott ignored him.

"With Freya in charge very few things are safe. But doing what's right. Well, that has its own reward, and I refuse to do what I know is wrong just so things will be safe. Or easy." Nott said.

"I don't know if that's brave, or stupid." Dan commented.

"Or a trick." Gerard offered.

"I like to believe it's faithful." Nott said, "All the Creator expects me to do is the right thing. Beyond that, I'll trust that he has it in his hands."

"And you believe helping us is the right thing to do?" Gerard said doubtfully.

"I believe that wiping out an entire race of people has never been in the Creator's plan. Not with the Vanir. Not with the Jotun. Not with the Dwarves. Not with the Vatnfirar, and not with the Fenrir." Nott said.

Like Lofn, Nott was friendly. The type of person that Jem would have gotten on well with, back home, before all this Valkyrie stuff. The sort of person Jem naturally gravitated towards. Jem was at ease with her, despite the almost impossible intensity of her Aesir beauty. Dan and Gerard, on the other hand, were on edge. They didn't dislike Nott as such. But they didn't trust her either. It wasn't like with Lofn. She'd essentially saved their lives, and after that, they hadn't had much choice but to trust her. With Nott, they seemed extra nervous. She'd provided them with a safe place to stay, and food. But as far as they were concerned she could decide to turn on them at any moment. There was also the fact that they were in the middle of a town full of Aesir, and Nott had Aesir customers milling around downstairs. They were so close to home, and yet so far away. Anything could go wrong, and then they would be stuck in this place. Or worse, back in that dungeon with Freyr.

It was interesting for Dan being around Jemima. When he'd first imagined finding his mate, his expectations had been a little different than what he had found in Jem. He'd never considered that his mate wouldn't be found amongst the Fenrir. He'd imagined a dark-haired, tough as nails mate. Possibly even from his own pack. There was no doubt that Jem was tough, she had a core of steel. But she wasn't hard in the way he had anticipated his mate to be. She was strong. Resolute in her decisions, and at the same time, she was the sweetest, kindest woman Dan had ever met. Even Gerard was charmed by her, and Gerard was never charmed by anyone. Dan had never expected that his mate would be the type of woman who would put other people at ease. People like his best friend, who had always struggled to trust anyone from outside of their race. Sometimes struggle to trust anyone from outside of their pack. That she would be a listener. Someone who supported the people around her to achieve their dreams. Rather than someone who would take charge and have others help her achieve her own dreams. The mate Dan imagined had been a woman who worked alongside him while being a force to be reckoned with. He'd imagined a mate who was passionate, forceful, and instantly respected because of her tough exterior. He had no doubt that Jem would work alongside him. She would be a strong support. Backing him up and working her tail off next to him no matter what he chose to do. He had no doubt that she would be passionate. But she would never be the type of woman to earn respect through intimidation. Her kind personality would find the cracks in peoples armour and slip between them. She would love people so fiercely that they wouldn't even realise that she had gone from being just a person in their lives, and a Valkyrie at that, to someone they loved and respected. He only hoped that he would be able to support her in the same way. So far, in the time he had known her, Jem had sacrificed a lot. She had left the Valkyrie so she could save him and Gerard for one thing. If her being his mate meant he would need to leave his pack, his family, could he make that kind of sacrifice for her? He hoped that he would if that time came. He knew Jem was something special. That she was the right person for him. That she was his mate, and he wanted to show her that he was the right person for her as well. So far she seemed to accept him. But accepting someone, and loving them. They were two different things. It had only been a short stretch of time. But Dan knew. Even without the mating call, he didn't doubt that he would have eventually realised she was his mate. Just being around Jem was enough. She wasn't just beautiful. She was intelligent. Thoughtful. Resilient. Brave. Even the bravest of the females in the Lovell den would have felt intimidated by the journey they were on. Heck, he was intimidated by it. But Jem. Whether she was frightened or not, just kept pushing on, and somehow she was managing to make friends on the way.

Nott farewelled them after a breakfast of the best bacon Dan had ever eaten. She'd advised them to hold off leaving and go with the crowd. They'd still stand out. But not nearly as distinctly as if they'd left while everyone else was still asleep inside their homes. Nott's argument was that people with something to hide were the only one who would leave while the sun was still down, and so they had followed her advice, joining the crowds of Aesir making the pilgrimage to Heimdell's castle. Some of the Aesir were visiting the castle out of interest, like tourists, with no real interest in travelling across the Rainbow bridge, and some were putting themselves forward to be apprentices. Wanting to learn directly from Heimdell how to care for and protect the Rainbow bridge.

"We're here." Jem exclaimed with a puff, resting her hands on her hips and tilting her head back to look up the sheer cliff face of the Heimdell mountains, where presumably the castle sat atop.

Dan came up behind Jem and gave her a kiss on the back of her neck. He refused to give up any chance to be close to her. There was no guarantee any of them would live through this little adventure, and if Dan only had these few days, weeks, or minutes to be close to Jem, then he would take each and every one and live them to the full.

"Are you sure you want to fly up? I can still carry you." Dan offered, acknowledging to himself that he would rather Jem was close to him as they made this journey, rather than flying ahead of him and Gerard. He was loath to leave her unprotected. Even if she had proved time and again that she was capable of protecting herself.

"I'm too heavy." Jem said, to which he shook his head. She weighed almost nothing, and even if she had been heavy he wouldn't have rejected her comforting weight on his back if she'd accepted his offer. Keeping her close and safe was foremost in his thoughts.

"Besides, we have no idea what we're going to be up against when we get to the top. I can warn you. That way you'll be able to defend yourself a lot easier. Not to mention having me on your back will slow you down." She continued.

There was no point in disagreeing with her. She wasn't wrong. At the same time if she was killed or captured it would destroy Dan as soundly as if he'd been recaptured himself. If anything, he felt that the punishment she would get for betraying the Valkyrie, for betraying Freya, would be much more severe than what he received. He wouldn't allow that. Not while he had breath in him.

Jem took a deep breath, unclasped the swan

feather cloak and looked at him with a nervous smile.

"Let's do this." She said, her attempt at sounding cheery falling a little flat.

Gerard nodded and returned her smile. Dan stepped close to her and gave her a kiss on the forehead.

"Be careful." He said to her.

She had a genuine smile. "I will be. You too." She said giving him a quick kiss on the lips.

She threw the swan cloak back around her shoulders, her lips moving, though even with his Fenrir hearing he struggled to discern what she was saying. Her body shimmered as though she were coated in gold dust, blinding him momentarily as her body shifted and changed, and then she was standing before him as a large pure white swan. It struck him that a Valkyrie shifting into a swan was much like Jem. Unexpected, and beautiful. She spread her wings wide and began flapping, running to assist in launching her body into the air, and then she was airborne. Dan took a few moments to watch as she maintained an exhausting rhythm, flapping her wings.

"We need to move." Gerard said, "We aren't safe down here, and the longer she's up there alone, the less safe she is."

Dan nodded. Forcing a partial shift wasn't something he or any Fenrir did often. But it was a process Dan found easy. Not as painful as a full shift could occasionally be. But not without pain either. He felt his fingers and feet change, not to full wolf, footpads would be useless for climbing. But within moments he was able to release his claws.

"Well then brother. Let's give this free climbing thing another crack." Dan said.

Gerard laughed. "Try not to fall on your ass."

Dan walked closer to the cliff face and looked up. There was no way they weren't going to be exhausted when this was over. Then he saw Jem had landed on a ledge above and was waiting for them. He grabbed the first rock and began his ascent. He was relieved Jem wasn't just flying straight to the top. It could take them a fair while to get up the rock face, and every minute she was alone in the castle put her in more danger.

"Let's just do this before someone catches us." Dan said, with a laugh at his friend.

Being in swan form was different to say the least. It was remarkable to be able to fly. But what was most surprising to Jem was that she still felt like herself. The very first time she shifted she had expected to feel strange. As though she were wearing an ill-fitting outfit. It was nothing like that. Her swan legs, they felt like her legs. Her wings, they felt like hers. Every part of her was just a normal extension of who she had always been. Like a finger or a strand of hair. There was nothing in her swan body that felt out of place. It was all very natural and normal. Watching the ground disappear beneath her wasn't unsettling as she'd expected. If anything it was a thrill. She loved the height. She loved the feel of the air beneath her wings. It kind of reminded her of a warm summer's day, driving with the windows of the car down. The warm air making her feel light, free, and joyful. Only instead of a car carrying her, her swan body was what allowed her to travel. Even the flapping, that seemed like it should have made her exhausted, made her feel glorious and free. Who would have thought that she would like heights? As a human it had been far from her favourite thing. But with wings. With wings she was fearless. So fearless that she didn't even think twice about landing on the small ledge above Dan and Gerard. It would have taken her all of five minutes to get to the top. But even with the confidence she felt as a swan, it seemed like the height of folly to wait at the top of the cliff alone. It would be asking to get caught. Instead, she watched Dan and Gerard climb. They moved quickly, confidently. Not even using the claws that Jem could clearly see extended. They moved almost like crabs. Or at least like a crab mixed with a monkey. They were extremely large men. Gerard more so than Dan. But even though Dan was smaller, he wasn't small by any stretch of the imagination. Jem wasn't a tiny woman. She was a broad almost athletic build. But next to Dan she seemed almost petite, and next to Gerard. Well, he left no doubt that she was in fact feminine. She wondered if all the Fenrir males were as big as the two of them. Or if Fenrir were the same as humans, with people of every size, shape, and colour. Were Fenrir only in Germany, or were they all over the world? Were there actually lots of different humanoid races living in the world, and were the 'normal' humans just too blind to see them? Just like she had been until she found out she wasn't normal. Jem's life had changed dramatically from the moment she'd met Dan. She'd been hoping for a romance novel worthy love story of her own. What she could never have even thought to hope for, was an entirely new way to see the world. Her eyes had been opened to a completely new reality, and there was no way that could be undone. Jem still hoped that whatever she had with Dan, whether they were mates or not, would be romance novel worthy.

But even if it wasn't, she couldn't lose what she had gained through the process of knowing him. With every day since meeting him, and discovering her Valkyrie heritage, she had become more of who she truly was. It had been a terrifying few weeks. But she wouldn't change it. She hadn't just become a Valkyrie or the mate of a Fenrir alpha male. She'd found a strength she had never known she had. She had stood up and said no when what was going on was wrong. Even when she knew it would mean sacrificing something valuable to her. She would wager that over the last few weeks she had grown more in confidence, maturity, and spirit than at any other point in her life. She could honestly say, that at this moment when nothing was guaranteed, she trusted the Creator more than ever before to take care of what would happen next, and it gave her a sense of peace like she had never experienced before.

Dan and Gerard finally reached her at the spot she'd chosen to stop. Both of them were sweaty. But they didn't show any signs of fatigue, despite the sweat.

Keep going Dan. You can do it. I love you. She thought to herself. Though obviously she couldn't verbalise it. One of the limitations of being in swan form.

She nearly fell off the ledge when Dan shot her a grin, his eyes glowing golden, and she heard a whisper in her mind. *I'll climb forever if it means I get to hear you tell me you love me.*

She made a surprised honking noise, drawing Gerard's attention. He spun around, searching for danger, and almost losing his grip.

"What's wrong?" Gerard asked, still searching for the danger.

You can hear me? Jem thought at Dan.

"I can." Dan said with a smile.

"You can what?' Gerard asked, now looking confused.

But he can't? Jem asked Dan.

"Apparently not." Dan said with a chuckle.

Gerard glared at Dan. "Explain."

"I can hear her." Dan said.

"I did too. Her honking was that loud I'll be surprised if everyone up there in the castle didn't hear her. Not to mention I nearly fell off the side of the mountain she gave me such a fright." Gerard said in annoyance.

"Not the honk." Dan said, "I heard her speaking in my mind."

And you could speak back. Jem added.

Dan nodded at her. "You're right, and I could speak back."

Now Gerard really did look confused. "What are you talking about?"

"I could speak to her like we can in wolf form." Dan said.

Gerard's eyes popped open in surprise. "Really? But she's not a Fenrir, you're not fully shifted, and I couldn't hear her."

Dan frowned and looked up at her.

Maybe it's to do with the mating bond? She suggested.

Dan smiled. "That would make sense." He said, then looked at Gerard. "Jem's suggesting it could be to do with the mating bond."

"But it hasn't been consummated." Gerard said.

"It doesn't need to be consummated to be a genuine mating bond with our people though Gerard." Dan said simply.

"True." Gerard agreed, "But Jem isn't Fenrir. No offence."

Jem shrugged. Well, she did the swan equivalent of a shrug. She wasn't Fenrir after all.

"Clearly that doesn't matter." Dan said.

Gerard nodded. "I'm glad you've found each other." He said, "And that you were brave enough to save us."

"Anytime." She said, and Dan relayed it to Gerard. "Maybe eventually you'll be able to learn to project your thoughts to others?" Gerard said.

"Maybe. It's definitely something worth testing out." Dan said. "But it might need to wait till we're safely back in the den."

"Agreed." Gerard said, hoisting himself far enough above Jem that she felt the need to fly up higher.

And on that note, I'll fly up a bit higher. Jem said to Dan.

Dan nodded. "We'll see you up there soon." He said.

Gerard nodded at her and returned his focus to the mountainside. Not that it could really be called a mountain. Jem tended to think of mountains as being slowly sloped. The Himinbjord Mountains, or at least this stretch of them, really was more of a sheer cliff face made up of stone that would occasionally break away as sharp shards of rock. More than once Jem had watched Dan or Gerard get a handful of rock only to have it crack beneath their fingers. Luckily in those cases, they were able to quickly use their claws to prevent what would be a guaranteed fatal fall. In all likelihood, both of the men would have cuts all over their hands though. She'd best hope that nothing, and no one nearby had a sense of smell strong enough to realise where they were or what they were doing. Otherwise, this perilous climb would have been for nothing. Jem trusted the Creator to take care of things. But that definitely didn't mean she wasn't scared. She'd never been more frightened in her life. She'd heard it said. Or maybe she'd read it. That bravery wasn't the absence of fear, it was having the courage to do what needed to be done. To do the right thing. Even when you were terrified, and the odds were stacked against you.

How are you going? She asked as Dan got a little closer.

He looked up at her and smiled. "Good my love." He said, though going by the sweat dripping off of him it wasn't exactly easy.

Nearly there. She said, trying to inject some positivity into her mental voice.

Dan laughed out loud. "Don't worry little dove. We're going fine."

Gerard looked at him, not voicing his question, though looking curious.

"She's worried about us." Dan explained.

Gerard laughed too. "Don't worry Jem, I won't let this idiot fall." He said.

The moment Dan and Gerard got equal to her position again Jem opened her wings wide, preparing to go to the top, but Dan looked at her, his expression dead serious.

"Don't go up there yet. Let us get most of the way. I want you safe." Dan said.

I'll be fine. Jem replied.

"I won't be." Dan admitted, "Please. Just to play it safe hang back until we're closer."

Jem nodded, her long swan neck bobbing. Dan smiled.

"Thank you." He said.

Jem stayed put for what felt like an eternity. Her long swan neck craned up so she could watch Dan and Gerard as they made their ascent. It was like a kind of torture watching them get steadily closer to danger while being far enough away that she'd be no help. She supposed that was exactly how Dan had been feeling imagining her up there without him to protect her. Still, whether he was ready for it or not, it was time. Jem leaned forward and leapt off the ledge, allowing herself to free fall for a few moments, then putting a little bit of distance between herself and the cliff face before opening her wings, feeling the air fill them and allowing it to buffer her upwards. She flapped her wings hard, lifting herself up above Dan and Gerard, and settling herself on the ledge.

"How does it look?" Dan's voice came to her.

Clear for now. She said, looking across the empty courtyard. *It's really exposed though.*

"Don't shift back." He said, "Find somewhere out of sight to sit. On a roof nearby or something."

Okay. She said, jumping off the ledge and flying up to sit on the roof behind what she would have called a gargoyle. If it weren't for the fact that it looked more like a dragon, or maybe a massive snake. Whatever it was, it hid her well.

"Okay. We're almost there." Dan said a while later. "What do you think our best option is now?" he asked.

Jem looked around. She'd been thinking about it for a while. The area where they'd climbed had them coming up over the edge right into a wide-open grass area surrounded by buildings that were all linked together. If they wanted to go unnoticed they needed to get into one of the buildings before anyone saw them.

Run straight to your left. There's an entrance there. It seems to be empty. Creator willing it's not a room with someone very quiet, or someone sleeping. But even if it is, it's our best option for now. Jem said.

H

eimdell's castle

Dan and Gerard leapt over the ledge, making surprisingly little sound. They quickly spotted the doorway Jem had mentioned, sprinted across the courtyard, burst through the door, and shut it behind them the moment Jem waddled through.

It was a classroom. Or at least it seemed to be. Jem was very thankful the room was empty. If they'd burst in on a class in session there was no way they would have been able to explain why they were there.

Jem had just finished transforming back to her human form when Dan and Gerard pushed her behind them, placing a wall of Fenrir fury between her and whoever had just stepped out from the side room.

"So." The gravelly, masculine voice said. "You must be the two Fenrir Freyr is so angry about losing, and the Valkyrie who helped them escaped."

Dan and Gerard growled, allowing another partial change, their claws and teeth extending.

Jem popped up on her tiptoes so she could see the man. He was painfully thin, his hair white and scraggly. His skin was a muted brown, as though at one stage he had been very dark, but his skin had dried out creating a powdery film on top. His eyes were wide open as though he had been surprised suddenly, and were much like his skin, dark, yet muted. As though cataracts covered not only the pupil and iris but his entire eye on each side. Jem would have assumed he was blind if his gaze didn't travel between each of them. One by one, clear intelligence and awareness evident on his face as he took in each of them individually.

"Calm yourselves." The man said. "Lofn and Nott both let me know you were on your way. Daniel, Gerard, Jemima." He said.

The men didn't relax in the slightest.

"Who're you?" Dan asked, his elongated teeth slightly slurring his words.

"Oh, I apologise." The man said, "I always assume people know. I'm Heimdell. It's a pleasure to meet you." He smiled.

"Heimdell." Jem said in surprise.

Finding out who the man was, did absolutely nothing to help the guys to dial back the aggression.

"Freya." Dan said.

"Isn't anywhere near here. Nor does she bother to come this way if she can avoid it." Heimdell said.

"She's your Queen." Gerard said.

"Is she." Heimdell said.

"You don't work for her?" Jem asked.

Heimdell shook his head. "Freya is like a rotten apple. Once, a long time ago, she was beautiful. Sweet. She brought health and vitality to all those who came into contact with her. She hasn't been that woman for a very long time. She's managed to maintain her appearance. She still appears beautiful on the outside. But there are some of our people, those like yourself Jemima, or like me, who have the ability to see through the persona she shares with the world."

"You'll help us escape?" Jem asked.

"And anyone else who wants to leave Asgard and help in the war against Freya. She is poisonous, and it won't be long before she sacrifices every Aesir to get whatever it is that she is really after." Heimdell said.

"I don't trust him." Gerard said.

"I wouldn't trust me either if I were you." Heimdell said, "But if you want to get out of here and back to your people, you're going to have to."

"Freya will figure out what you've done." Dan said, his claws and teeth retracting.

Heimdell nodded. "She will. Unless I announce to her that the three of you got in here, knocked out some of my guards and passed through the bridge before I could stop you."

Gerard glared at him, but his claws and teeth retracted. "How much time can you give us?"

"Enough time to get through the bridge. Maybe ten minutes before I have to tell her. I won't risk the safety of my students." Heimdell said. "Once you start running you won't be able to stop until you get to your den, or somewhere else she can't find you."

"How long will it take her to get to us?" Jem asked.

"It depends on whether she has a fully charged piece of the bridge or not." Heimdell said, "She hasn't recharged the piece I gave her in a while. But I have no doubt she has more than one piece. Every time a new piece is harvested she expects to be supplied with one to complete the tasks she has in Midgard. I have always said no, but individuals wanting to garner her favour find a way to get them for her."

"Helping us get through." Jem said, "It'll make it harder for you to get anybody else out, won't it?"

"Perhaps." Heimdell agreed, "But I won't let that hold me back. You can't guarantee tomorrow my dear. All I know is that I can help you now. The Creator's given me a chance to do the right thing, and I won't give it up in hopes that some bigger grander task will come along."

"Thank you." Jem said.

Neither Dan or Gerard thanked Heimdell verbally. They were still wary. But they nodded, and Heimdell seemed to accept that.

"Where are you going to get these guards that we have to knock out? Or are you just going to say we did it, and hope no one wants to speak to these guards?" Gerard scoffed.

"I have some guards who know what's going on." Heimdell said, "And I know most of my students well enough to know that even if they were aware of what's going on they would never tell

Freya. They would never betray me."

"How long have you known about us?" Dan asked.

"Lady Lofn contacted me as soon as you arrived at her home. I'm actually the one who suggested that Lady Nott be a part of the plan to help you leave Asgard." Heimdell said.

"So you've known a few weeks then?" Dan said.

Heimdell nodded.

"Alright then. Let's do this." Dan said clapping his hands together as if the gesture would stir them into action.

"Will we actually have to hit them?" Jem asked. "The guards that is."

The last thing she wanted to do was beat up on somebody who was helping them.

"If you want to keep us safe. Yes. We may even have to damage some of the rooms so it looks as though we put up a fight." Heimdell looked around. "Though maybe not this one. Some of these ingredients were very hard to come by."

Jem looked to Dan shaking her head. "I don't think I can hurt them." Jem said.

Dan placed a hand on her cheek. "Don't worry little dove, Gerard and I will take care of that."

She felt her eyes widen in surprise.

"We'll only do what's necessary to make it look genuine. Nothing more." Dan continued.

"Fenrir aren't violent Jem. We spar for training, and we protect our own. But we don't fight without good reason." Gerard said.

Jem sighed. "I know. I just. You're so prepared to do it." She said.

All of the men nodded.

"It has to be done, or even more people will be put at risk." Heimdell said.

"We wouldn't do it if it weren't necessary." Dan said, "I promise."

Jem lifted up on her tiptoes and gave Dan a quick kiss. "Okay." She said, and that was it. They were off again.

For a man who appeared so old, and had cataracts that seemed like they should render him completely blind, Heimdell was fast. Like super fast. He essentially ran the entire way from where they had met him to the rather large room where the guards waited on high alert. He wasn't even short of breath, despite the frantic pace, and Jem's own pounding heart. As they stepped over the threshold into the room the guards spun, their swords were drawn, ready to fight. Dan took Jem's wrist loosely, pulling her behind him as he prepared to fight. Even knowing she was quite capable of defending herself, she thought it was unlikely that he would ever be able to stop himself from acting out on his instinctive urge to protect her. Much as Jem felt as though she should have been one of those women who insisted she didn't need protecting, that she could take care of herself, Jem didn't think Dan caring enough to want to protect her would ever grow old.

Dan and Gerard growled at the guards, who on seeing Heimdell sighed with relief, and lowered their swords.

"Thank the Creator Lord Heimdell. We were getting worried that Freya had discovered your intention to betray her." One of the men said as he slid his sword back into its scabbard.

"Not yet." Heimdell said, "But she will if we don't do this just right."

The guards nodded.

"So." The same guard said, looking at Dan, Gerard and Jem with interest. "You're Fenrir."

Gerard grunted, and Dan just stared at the guard, still planting himself solidly between Jem and the men. Clearly not ready to risk her getting hurt.

The guard laughed. "Well, you're about as talkative as I was expecting." He said, which had the other three guards smirking.

"You're Einherjar?" Jem asked moving to Dan's side, her hand still holding his to show she wasn't going anywhere.

"And you're our resident Valkyrie defector." The guy said with a smile. "I'm Aidan. It's nice to meet you."

Dan growled at him.

"Jem." She said, then added. "This is Gerard, and my mate, Dan."

She felt Dan's hand stiffen, and his head shot in her direction for the first time since stepping into the room taking his attention off the guards. She hadn't called him her mate before. Not in conversation with others at least, and not without a question mark attached to it. She had claimed him in public, and for whatever reason, he clearly hadn't been expecting that.

"Is that right?" Aidan said, "This all just gets more and more interesting."

"How so?" Gerard asked out of the blue.

Aidan looked over at him. "Freya's been telling people in Asgard for years that Fenrir are just savage beasts. That they don't understand love and loyalty. That they only understand vengeance and have a thirst for Aesir blood. You breaking him and his friend out of that Aesir prison is one thing, but being his mate. Once this gets out, and we will make sure it does. Freya's position as Queen is only going to destabilise more." He said with a smile.

"She's really been that bad to the people here?" Dan asked.

"Most people are completely oblivious to what she is up to. But anyone who steps outside of her favour. They know the truth of who she is." Aidan said.

"You've experienced it first hand then?" Dan asked.

Aidan shook his head and pulled off his helmet, his hair was almost white blonde, his eyes a striking blue. "I've lived under a corrupt ruler before. I've seen the way they twist and distort the truth. How they turn good people into monsters. I almost became one of the monsters, and I can tell you now, that you don't have to be on the receiving end of evil to know it's bad."

Another guard with dark brown, almost black, hair and olive skin squeezed Aidan's shoulder in a show of solidarity.

"We will fight evil in all its forms." The other young man said.

"Until the Creator leads us home." The four Einherjar said in unison.

"Which means we need to make this look as real as possible." Aidan said, clearing his throat.

"If we plan on building any kind of resistance against Freya then we need to be able to get more people out of here. Preferably under the radar." Heimdell said.

"We don't exactly have time to spar." Gerard said.

"No." Aidan's dark-haired friend agreed. "Which is why we're going to rush at you, and you're going to do your best to knock us out with the first hit."

Gerard laughed and looked over at Dan. "I might like these Einherjar after all."

Dan smiled. "Fists only." He said.

"Agreed." Aidan said, "No swords, no claws."

The men nodded at each other, and then it was on. Considering they said there'd be no time for sparring, neither Dan and Gerard nor the Einherjar guards were going easy on each other.

"They need to make the scuffle look real." Heimdell said, coming up beside her.

Jem just nodded as she watched body parts connecting aggressively. Meanwhile, the men were laughing.

"One day we'll spar for real Dan." Aidan said.

Dan grinned. "I looked forward to that day my friend." He said, before soundly punching Aidan in the head and sending him sprawling unconscious across the room.

Heimdell pulled Jem into a hug. "Go now. Run as fast as you can. Shift if you must. I need to start calling out for help. Make it seem realistic. It was lovely meeting you, I have no doubt that we will meet again in the future." He said, slipping something into her hand, and then he began yelling at the top of his lungs.

Gerard suddenly had his hands around Jem's waist and was depositing her on Dan's back. Some time between knocking out Aidan and Heimdell speaking to her Dan had shifted into wolf form. It was a good thing Gerard had lifted her onto Dan's back. Dan was as tall as a human, but in wolf form he was simply enormous. Jem wasn't entirely certain she could have climbed up without help. Then they were off, speeding down the stairs at a breakneck pace. It was terrifying, and for a while, Jem simply closed her eyes and prayed that they wouldn't slip, trip, or fall.

"Little Dove." Dan's voice came to her mind.

Who would have thought they could communicate mind to mind even when she wasn't a swan? Of course, who would have thought that they could transform into animals in the first place, let alone talk in their minds?

"You need to see this my love." He said.

Jem opened her eyes and gasped in surprise. They were running down a staircase still. Only now it looked like the walls, ceiling, and the floor had been perfectly carved from an impossibly large opal. Rainbows zapped across the walls as though light was shining into them. Only the light wasn't coming from some external force but from the walls themselves.

"Wow." Jem said aloud, and she felt Dan smile, even if she couldn't see it.

GUESS WHO'S BACK

The journey down the winding Rainbow stairwell was a lot faster than they had expected. Which was probably why Murphy's Law came into effect. Because if their journey to Midgard was quick. Freya and Freyr's was quicker. Jem, Dan and Gerard had no sooner stepped foot on the dewy grass of the dusky earthen realm than they heard the stretching of leather and the gentle clanging of metal on metal coming from behind the freshly scented pine trees.

Freya must have had more than a few fully charged travelling gems after all. Jem had been living in hope that Freya only owned a few of the rare gems. How many of them could Freya possibly have when, as Heimdell said, they weren't all that common, and they weren't all handed over to Freya. Then Jem had put stock into the fact that surely, even if Freya did have more than a few of the travelling gems, she would only be able to send a few people after them. It took only moments to dash Jem's hopes. Freya either had a few handfuls of the travelling gems, or each gem could carry a dozen or so people. Whatever the truth was, it seemed as though the forest they had emerged into was practically crawling with Einherjar and Valkyrie. *We have no choice. We don't stand a chance against all of these troops.* Dan said. *We need to run.*

Dan was clearly talking to Gerard, not her.

The change was small, but in seconds Jem could clearly see that both of the Fenrir were pushing themselves even harder. Which seemed impossible given the pace they'd been maintaining while descending the Bifrost had been faster than anything Jem had ever experienced. But somehow they managed it. Thanks be to the Creator that the trees and bushes, even with Einherjar and the occasional Valkyrie hiding behind them, didn't slow Dan or Gerard down at all. If anything the familiarity of running through a forest actually allowed them to increase their pace and dodge Freya and Freyr's troops more easily. That, and if Jem wasn't mistaken, there were a few of the Einherjar and Valkyrie who lowered their weapons and bowed their heads just slightly as the three of them passed. Every now and then one of the obviously skilled warriors would appear to trip over nothing knocking into one of their companions, sending both of their weapons sprawling to the ground. Or they would shoot at one of the Fenrir and miss entirely, even though they were painfully exposed.

"Get them!" Jem heard the clearly frustrated Freyr bellow.

"I know where we are!" Jem said aloud as the sudden realisation hit her. "We're in Barri reserve." She said just a little bit quieter.

Do you know where that is in respect to home Gerard? Dan asked.

Gerard's head bobbed up and down in the murky darkness.

I know roughly where that is. Dan thought to her. *I don't come this way often though. Gerard does a lot more work on four paws, tracking lost Fenrir and checking up on rogues. He's saying he knows how to get home.*

Jem sighed. "We've just got to get past all of Freya's people." She said.

The boys somehow managed a noise that even in wolf form, with their sides heaving and froth starting to form at the corner of their mouths, could be distinctly identified as a chuckle.

Jem rolled her eyes. "If we get caught I'm officially blaming the two of you." She said.

They laughed again pushing themselves even harder. Jem was expecting them to run into a patrol of Valkyrie or Einherjar at any moment. Every time they turned a corner she realised she'd been holding her breath. It would be just her luck for them to be caught right before they got to safety. But it never happened. It was a little anticlimactic actually. They had no battle royale. No final confrontation with the big bad. All of a sudden Gerard and Dan just slowed down. Though not before releasing what Jem had thought was a victory howl, but in actuality was to let the pack know that they had made it back into pack lands and that Freya along with her people could be on their tails.

One by one Jem watched as massive black wolves stepped out of the forest, and for the first time since meeting Dan and Gerard, she understood how the Aesir could find them intimidating. She could understand why they would be frightened. As soon as they saw her the individual wolves moved, grouping closer together, approaching Jem, Dan and Gerard as a pack. A pack ready to fight. More than one of the wolves growled at her as they approached, their lips raising and their sharp white teeth exposed. Jem pulled her body in closer to Dan's, unsuccessfully attempting to hide, burying her face in the fur at his scruff. It was fairly close to the reception she had expected. But expecting something and experiencing it were two very different things.

Dan. She mind spoke to him. *I don't think this is a good idea. I should leave.*

One of the bigger wolves took a step forward, leading the others towards them, towards her, and to Jem's surprise, Gerard stepped in front of her and Dan, his lip peeling back as he growled at the other wolves.

You're my mate. You're not leaving. Dan said to her. *You're coming home.*

And clearly what he meant was that this was now her home.

This is Jem, my mate. Dan mind spoke, including not only Jem but all the other wolves.

All of a sudden something, though Jem didn't think it was possible to explain what, slipped into place and she could hear them. Not just Dan. She could hear all of the Fenrir, and all bar Gerard were protesting her presence near the den. It was a cacophony of noise. Men's voices. Women's voices. They were speaking over each other, and yet she could distinctly identify where each voice had come from. As though they had simply been speaking rather than making growly wolf noises. *Ridiculous.* The massive male at the front said.

Dan growled. *I told you before Drew. Jemima is my mate. I was right then, and I'm right now.*

She's Valkyrie. One of the women practically spat. *She can't come into the den.* Another male said. *She's a threat to our people.*

I have a few questions for her. Drew said. *So the only way she's getting in here is as our prisoner.*

Gerard growled louder and began pacing in front of Jem and Dan, protecting them.

Stand down Gerard. The male Dan had called Drew said.

Gerard growled louder and snapped his teeth together sharply, refusing to give up his position in front of them. Drew was clearly confused by Gerard's refusal.

You don't need to do this. Jem said to Dan. *You're safe now. You're home. You don't have to protect me anymore.*

You're right. Dan agreed, and Jem's heart dropped. *I don't have to. I want to. I love you Jem.*

Jem's heart skipped a beat. "I love you too." She replied, only this time she said it out loud without thinking.

All heads spun in her direction, and Jem couldn't help but feel as though she were facing a firing squad. Not that a pack of enormous wolves were any less intimidating than a group of people with guns.

She's lying. The female who had spoken earlier announced.

I'm not lying. Jem replied, mind speaking to the group.

A few of the Fenrir yelped in surprise, while the others growled.

How did she do that? a second female asked, her white coat making her stand out from all the other black wolves.

Dan sighed. *I told you. She's my mate.*

You can hear us? The white female asked, ignoring the others and speaking directly to Jem. Jem nodded. *I can.* she replied.

Since when? Drew asked, his voice had softened.

She's been able to hear me since she first shifted into swan form. Dan said.

Was she able to hear Gerard then? Drew asked.

Both Jem and Dan shook their heads, while Gerard continued his pacing.

No. Dan said.

So how is it that she can hear us now? Drew asked.

When did you start hearing them Little Dove? Dan asked her. Though this time he was clearly speaking to the entire group.

As soon as you told them I was your mate. Jem said,

and she could practically feel his satisfied smile at her answer because she certainly couldn't see it from up on top of him, and she wasn't convinced you could tell a wolf was smiling, not with all those teeth.

What more proof do you need Drew? Dan said smugly.

It could easily be some kind of Valkyrie trap. She's probably just using you to lead the rest of them here. Drew said, his eyes darting around, as though searching for an incoming Valkyrie army.

Gerard growled again pausing in front of Drew before he resumed his pacing.

Jem climbed down from Dan's back, her eyes fixed on Drew. She was staring him down now. Her courage had come right to the forefront, and though she was meant to be descended from a Valkyrie who brokered peace she was more than a little irked at his accusation. She was fighting not to use the other skills she'd been taught and start beating the tar out of him.

"It's not a trap." She said simply, managing to keep her voice level despite her anger. "There are no Valkyrie besides me anywhere near here. Not unless they followed us through the spells that are meant to protect this place, and though it is absolutely none of your business." She said staring each one of the wolves down. "I do love Dan. He is my mate." She announced.

Prove it. The angry female said.

Jem shot her a blood-freezing glare. "And how

exactly do you propose I do that?" she said coldly. The female stayed silent, so Jem kept speaking.

"For one thing. The only person I have to prove my love to is Dan. Not any you. And for another, real love can't be proved in one action. Love isn't just one thing. One action. Or some grand gesture. Love is patient, kind, honest. It puts the other person first. It isn't jealous or resentful. It forgives mistakes. Real love is developed over a lifetime. Expressed over a lifetime." Jem said. "The only way to 'prove' love like you want me to, is over a lifetime."

Exactly. Said Drew *And you haven't known him nearly long enough to build that kind of love.*

Dan exposed his teeth, snapping and growling at Drew, before shifting into his human form.

"It was long enough for her to sneak us out of Freya's dungeon." Dan growled.

Drew scoffed at Dan's answer and shifted into his own human form, as did the rest of the Fenrir. It took all of two seconds for Jem to realise that Dan and Drew were related, and she would wager the white pelted female was related to him as well. Dan's brother and sister.

Jem put a hand on Dan's arm, holding him back.

"Dan. This isn't just your pack. They're your family." She said, in particular indicating Drew and his sister. Dan had spoken about his sister, Peta, the only female in his family besides his Mum. Which was saying something given he was one of eight.

Dan looked at Jem, his face softening. "You're my family now." He said, "Even if it means I have to go rogue."

Every single one of the pack members gathered in front of them looked surprised.

"He wouldn't be going alone." Gerard added crossing his arms over his broad, solid chest.

Jem turned away from the pack, exposing her back. If they chose to shift and attack her now she would be an easy target. But she didn't even think about that. All she could think about was the pain Dan and Gerard must have been experiencing at the thought of leaving their families.

"You can't do this for me." Jem said.

Dan smiled at her. "I'm not doing it for you." He said, "Or at least I'm not doing it just for you. I'm doing it for myself."

He took Jem's face in his hand. "My love, for Fenrir mates and marriage aren't like with humans. Mates aren't so easy to find. Not true mates. We all only get one. You're it for me, and now that I've found you, there's no way I'm just going to let you walk away." He said, dropping a kiss on her lips.

Jem felt moisture on her cheeks and realised she was crying. She'd never considered that she would ever find someone who would love her like Dan did. She'd hoped of course, and dreamed. But never in a thousand years had she expected to actually find a love like his.

"If it weren't for Jem, Dan would have died." Gerard announced.

"I'm surprised she was able to convince you Gerard." Drew said, though now he had deep frown lines etched into his forehead. Like maybe he was questioning his stance on her being, or not being, his little brother's mate.

"Did she cast a spell on you or something?" this from the angry female who had spoken earlier.

She was a surprisingly short woman now that she was in human form. When she had spoken at Jem while in wolf form Jem had expected a big woman. Someone tall and solid. Instead, the woman was short, almost willowy. With light brown skin. Long, wavy, pitch-black hair. An angry expression to go with her tone, and dark brown eyes to go with the glare she directed at Jem.

Gerard laughed.

"What do you mean Dan would have died?" Peta asked. "In the dungeon?"

Gerard shook his head. "No. At least not just there. Dan was in bad shape when she got us out of the dungeon. But by the time we got to Lofn's home Dan was..." Gerard took a deep breath. "He was so broken there was no way even being a Fenrir could have healed him. Even if he'd had a week to recuperate."

Gerard explained not only who Lofn was, but the state Dan had been in, and for the first time Jem got to hear about those couple of days from

Gerard's perspective. How he didn't want to trust her. How he hadn't fully trusted her. How there was no way he would have trusted her if it hadn't been for Lofn healing Dan. The way Gerard explained Dan's healing made Jem's heartbreak anew. She had been terrified. But clearly so had Gerard. Terrified he would lose his friend. He explained the singing. An experience that Jem doubted she could have explained as eloquently as this usually silent sentinel of a man was, and then he explained what he had heard. What he had seen when Jem had started singing, and she wanted to cry again.

"If there was ever a way to see a mating bond." Gerard said, "Then that was it. Dan and Jem weren't just joined heart to heart. They were joined spirit to spirit. They were made for each other, and if seeing that hadn't been enough, I heard what she said."

"She could have lied." The dark-haired woman said.

Gerard gave her a death stare. "The language we all spoke wasn't one you could lie in." He said dryly. "It was as though we were communicating in the purest way possible. It was a secret language. One you recognised instinctively, but couldn't replicate if you tried. It was as though the Creator himself were right there, crafting each word we spoke, and he was only allowing the truth to be spoken. Whether you like it or not, Jem is Dan's mate. She's the only reason either of us are alive right now, and if you make her leave, then all three of us will be going."

"She's the reason you ended up in that dungeon in the first place!" The dark-haired girl exclaimed in angry frustration.

Dan glared at his older brother. "No. She's not." He said, his voice hard. Then he sighed. He wasn't going to accuse his brother. "We'll either be returning to the den with Jem at my side as my mate. Or we'll be leaving. Gerard knows plenty of rogues. We'll have someplace to stay."

"Dan." Peta said, her voice pleading.

"I'm sorry Peta, but that's how it's got to be." Dan said.

"We can't let her in without the Alpha's permission." One of the men said.

"What makes you think the rogues would accept her. She's Valkyrie no matter where you go." The angry woman hissed.

"That's enough Naomi." Drew said, then turned to one of his men, "Run back to the den and see what Alpha Lovell wants to do."

Dan's Father was an enormous wolf. He was bigger than either Dan or Drew while in his wolf form, and that was saying something. But what shocked Jem the most about him was that despite his size, she wasn't afraid of him in the slightest. When Dan's brother Drew and the rest of his group had arrived she'd stood tall and completely faked being unfazed by them. But when it came down to it she had been absolutely terrified. Then the moment Jem saw Dan's Father approaching she could feel her muscles relaxing, and her heart rate slowing. In short, she had that same feeling you get when you arrive at a place where you know you're safe. Like your favourite chair. The beach. Or maybe your bedroom. Without any clear idea of what she was doing, or why, she walked through the crowd of Fenrir and made a beeline directly for him. Dan strode close by her side. But for the first time since she'd realised she loved Dan, she barely noticed his presence. The Fenrir around her growled, and she simply ignored them. The pull to approach and greet Dan's Father was magnetic in its intensity. She didn't just want to meet him. She needed to meet him. It wasn't some kind of weird attraction. There was no love. No lust. Nothing like that. When it came to that sort of thing there was only Dan. But this man, this wolf, this Fenrir Alpha evoked a sort of instant, instinctive respect. He was terrifying, and yet Jem didn't feel an iota of fear. He was enormous. But Jem didn't feel small. For all intents and purposes, he was dangerous, and yet Jem had only ever felt this safe when she had been a child, sitting on the lounge floor with her family around her at some massive gathering, knowing without hesitation that she was perfectly loved. He wasn't a threat to her. Every fibre of her being echoed the word safe.

Alpha Lovell watched with interest as Jem approached. The Fenrir around her shifted back to their wolf forms and growled. But Alpha Lovell continued to just watch her. Never making a single hostile move towards her. When she finally reached him she lowered her head, pressing her nose and forehead against his. When she pulled away moments later she found herself sinking gently to her knees, looking up at him, her neck extended slightly to the side, offering her throat. She had no idea why she did it. There had been no kind of prompting. She and Dan hadn't spoken about what to do when she met his Father, the pack Alpha. As soon as she offered her throat every single one of the wolves behind her stopped growling. They were so quiet they were barely even breathing. Dan's Father lowered his head to hers, touching his cold Fenrir nose to her exposed neck.

Welcome to the Lovell den little Valkyrie. Dan's Father said. His voice was soft and full of kindness. Much like she remembered her own Father's voice being. *I'm Eric Lovell, Alpha of the*

Lovell pack. But more importantly for you, I am Daniel's Father. I can see we have a lot to talk about. How about you come inside and meet my wife Elaine and we can get to the bottom of all this shall we.

Thank you. Jem mind spoke to him in return.

Dan took Jem's hand and gave it a squeeze, before giving her a quick kiss and shifting back into his wolf form. At his prompting, Jem climbed onto his back. It amused her how she had only ever ridden a horse a few times before all of this had happened, and she hadn't exactly been particularly fantastic at it, yet riding on the back of a massive human turned wolf, without a saddle was quickly becoming a normal part of her life. Clearly, her perception of normal had shifted. Whatever she would think of as normal from now on, she had no doubt that this mode of transportation would be something she could expect to enjoy regularly for many years to come. Assuming, of course, Dan's parents didn't hate her, and you know maul her, or send her away. Though going by Alpha Lovell's reaction to her, she might just be okay.

Jem must have looked like a complete idiot riding into the Fenrir den that very first time, and not because she was riding Dan like he was a horse. Though that was an odd thing in and of itself. But more because for the entire ride her mouth was hanging open in an 'o' of surprise. In many ways she was mimicking the reactions of the Fenrir they passed. All of them appeared to pause whatever they were doing as their party made their way past, presumably because they could smell Jem. Either that or maybe to stare at their Alpha, who was being trailed after by some of what had to be the most accomplished fighters in the Lovell pack. Meanwhile, to add to the intrigue, the Lovell fighters were all watching her being carried in on the Alpha's youngest sons back very closely. Dan was flanked by Gerard who was clearly protecting her and Dan, rather than their Alpha. It was a sight that had likely been unheard of up until this point.

Jem was beyond surprised when the dark, dank tunnel their group had entered through quickly transformed into a series of light, bright, and surprisingly open tunnels. Some of the walls were painted beautifully, others had been left plain. They passed doorways that clearly led to homes and archways that seemed to go towards an underground town. A reasonably big town at that. There were Fenrir everywhere. Young and old. Of all different colours, sizes and shapes, and all with varying tastes in fashion.

They were all so different, and yet there was something about them. Something aside from where they were and how they looked that gave Jem the distinct feeling of sameness. They were different. But they all went together perfectly. She surmised that the dual sense of individuality and sameness must have been to do with what it meant to be part of a pack. Each pack member was different. They were all unique, and yet they belonged. They were part of a greater whole.

This place is amazing. Jem mind spoke to Dan.

It is, isn't it? He replied in satisfaction.

I've always thought so. Dan's Father said.

Jem's eyes darted to Alpha Lovell. *You can hear me? Even though I was only speaking to Dan? Can the others hear me too?* She asked in embarrassment, feeling her cheeks flush.

Alpha Lovell, Eric, laughed in that way that only a Fenrir could. Both human and animal at the same time. A chuckle that was uniquely his, projected both through the mind link and released audibly in his wolf form.

I can hear you. But only because you are clearly still learning how to project your voice, and because as Alpha, and Daniel's father I have an innate ability to hear each member of my pack. You don't need to worry though. I won't share anything you don't want to be shared, and the others can't hear you. Not unless you want them to. Alpha Lovell said.

There it was again, that feeling of something slipping into place.

Alpha Lovell laughed again, though neither she nor Dan had actually said anything. She felt a strange feeling of connection. Up until now, she had only found that connection with Dan and at a stretch Gerard. But now she felt it towards Alpha Lovell. She felt accepted. As though she were part of the pack at his declaration, rather than an outsider.

Another of the benefits of being Alpha. Once you offered your neck, accepting me as your Alpha I could see the mating bond forming between the two of you. It's a surprisingly strong bond given you haven't consummated the pairing. He said *I imagine you have quite a story to tell us.*

"You have no idea." Jem sighed.

Alpha Lovell kept laughing. It was as though a weight had been on his shoulders and it was finally lifted. The fear of being kicked out of Dan's home seemed to Jem to be growing smaller and smaller with every passing moment.

"Daniel!" A woman exclaimed, running from an open doorway, her chestnut hair streaming behind her as she threw herself at him, her arms wrapped around his wolfy neck.

Jem sat up straighter. If this woman were anyone other than Daniel's mother Jem would have been shocked. But the intimacy of the greeting was still a little awkward for her. She felt as though she were intruding on a private moment. Dan's mother pulled back and frowned at the parade of Fenrir following Alpha Lovell and Daniel.

"What on earth do you all think you're doing here? Get back to your posts." She said, and a strange stirring of command wound its way through her voice.

They all shuffled from side to side, not a single one leaving, but looking increasingly uncomfortable at disobeying a direct command from the Alpha Female. They turned toward Jem, pointing her out to Dan's Mum, their lips pulling back, and a few snarls being dropped.

"Do you really think one Valkyrie is going to be able to kill Alpha Lovell or me with two of my son's and my daughter here? Not to mention neither of us is so old that we don't still have the ability to kick each of your butts soundly and send you home to your mothers. Now go!" She demanded. This time her voice was physically louder, and the command that had leached into her voice earlier was an almost tangible thing. No, it wasn't almost tangible. It was completely tangible. Right before Jem's eyes, a thread of gold light shot from Dan's Mum into and through each of the Fenrir behind her, sending them scurrying on their way.

"Your mother has been sick with worry about you Gerard." Dan's mother said. "It might be a good idea to let her know you're back."

Gerard shifted. "If it's alright with you Elaine. I'd like to stay with Dan and Jem." Gerard said. He was standing his ground firmly. He would no doubt fight against that strange gold thread of command if she released it on him. Actually, when the first command had been given it had rolled right off of him.

Elaine smiled. "Of course Gerard. The three of you have been through a lot. We're just relieved to have you home." She said.

"Um Elaine." Jem said, drawing Dan's mother's attention, and climbing down off of Dan's back so she wasn't towering ominously over everyone, "I'm Jemima. It's nice to meet you." She said offering her hand nervously.

Elaine smiled brightly. "I can't say I'm not surprised to have you standing here in front of me Jemima. But going by how worse for wear you all look I imagine I have a great deal to thank you for." She said offering her hand. "I'm Elaine Lovell. Alpha female of the Lovell pack, and Daniel's Mother. Come on inside. These five can go change and maybe Gerard can get his Mother over here to look each of you over."

Jem frowned.

"My Mum is one of the den's doctors." Gerard explained.

"She's one of our best doctors." Elaine said, "Probably even one of the best in all the packs."

Jem nodded nervously and followed Elaine inside.

The boys made their way down the hallway to where they would no doubt get dressed. Each of them, Peta included, completely unaware of Jem's growing embarrassment at their nakedness. It was interesting how outside of the little underground house them being entirely naked seemed fairly normal. But inside it seemed strange. A bit like the whole togs and undies debate. How far into civilisation can you go before something that wasn't inappropriate in one place becomes inappropriate? Jem wasn't certain she would ever fully get used to it. Being around the Fenrir really showed her how private she was when it came to her body. The idea of others seeing her nude after she shifted between human and swan made her feel really exposed and pinpointed her apparent issues with her body. It was quite possible that she would need to work towards being comfortable with nudity. Especially if she planned on using the swan cloak ever again.

"So." Elaine said, indicating for Jem to sit down on a big couch in what had to be their family lounge.

Jem pulled the backpack she'd been carrying into her lap and hugged it nervously to herself.

"So." Jem repeated after her.

"You're Daniel's mate then?" Elaine asked.

Jem felt her face flush impossibly deeper, but she managed to make her voice firm. "He's mine, yes." She said.

Elaine smiled. "Good girl." And when Jem's eyebrow raised in question Elaine continued on. "With the Fenrir people, it has never been the males choice when it comes to finding a mate. One of our males could be completely convinced that a certain female is meant to be his mate. But if she doesn't agree, his opinion on the matter is completely moot. Of course, it works the same way for our females. A mating bond cannot be forced. It has to be not only accepted but claimed, and I can see you have claimed each other." She smiled.

Jem sighed. "You and Eric, um Alpha Lovell seem to be the only ones who feel that way." She said, just in time for a dressed and still hostile looking Drew to step out of the doorway behind his Mother. Clearly, his bedroom was not off of a hallway but directly off of the lounge.

"You're a Valkyrie." Drew announced, as if that explained it all.

Jem slid the backpack off her lap onto the couch and stood so that Drew wasn't towering over her. "I've known I was a Valkyrie all of a few weeks, and I spent most of that time either hiding or running in an attempt to get Dan and Gerard away from Freya and her people." Jem said, "But yes I'm a Valkyrie, and you can change into an enormous wolf. A creature that not only the Valkyrie but the Aesir people have been indoctrinated into thinking will kill them on sight. I only experienced a few weeks of

Freya's anti-Fenrir propaganda, but the rest of those people have experienced it for years. Some have had an entire life's worth of teaching about how all you want to do is kill them. Where you Fenrir had stories of Freya and her evil Valkyrie, the people in Asgard had the Fenrir as their bogeyman. For them, you're the creature under the bed. You're the reason Odin is gone. You're their equivalent of the grim reaper."

Drew stared at her dumbstruck.

"Just because you've been told something, or thought something your entire life doesn't make it true." Jem continued. "I'm taking my life into my own hands. Or at least putting it into Dan's. He's told me that what Freya says about your people isn't true. That like any other people the Fenrir are individuals. Sure some are bad. But overall Fenrir are good people, and every one of you can't be judged by a few stories about bad ones. That's assuming the stories she told were true. I'm going to suggest that you might want to think about the Valkyrie and even the Aesir the same way. I don't doubt that there have been evil things done to your people by theirs. But not every one of their people were involved in that, or were even aware of it."

Jem felt Dan's warmth and smelt his unique scent before he even reached her. He wrapped his arms around her and she leaned back into his comforting mass.

"The only reason we were able to get home was

because of the efforts of Jem, and a handful of Asgardian people." Dan said.

"And Jem wasn't the only Valkyrie to help us." Gerard said as he made his way through to what Jem assumed was another room. Maybe a room where he had access to a phone.

Elaine cocked her head to the side in question. "Other Valkyrie helped?" she asked.

Jem nodded. "Reyna. Leader of the negotiator Valkyrie."

"And from what she said, she isn't the only one who believes that Freya is feeding the people dangerous lies." Dan said, "There are more Valkyrie who don't follow Freya, but they have nowhere else to go." He took a deep breath. "Which is why Jem and I are going to create a safe place for the Valkyrie who oppose Freya to go."

"I'm sorry, what!?" Drew said.

Eric chose that exact moment to walk in.

"What's all this then?" he asked. "Are you starting this discussion without me."

"Daniel wants to bring the Valkyrie who are supposedly against Freya here!" Drew exclaimed.

"Actually." Dan said, keeping his voice surprisingly neutral, "I was starting to think that Jem and I might need to leave the den."

Drew's mouth hung open in shock. "You'd leave the pack. Go rogue for her?" he said in surprise.

Dan glared at his brother. "I'd go back to that dungeon for her if I had to." He said.

Jem trembled at the idea of Dan being back in

Freyr's clutches, then turned in his arms. "You can't leave your pack Dan."

"If they all react to us like Drew and the others. Then yes, I can." Dan said.

Jem looked around the room at Dan's family. "Dan, the only person they're reacting to is me. They're all relieved you're home."

Dan tipped Jem's chin up so that she was looking into his eyes. "Do you really think I'd want to stay here without you. I've told you this a dozen times Jemima. But I'll keep telling you for as long as I have to. You're my mate, and now that I've found you I'm not letting you go." He said, then kissed her softly on the forehead. "Besides. Like you said. Most of the Valkyrie are terrified of the Fenrir. If we're going to help them get away from Freya, then we're going to need to have someplace for them to go."

"True." Jem said. "But leaving your pack. Your family." She sighed.

"I told you. You're my family now." He said.

Dan's Father walked over and put his hand on Dan's shoulder. "Our people will get used to the idea of Jem being a Valkyrie. I've accepted her as a part of my pack and they will too."

"That's really kind of you." Jem said, though she really didn't look forward to the transition period. The type of acceptance that she would get from the pack and the type she would prefer were oceans apart.

"Don't worry Jem." Peta said,"They really are

good people."

"Once they know what you did to get us out of Asgard they'll understand." Gerard offered, more than that he gave the distinct impression that anyone that had a problem with Jem was going to have a problem with him, and given how long it had taken Gerard to warm to her, even with her saving their lives, she appreciated the loyalty that he had towards her now.

"Perhaps you should tell us what happened after you left the den?" Alpha Lovell said.

PROPHECY, PLANS, AND PROPOSALS

After they were all seated, with Jem squished protectively between Dan and Gerard. Gerard's Mother Hazel arrived and insisted on giving all three of them sound check-ups, including Jem. It became quickly apparent to Jem that Hazel was singularly focused on helping the people in her care, no matter who they were. Meanwhile Hazel was completely unable to confirm the injuries that Dan had sustained from Freyr during his time in the dungeon. According to her, it was thanks in large part to the incredible Fenrir ability to heal. In both Jem's and Gerard's opinion, it was mostly due to the healing that Lofn had assisted them with. Without it, they were both convinced Dan wouldn't have even been capable of walking yet. No matter what healing had or hadn't happened. By the time Gerard and Dan had explained everything that had transpired since they left the den everyone in the room was staring at Jem. Some as though she had grown a second head. But mostly with surprise, and possibly a little bit of awe. Everyone seemed to have gained a new sense of respect for her. Except maybe Drew, who paused for a moment before asking her a question.

"You said something about a prophecy?" He asked.

Jem nodded and opened her bag.

"You might need to get Dante, or maybe Jordan to check this one out." Dan said.

"It got a little damaged before I could save it." Jem admitted, carefully pulling the cloth wrapped prophecy from her bag, "Hopefully it's still in one piece. I haven't exactly checked it since I grabbed it, and we've done quite a bit of travelling since then."

Jem carefully unrolled the material she'd wrapped around the paper. Or at least what was left of the paper she'd salvaged from Freya's fireplace. As she rolled it out pieces of parchment tore, and a few parts crumbled away into black ash.

Drew and the others moved closer so they could look at the prophecy more closely.

"It's quite damaged." Elaine said.

Jem nodded.

"It's in old Norse." Peta said.

"Drew can you please call Dante?" Eric asked.

"I'm already on it." A voice called over a speaker

in the wall.

Jem jumped in fright.

"That's my brother Nicolai." Dan explained, then grinned, "He's a bit of a recluse. Aye Nick?"

"Thank you Nick." Eric said, completely ignoring Dan's teasing, "Will you be joining us?"

"Maybe later." Nick said, "We have a team on their way in, and I want to make sure they get here safely."

"Can you send along Bobbie and Ben then please." Eric asked.

"Of course. They look like they're in the movie theatre at the moment. I'll let them know." Nick said, "Oh, and it's nice to meet you Jemima." He said.

"Umm. You too?" Jem said.

Dan laughed. "Nick you do know Jem can't see you right?"

"Of course. I mean." Nick paused, "I look forward to meeting you in person Jemima."

"I look forward to meeting you in person too Nicolai." Jem said.

Before long a set of identical young men stepped through the doors. Well, they were almost identical. Almost. They had the same face. The same hair colour. The same cheeky smile. The same look of mischief about them, as though they were very rarely without a smile. The only noticeable difference between the two of them was that one of the twins, the quieter one, though not by much, had shorter hair than his brother. He was introduced as Ben. While his twin, with chest-length hair, was introduced as Bobbie. They apparently thought being pulled out of the movie to meet a Valkyrie, who was, in their words, their 'new sister in law' was the most hysterical joke ever, and despite both Dan and Gerard's clear stay away demeanours, somehow they managed to sit themselves either side of Jem and began their own very special 'new family member initiation'. Which mostly consisted of light-hearted teasing around if she could fly. Questions about if she wore that kick-ass armour from all the paintings? What could she possibly see in Dan when his twin brothers were clearly not only more intelligent but obviously more attractive as well. And if Freya made Jem and the other Valkyrie dance naked under the light of the full moon while reciting the alphabet backwards as part of her 'super-secret' Valkyrie initiation. Without even trying to, the twins effectively sucked the stress right out of the room. Even Drew seemed to have mellowed out a little. Though to be fair his mellow was still pretty high strung. At the moment he was staring at the parchment so intently she thought his eyes might pop out. Either that or the parchment would burst into life and reveal all its secrets just so that he would look away.

The twins were at the point in their

interrogation where they had announced that she was too nice to be a Valkyrie, and suggesting that she should prove it by putting on her swan cloak and transforming when yet another of Dan's brothers arrived. Dante was very briefly introduced to her before he went straight to work on the scroll. Pausing momentarily to call another pack member named Jordan to confirm his translations. Jem sighed softly, completely oblivious to the Fenrir's incredible hearing. They all paused to look at her. She felt like prey right up until Dan's Mum asked her if everything was okay.

"It's just. It must be nice having a big family." She admitted.

"Are you kidding? Having to deal with all these idiots day in and day out." Peta said although she was grinning enough that Jem could tell she was joking.

Dante looked up from what he was doing. "You don't have any brothers or sisters?" he asked.

Jem shook her head. "It was just me and Dad when Mum first died. But after he married Jodi he stopped having time for me. At least beyond a Birthday or Holiday phone call. He probably hasn't even noticed I've gone missing." She said.

Elaine looked stricken. "I can't imagine that's true Jemima. You don't stop loving someone just because a new person comes into your life." She said.

"Having no siblings is pretty normal for Fenrir."

Gerard offered with a shrug.

Jem looked around, how could that be true when Dan's family was so big?

"Our family is, unique, to say the least." Dante said, "Ours is the biggest family unit in all four packs. It's actually one of the only families in generations to have more than one or two children."

Jem frowned. "Really?"

Dan nodded along with Dante and his parents.

"But. I mean with everything else going on with Freya and the Aesir. Isn't that weird?" Jem said.

"How do you mean?" Drew asked looking at her thoughtfully.

"Well, from what Reyna told us Freya has been getting more and more insistent on wiping out the Fenrir over the last few hundred years, and then there's your family that is somehow getting bigger and bigger despite the fact that families with multiple children are almost unheard of. It just seems strange." Jem said.

"It sounds like yet another thing I'll need to look into." Dante said.

The front door creaked and a young man, that Jem had to assume was Nick, stepped into the room with a guy who had sandy blonde hair and an expression of both surprise and awe.

"There really is a Valkyrie in our den." He sighed.

Dan released a low growl.

Jem stood up and offered her hand nervously. "Um. Hi. I'm Jem, Dan's mate." She said.

"Jordan." He said reaching out timidly. "I understand you have a prophecy for me to look at?"

"Over here." Dante said from the coffee table where he was crouched over the brittle, burnt piece of parchment.

"Man. This thing has seen better days. What happened to it?" Jordan asked.

"Freya and a fireplace." Jem said.

He looked at Jem with wide eyes. "You stole this from Freya."

Jem nodded.

"Man, you must have a death wish." He said, "Quick thinking though."

Jem laughed. "Not quick enough." She said indicating what was left of the paper.

Jordan shook his head. "Once I get this back to my lab, into one of my machines, and scanned, we should be able to get most of what was lost back." He said.

"This could be nothing though right?" Drew said.

"Or something big." Dan said.

"Or Freya's shopping list." Drew grumbled.

"Either way we need to be careful with it. We don't want to run the risk of losing any more of it, especially before we translate it. What have you got so far Dante?" Jordan asked with a chuckle. "Usually it's me coming to you for translations."

Dante frowned. "I didn't want to get anyone's hopes up before I confirmed it."

The two men put their heads together and proceeded to point and nod. Occasionally one of them would drop a 'do you see it?', 'I thought that too', or 'there's not enough visible to tell but I think, yeah me too'.

Jem turned to Dan. "Do they realise that they're not actually speaking in full sentences?" she asked.

Bobbie and Ben snorted back laughs. "Those two do it all the time." Ben said.

"It's almost like they're twins." The twins said in unison, with massive grins on their faces.

Jem laughed. "You're idiots, you know that right?"

Dan burst out laughing, and even Nick who had been watching their interaction from the corner was smirking.

Both of the twins held hands to their hearts.

"I'm offended, aren't you Ben?" Bobbie said.

"Deeply offended Bobbie." Ben said, "Clearly Drew's right. Jem is the most evil of the Valkyrie, we must end her now."

"Agreed." Said Bobbie. "To the dungeon with her!" he exclaimed.

Drew shot the twins an annoyed look then turned to Jem. "You're right, they are complete idiots. I can't believe I'm related to either of them." He said, and Jem felt some of his iciness thaw.

"Don't worry Drew." Bobbie said, "Ben and I have talked about it a lot, and we agree with you.

There's no way two such impressive, funny, and all-around amazing Fenrir as us are related to you. We're pretty sure you're adopted."

"Now boys, you know we were waiting for the right time to tell him." Elaine said with a glint in her eye, clearly trying desperately not to laugh.

Drew rolled his eyes. "Welcome to the family Jem and good luck. I don't know that I'd wish this madhouse on even Freya herself." He said.

Dante looked up, nodded at Jordan a few times before turning first to Jem, and then to his Dad. "It was worth saving." He said suddenly.

"It's going to take a while to translate it all. What with all the damage. Plus most of the language is in an older dialect than we've seen before." Jordan said.

"But the lines we can confirm at this point make it clear that this is a big prophecy. An important one." Dante said.

"What do you have?" Eric asked, smoothly transitioning from Dad and into Alpha.

"See here?" Dante pointed to a spot on the parchment that had survived largely unscathed. Alpha Lovell nodded.

"Assuming we've translated it correctly, and we believe we have. This says 'The witch twins rise to seats on high'." Dante said.

"Who are the witch twins?" Jem asked.

"The witch twins is another name for Freya and Freyr." Nick said, "It's not a name they particularly like though."

"I can't imagine why." Jem said.

Dan laughed.

"This line here says 'A war will come'." Jordan pointed out. "Obviously there are quite a few lines missing before it, so we don't really know the context."

"Given the way the Aesir have hunted us for as long as we can remember, I would have said the war had already begun." Dan said.

Gerard nodded.

"Only, wouldn't a war include, and affect everyone." Jem offered nervously. "I mean. Not just the Fenrir and the Aesir. But, everyone. Humans as well."

"Who knows." Jordan said, "What we can translate here isn't particularly specific."

"This here is though." Said Dante. "The maidens born to bird of white. Will help secure the final fight."

"You think it means the Valkyrie." Jem said.

"They're the only ones I can think of who have any historical relation to white birds." Dante said.

"There you go then." Drew said.

Dan glared at his brother. "The Valkyrie, Jem included, could be the thing that secures the battle for us." He said, "If we can get enough of them away from Freya."

"And I think we can." said Jem.

"But how could we ever trust them?" Drew said.

"How can they trust you?" Jem retorted. "Most of them are terrified of you, and that hostile attitude of yours is hardly going to shift their perception."

"Maybe I don't want their perception to shift." Drew growled.

Jem sighed. "Then you're short-sighted."

He growled at her.

"Most of those women are just like me." Jem explained, and Drew went quiet, "They didn't know they were Valkyrie until they were swept up to Asgard. A lot of them have felt powerless and even worthless for most of their lives. Then suddenly they're told that they're special. That there's a special call on their lives. Most of them have never even seen a Fenrir let alone hurt one, and if they knew what Freya was up to, whatever it is, they wouldn't stand with her. If they knew the lies she was telling about the Fenrir they would never help her capture them."

"Maybe." Drew grunted.

"I think it's worth finding out." Alpha Lovell said, and they all nodded along. "Somewhere outside of pack lands." He continued. "Until we know we can trust them."

"I'm not suggesting we bring them all here, even if they were comfortable coming." Jem said, "I'd never want to put your people at risk. It's just. It's like they're my sisters, and I want to help them. I want to save them."

"As long as they are out of the den, and I or one

of my security team can screen them before they come here I'm good with that." Drew said.

"Thank you." Jem said.

Drew looked at her and sighed. "I'm not going to pretend having a sister-in-law who's a Valkyrie was ever at the top of my list of things I wanted for our pack." He said "But it's happened, and as far as things go, I like you Jem. More importantly, Dan likes you. So as long as you don't hurt our people, I'll defend you the same way I would any other member of our pack." He said.

"I. Um. Thank you." Jem said.

Jordan cleared his throat. "The last line just says 'Lest this battle be your last'." He said. "I know there's a lot more here. A lot more to this prophecy. But I think we're going to have to get it scanned."

"It might be worth going through the pack histories. All of the old prophecies." Dante said. "See if there are any other links. Maybe this prophecy has already happened."

Jem shook her head. "If it had already happened then Freya wouldn't have been so upset with Hod and Elena. She was fuming, and she said something about wiping their memories. Making them hate each other."

"Hod and Elena?" Dante said. "You mean her son Hod, and Elena daughter of Sol."

Jem nodded.

"The only reason she didn't kill Elena is because Hod said she was his soulmate, that and I think she wanted to punish her a little bit. She really didn't like Elena."

Conversation amongst the Fenrir got a lot more frantic from there on. They made plans for Dante to visit the other dens so he could go through their archives. They discussed what they would do for any rogue Valkyrie they were able to get to come over to the Fenrir's side. One thing was for certain though. Despite Jem's reception at the Lovell den, she couldn't help but feel she had been accepted, and if Dan's family had accepted her then the rest of the pack would too. Eventually. She had not only saved Dan and Gerard but in grabbing that prophecy before it was destroyed she may just have helped to save all the Fenrir. Maybe even the world.

BOOKS BY THIS AUTHOR

Second Chances: A Kiwi Romance

When Katy's husband walks out on her with his mistress all her hopes and dreams are shattered. Then her Aunt Connie dies leaving her a run-down house that she instantly falls in love with and it seems like she finally has the chance to make a fresh start. If only the builder she has been forced to work with wasn't trying to snake it out from under her. Rick thinks he'll finally be able to get back his family homestead after the passing of local recluse and current owner of the now run-down house Connie Pride. Then he meets Connie's niece Katy and all hopes of ever having the home returned are destroyed. It's clear that she's as in love with the old house as he is and has absolutely no intention of selling it back to him. Can Katy turn this old broken house into something beautiful with the help of her surly builder, or will working with Rick end in not only the loss of the house she's fallen in love with but also a broken heart.

Trusted (The Fenrir Series)

Peta isn't normal. She's not even human all of the time. Of course no Fenrir is human ALL of the time. Not when they have the option of shifting into a wolf. Too bad she hasn't had the option to shift in ages. Not since she hit her first heat and all the males started losing their minds. Her Dad's refusing to let her leave the den and she's going stir crazy. Luckily Peta's Mum and brother have found a way to sneak her out so she can have the freedom she so desperately needs.Ryder's alone. Rejected by his people. Outliving every human he's ever met by thousands of years. Then there are the Fenrir, they hate the Aesir, and in particular they hate Ryder. He would never have anything to do with them, except for the fact that he just hit one of their females with his motorcycle. He knows he can't leave her injured on the side of the road, but helping a Fenrir isn't easy, and he has the bite to prove it. With Ryder's help Peta is quickly back on her feet, but now the Aesir is sick and he's following her around like a love sick puppy. Peta is unnaturally protective of Ryder, her family is freaking out, and the only solution to their problem is to get him to the Dwarves, a race of people Peta didn't even believe actually existed. Can a Fenrir and an Aesir be anything other than enemies? Is Ryder simply sick, or is something else going on? Can the pain of the past be erased by love, or are some pains too dark and too deep to heal?

Wanted (The Fenrir Series)

Molly's life is a living nightmare at Valker Women's home, she's bullied daily and can't find a job anywhere. Things are looking bleak, and then to top everything off she gets bitten by a wolf and starts losing her mind. At least she thinks she's losing her mind. It's either that or she actually changed into a wolf herself and is now naked in a cave full of wolf people. Drew just wants to work his way to become Alpha of the Lovell pack. He doesn't want a mate, he's not ready for it. He's certainly not ready for Molly, the Fenrir who doesn't know she's Fenrir. Can Molly adjust to her new life as a Fenrir? Will Drew admit his attraction to the new addition to the Lovell pack? Or will outside forces steal their chance to know each other and destroy the pack in the process.

ABOUT THE AUTHOR

Karla Rose

Karla Rose is a wife and mother of two,
living in the Waikato, New Zealand.

She spends her time, helping where she can, loving her husband, and supporting her children as they learn and grow.

She has a love of food, movies, music, TV series, the beach, friends
and family.

You can find her on her website karlamrose.weebly.com, or her Facebook page Karla Rose - Author.

A MESSAGE FROM THE AUTHOR

Thank you so much for reading my book.
I really hope you enjoyed entering the
world of the Fenrir and the Aesir!

If you enjoyed this book then I'd
love for you to review it.

Your review goes a long way to getting my
stories into the hands of readers and book lovers
all over the world, and I appreciate not only
your review, but the time you take to write one.

Thank you again sweet reader.

Karla Rose.